after hours at the
almost home

after hours at the

almost home

tara yellen

unbridled books

Unbridled Books
Denver, Colorado

Library of Congress Cataloging-in-Publication Data

Yellen, Tara.
After hours at the Almost Home / Tara Yellen.
p. cm.
ISBN 978-1-932961-48-5
1. Bars (Drinking establishments)—Fiction.   2. Colorado—Fiction.
I. Title.
PS3625.E455A69 2008
813'.6—dc22   2008000462

1   3   5   7   9   10   8   6   4   2

Book Design by SH • CV

First Printing

For my mom, my dad, and Betsey

When the blackbird flew out of sight,

It marked the edge

of one of many circles.

— WALLACE STEVENS,
"Thirteen Ways of Looking at a Blackbird"

after hours at the
almost home

The Almost Home, the bar and grill at 2nd and Middleton, was not an old building or a new building, it was somewhere in between—built quick and sturdy, gray brick, steel trim, the type of place you'd overlook if it wasn't smack-dab in the middle of Cherry Creek, Denver's affluent shopping district. In a row of mostly shoe and stationery stores, the Almost Home stood out unapologetic, chugging smoke, its beer signs the first hint of twilight in the neighborhood—coming to life, it seemed, suddenly, though really they were on all day. Even from the outside, even without seeing anyone enter or exit, you could tell this wasn't where the businessmen and women and the Dolce & Gabbana shoppers went for lunch. It was the kind of place a person could go to drink before noon. Maybe stick around for the burger special, watch the news.

On certain days, however, for court verdicts or important games, everything was different. People came from all over and the Almost Home transformed. Nothing *technically* changed, of course, aside from the occasional plastic banner or two, but it was as though, in an instant, the bar would step from its own shadows to assume center stage in Cherry Creek. Like the beer lights: before you knew it, there it was.

Tonight was the Super Bowl. This was the second year in a row Denver was playing. Last year they'd won, and this year they were expected to win again. At 3:30 in the afternoon, an hour from kickoff, the Almost Home was filling up. Throngs of people arrived in clumps. Families and college kids and fans and friends of fans—anyone you could think of.

One of them was JJ.

She stood outside. People passed her by, entering the Almost Home in flashes of orange and blue—hats and ski coats and face paint. It was winter. She was in Denver. Exactly on time, JJ was prepared— she'd stocked her purse with pens and breath mints, was wearing the brand of no-skid sneakers the manager had suggested—but she didn't go in, not yet. Instead, she took a few seconds to picture it clearly: one day far in the future, while strolling past this corner, coming from brunch or maybe the symphony, she'd catch a waft of french-fry grease. She'd stop. She'd pull in the smell and think, *I remember that first day.*

It was exhilarating now to conjure it in the then, and it gave JJ perspective on the past year. Failed beginnings made you more interesting, she thought, not less. She'd gone places. She'd moved five times and worked at six jobs. She knew exactly where to find the most economical garbage pail, dish drainer, and bath mat in any Target, anywhere in the country; she knew how to disinfect a secondhand mattress. If nothing else, disorientation gave her this: the drive to propel herself from disorder to order. It gave her antsy hope.

And now, finally, standing before this building—which was otherwise unremarkable in its boxiness, in its blank slabs of chipped and salt-stained brick—it seemed to JJ that things could actually fall into place.

There was an advantage to such foresight. It offered a warning: *Don't mess this one up.*

part one

These frogs
do not get
lonely.

1.

JJ was in the way. The aisles were crammed, people bumped into her—there was no place to stand. "Excuse me," she said. She squeezed her elbows close to her body, then tripped through a jangle of chairs. She'd never waited tables before, and so far all they'd had time to show her were how to change the soda syrups and where to find napkins. Customers grabbed her arms and asked her for things she couldn't hear or didn't understand. "Go Broncos," she said.

"Do something," a tall waitress hissed as she passed, her ponytail whapping JJ in the mouth. The waitress was carrying a tray of drinks high in the air and was moving fast without looking like she was moving fast. People got out of the way. JJ tried to follow her, to ask what it was exactly she should do, but the waitress was already far ahead, the crowd filling in behind her, the tray of drinks traveling over heads the only proof she hadn't vanished entirely.

JJ did her best. She handed out napkins, refilled waters. Tried to keep track of the servers. There were three of them: the tall blond waitress, another waitress who was older, in her thirties or forties, and a waiter who'd given her a quick tour earlier and told a funny joke about a goat that couldn't spell. His head was shaved and he was big. Really big. Tall and overweight both. He wasn't the type you'd imagine waiting tables—maybe not even someone you'd want around food. But the customers seemed to like him. One table applauded when he brought them pitchers of beer, another chanted his name. As for the bartenders, JJ couldn't see the one working now, way back there behind the swarm of customers—and had only briefly met the lanky, dark-haired guy who'd been behind the bar when she first arrived. He hadn't had time to say much.

It was fun, JJ decided. Or it looked fun: the activity, the purpose. How the servers all held their mouths in the same fixed manner. The way they balanced trays and carried plates across their wrists and up the insides of their arms. The food slid a bit on the plates, and the ketchup bottles that they stuck heads-down into their aprons waggled dangerously with every step, but nothing fell. Not even with the tall blonde and her cloppy heels. Amazing, JJ thought, watching her swoop a tray of bottles over someone's suddenly raised arm.

Something good happened in the football game. People jumped up and cheered. It was a strange mix of people. A woman dressed like a witch stood up and covered her ears. Across the room, at the midpoint of the long, boomerang-shaped bar, the big waiter—Keith—waved his tray and hollered for the bartender. "Order up!" The servers got their drinks there, at the *wait station.* It was marked by two silver handlebars curving into question marks. Like the kind you saw going into swimming pools.

Customers yelled, "Beer!" "Shots!" "Grandma," a woman called and held up her glass. *Grandma.* Maybe JJ'd heard it wrong.

The older waitress came up and touched JJ's arm. "This way," she said. Her face was wet and splotched, and her short orange hair stuck out in funny horns like she'd been yanking it. "I'm Colleen," she said, catching her breath. "Here—please—follow me."

JJ helped Colleen bring food to the tables. It wasn't as easy as it looked. The plates were hot and the cooks expected you to grab three or four at a time—which, for JJ, made it just about impossible to move, let alone cross the room. It proved far simpler to take things off the tables than to put them on, so she slipped away and busied herself with clearing used napkins and dishes and glasses, scooping them up and depositing them into plastic tubs by the kitchen doors. Just as she was getting the hang of it, though, just as she was starting to enjoy the stacking and weaving—it was almost like a sport—she went and dropped a chicken wing into someone's full mug of beer.

The beer's owner held it up. "What's this? Whatcha tryin' to give me? A *wet boner?*"

Laughter from the rest of the table.

"No," JJ said quickly, without thinking.

More laughter. In college, they were the type of guys who'd never given her a second glance: backwards baseball caps, smirky smiles. She resisted the urge to touch her hair.

"And where're my cheddar fries? It's been, what, hour and a half since we ordered? And now I don't even have a freakin' beer?"

"I'm so sorry," JJ said. "Maybe I could—"

"On the house." The tall blond waitress reappeared out of nowhere and set down a fresh mug and a full, foamy pitcher of beer. "See," she said to the guy, laying a hand on his shoulder, "we got you covered,

9

sweetie"—then she pulled JJ away by the wrist and backed her against a wall. "Who told you to come in?"

"I don't remember his name," JJ stammered. "I think he's a manager—"

"He said tonight."

"Yeah."

"Tonight?"

"Yeah."

"Wonderful. That's just terrific." The pendant around her neck read *Lena* in gold block letters. That seemed right: sharp and direct, like her voice. And her stare. And her breath—she was so close, JJ could taste the menthol of her chewing gum. "Maybe you haven't noticed, but it's Super Bowl Sunday. Welcome to Madison fucking Square Garden. If you're looking for a Girl Scout badge, try some other goddamn place."

And she was off.

She could be a beauty queen, JJ thought, still frozen there, getting an image of one of those frosted dresses with tight shoulders. Or maybe not the queen but a runner-up, a very close second.

Then it struck her: maybe she did have the wrong day.

Maybe she'd heard it wrong or written it down wrong, and really she was supposed to come in *next* Sunday. Or maybe—oh god—even yesterday. JJ tried to rethink the conversation and remember exactly what it was the manager had said.

"More beer," a nearby table hollered. "More everything!"

Game music blasted from the TVs: *dah nah-nah-nah, dah nah-nah-nah. . . .*

Of course, it was too late anyway. It no longer mattered. It wasn't tomorrow or yesterday. She was here now.

Across the room, Lena was charging toward the bar—her spine straight, her chin up, like she was wearing that pageant gown. Like she was off to beat up the queen.

JJ squared herself. She took a breath. She could do this.

Lena ducked behind the bar, leaving Colleen and Keith to work the floor. *Why is it,* she wanted to know, *that when something goes wrong, I'm expected to fix it?* She poured beers, poured drinks, slammed off taps just in time.

"Hey, we got a bartender," someone yelled. There was a spatter of applause.

"Right here! Another round!"

"Six kamikazes!"

She didn't look up. She tipped the vodka upside down. One two three, across to the next glass of ice, one two three, next.

Where the fuck is Marna?

Keith came barreling behind the bar and started knocking things over in the beer cooler. Lena swatted him away. "I'll do it! Just get your tables."

"Seven Heinekens, pitcher Bud, pitcher Coors, double Jack and Coke." He hiked up his jeans and pushed himself out into the crowd, toppling a stack of napkins with a beefy elbow. "Who's thirsty?" he bellowed.

"Hey, Lena." Colleen grabbed both handrails. Her face was gummy with sweat. "She's not in the bathroom and I checked downstairs. Can I get two Long Islands? Also four ciders? Please? I'm in the weeds."

"Oh service," someone singsonged down the bar. A regular. Not yet, Lena thought. If they caught your eye, they had you. She ignored the whole idiot lot—raising their empty glasses like a bunch of Statues of Liberty. "Hey," one of them called, "*I might as well be home.*"

Lena hadn't even worked here the longest. February would be three years—and that was counting the six months she'd quit and worked at Retox. Three years was a long time—much longer and they'd call her a Lifer—but not compared to some of the others. Denny'd started as a dishwasher back when he'd first moved here out of high school, more than ten years ago. And Keith—who'd, Christ, been named Best Server of Denver by *Westword* last spring and was still acting like he'd won an Oscar—well, he was going on at least four. So why was it, when the shit flew, *she* was the one that got the mop?

"Goddamn Super Bowl," she said to Colleen. She got Keith his pitchers, filled three Cokes and a Diet, stabbing the last with an extra straw to mark it. "Goddamn Marna. Unbelievable. Every other bar, double, triple staffed, right? A little planning involved, god forbid, bar backs, bussers—but what do we have? Who do we schedule? One flaky-ass bartender? And what? Three on the floor? And a *trainee*? A fucking deer in headlights?" She smacked an empty cardboard box out of her way and grabbed a cluster of ciders. This was what happened when you worked at a place with *no management.* As long as the doors stayed open and the register rang—and his asshole friends were accommodated—Bill could give a shit about the goings-on. Which, sure, led to certain perks. Free drinks, flexible hours. None of the corporate rigmarole you got at chain restaurants.

But there were also some big fucking drawbacks.

Lena swung open the cooler and grabbed the sour mix. It was sticky, a line of fruit flies glued to the rim. "*I* should just walk off. Don't think I haven't considered it. Don't think I don't consider it every goddamn day I have to be here."

"Want me to make the Long Islands? It's just the two."

"I *got* it, Colleen." *Just.* Colleen couldn't mix a gin and juice without a recipe. "Be useful," Lena told her. "Go deliver my drinks. And see if someone can come in."

"You don't think Marna's coming back? I'm sure she's coming back. I know it for a fact, Lena. It's her divorce night and she and Lily have plans later—"

"I don't *care* if Marna's coming back, I don't *care* what your daughter's plans are. I just want some fucking help."

"Hey, Lena," someone yelled, "we need to discuss the beer situation."

"Yeah, Lena, give us beer!"

"Grandma."

"Hold your goddamn panties, I'm catching up." She scooped ice, poured, scooped ice, poured.

"I left messages," Colleen said when she returned. She dropped cherries into a cherry Coke and licked her fingers. "What about Denny? Shouldn't I call him back in?"

"Well, let's see. He worked all day—and a double yesterday and a double Friday. And he's the only one of us who cares about the goddamn game. So, hmmm . . ."

"I know, but it would probably only be for a little while, right? Through the big rush or until Marna—"

"No." Lena topped off a Guinness with one hand and plunged a plastic sword into an olive with the other. It wasn't that she hadn't considered it. But right after she considered it, she pictured Denny now, this instant, in his living room—in *Stephanie's* living room, though that was beside the point—bent into the screen, eating fast-food burgers and fries and drinking a tallboy. She could see everything:

his one-dimpled grin, the way he'd punch a fist into his open palm and mutter at the bad plays. He would have flattened the paper bag into a plate and squirted ketchup in a careful mound, not too close to the edge. That's what was so funny about Denny: within his messiness he was somehow *tidy*. He had these small pockets of order.

What did they expect her to do—call him and beg? *Please save us? We can't function without you?*

Fuck no.

She stared down at the muck of drink tickets. Hopeless. The ink had bled into furry blots. She grabbed empty pitchers and began pouring. Bud, Bud Light, Coors. "Here," she called to Keith and Colleen, slopping down the pitchers, foam everywhere. She shook it off her wrists. "Give these out for now. I got the bar to deal with."

"Great," they each said. But they didn't move. They stood there looking at her, their faces like open coconuts.

Keith: "But I also need a daiquiri and a perfect Manhattan straight up extra bitters and seven butter Crowns. Oh, and sixteen lemon drops."

And Colleen: "I'm really slammed. Can I get four more Long Islands?"

JJ overheard the last of this and caught up with Colleen. She offered, "I'll help." Colleen was like an aunt, she decided. Not *her* aunt—who was older than this woman and certainly wouldn't have plucked out then drawn back in her eyebrows—but an aunt sort of person: quick-smiling and warm.

"With taking orders?" They'd stopped at a computer and Colleen began poking at squares on the face of the monitor. Fast. Menu items and modifiers. *Burgers. Fries. On the side. Bourbon, Makers, rocks.*

"Sure."

"Oh god, JJ, I wish you could." Colleen's voice was up an octave. She kept poking the screen. "I know you're trying. I wish Denny was still here to show you what to do. I don't have time. Crap, I can *never* find the *untoasted bun* key, it's not where you'd expect it. It doesn't make any sense! And it's a ridiculous thing to ask for anyway!"

"Denny? The daytime bartender?"

"Denny. Yeah. He's good at explaining. Wait. No mayo or extra mayo? *Crap.* I have no idea. Extra mayo. I'm deciding. Mayo tastes good."

"Isn't that him over there?"

"Who."

"Denny."

Colleen looked up, confused. "Denny? Where?"

JJ pointed toward the far end of the bar, by the restrooms. "I just saw him. Kinda slouchy, choppy dark hair—"

Colleen stood on her tiptoes and scanned the crowd. "No kidding?"

"Just two seconds ago. He was right there, he must be in the bathroom. He was kinda behind the video game. . . ."

"Hiding! He does that! He stayed to watch the game. Perfect. Okay. When he comes out, have him find you a book and an order pad and make him show you real fast how to write up tickets. Just the basics. I'll tell you one thing, don't *even* let him complain because, you know what, he's lucky we don't call him back on. Seriously. I am *this* close to calling him back on. And you can tell him I said that. Actually, wait, no." Colleen sighed. "Don't tell him I said that." With that, she turned back to the monitor.

"No worries," JJ said. "I'm on it."

15

. . .

"Grandma."

"All right, all right." Lena poured Grand Marnier into a shot glass and slid it down to Fran—who used to work here and was now the most regular of the regulars.

At every bar Lena had ever worked, the regulars were the same. Like from one sitcom to another. Fran with her *Grandmas*—and her barnacle husband, James. India the fake gypsy. All of them. Hammer the bookie; Spencer, who sold cheap weed and supposedly played for the Raiders for about five minutes in the '80s—which was why no one would sit next to him, you had to hear the same stories over and over. And then there was Old Barney, who left his big mangy dog outside in the way of customers. Just left it standing there, not even tied up, its nose pointed in.

It was five minutes to halftime. Most of these guys had been here since open, Lena knew, though she hadn't been around to see it. The reason they showed up so early on game days was to squeeze out the frat boys who would stream in from local colleges, who would elbow in to drink ridiculous vodka drinks and shout at the TVs. You really couldn't blame them, the regulars. The frat boys even smelled young, like lemon cookies and mouthwash.

She opened tallboys, set them down with a clunk, ignored requests for fresh frosty mugs.

"Hey, Lena," Colleen said. "Denny—"

"*No.*"

"Lena, you're not listening," Colleen whined.

"That's right. I'm not." Lena handed Keith a mind-eraser and a rum and Diet and began shaking a margarita.

"Denny's still here, Lena. He never left. He stayed to watch the game."

Lena stopped. The lights seemed to dim. She squinted at Colleen, who was trying to fit three drinks into one fat palm, her lips sucked in in concentration. For a moment Lena imagined grabbing the shaker— still half full of margarita—and whipping it straight at her. Instead, though, she stayed very still and kept her voice low, each word slow and separate like nursery school: "Denny. Is. What?"

"No kidding," Keith said.

"That's what I said! Yeah, down at the end somewhere." Colleen pointed.

Lena pushed herself up and forward to get a good view. No Denny. What she did see, however, sitting there on the last bar stool, chewing a swizzle stick, cross-legged and staring off like some *poetry reading,* was the new girl.

"Your idea of helping?" It was almost a real question, but if the new girl had a real answer, Lena wasn't going to wait to hear it. She took the girl squarely by the shoulders, guided her off the bar stool, and steered her through the crowd—stopping only briefly to let her grab her purse and coat—then into the kitchen, around the cooks and prep tables, to the back door. All the while, Colleen followed behind, whimpering about giving the kid a break. If you listened to Colleen, nothing was ever anyone's fault.

"Don't misunderstand me," Lena told the girl, unlocking the door, "you're welcome to come back. In fact, hey, here's a deal, if you can drum up a bartender—or someone with the *vaguest idea on how to wait tables*—we'd be delighted to see you again. Delighted." With that, she gave the girl a light shove out the door. It snapped shut behind her, whirling a few specks of snow into the hot kitchen air for an instant, like confetti.

2.

Denny rubbed his hands as the engine spat and sputtered. He flipped on the defrost. That was always the worst—the cold air before it turned, blasting at you. His left big toe was pinging, a constant high-pitched throb. The truck was an '86 Ram on its way out. It took forever to warm up. He'd barely make it home before the second half. He'd have just enough time to pull off his boots, open a beer. Call Steph. Maybe she'd pick up this time.

He rolled through the radio stations, passing the halftime crap, finding nothing but commercials. Lately he'd been listening to the religious shows. They reminded him of growing up. The soapy ladies ranting about sin, going on and on. And the men with their even angry keel. Talking in command. Denny remembered that. He knew exactly how these guys sounded at the breakfast table: *Pass that salt, son.* They had permanent echoes in their throats.

Denny closed his eyes and lit a cigarette, cracked the window. He had a bag of weed in the glove box, but he needed a minute, even for that. After a shift everything turned jelly. The rum and Cokes had kicked in too, and for a moment Denny thought about falling asleep. Just leaning the seat back a bit . . .

The Bible Man was on. Luke Lanko. A woman was trying to argue the biblical significance of vegetarianism. Ol' Luke was pissed. He got pissed at stupid questions. *You have it all wrong,* he boomed. The next caller knew better. *Bless you, Luke, I have your books.*

By the time Denny saw the new girl it was too late.

Or it was almost too late: if he really tried, he could leave. If he was fast about it. There she was, though, coming at him, red-faced and breathing clouds, her dark hair flopping in her eyes. *Now,* he thought. If he gunned it, he could scoot around her and make a straight shot of it.

"Denny?!" She slapped an open palm on his window.

He rolled it down.

"Oh. Good. Wow. Hi, it's *you,*" the girl said, out of breath. "You're still here."

He snapped off the radio, ground out his cigarette. Unlocked the passenger-side door. "Get in," he said.

"No, that's not what I mean. I have a car." She rubbed her nose with the back of her hand. It made a squishing noise and she sniffed.

"Get in, will you?"

She hesitated but ran around and did, then almost fell back out closing the door. "Yikes. Cold," she said, wriggling to show it. Thirty degrees out and she was wearing shorts. Denny watched her fasten her seatbelt.

"Going somewhere?" he asked.

"Oops! Sorry. Habit. Hey, um, it's really busy in there. Do you think—"

"Nope."

"But if—"

"Nope." He imagined what they'd told her inside: *No matter what he says, make him come in. He'll come in. He always comes in.*

"I don't think it would be for long, Denny, honestly. The bartender will be back soon, anyway. I mean, right?"

"Not if she's smart."

She waited. Rubbed her nose. Went at it with a knuckle, made that wet sound. "So . . . okay?"

He shrugged, grabbed another cigarette, thought about lighting it. Thought about going home to his new apartment. Steph had quit answering his calls weeks ago. She let them ring and ring until the machine would come on, and for a while there, before she changed the outgoing message, Denny was hearing his own voice coming back at him. The dog yapping in the background, some snippet of TV. An afternoon. Sometimes he called just so she'd see his name pop up on the caller ID. Other times he punched in the code to make it read *unavailable,* but mostly he just let it pop up. Either way, he didn't get her.

"Listen, Denny, Lena—" The new girl stopped herself and took a breath, like here was a place for courage. "I think they're having some sort of crisis in there. I think we should go in. Now. Seriously."

He didn't say anything.

"Lena—"

"That's really sick."

"What?"

"That thing you do. With your nose."

She froze. He could make her cry if he wanted to.

They were all the same, the girls Bill hired. She was just like the rest of them, guessing when to laugh, apologizing like crazy, complimenting shit for no reason. *Oh those are cool straws.* She'd ask for a ton of shifts and then a few months'd go by and she'd have finals or papers or something and she'd be freaking out, expecting time off. Expecting everyone to cover for her. Colleen's fourteen-year-old had more sense than this girl.

He stuck the unlit cigarette behind his ear and fished around on the seat beneath him for his pack of rolling papers. "You smoke?"

"No." She paused. "Sometimes, when I feel like it. I like Marlboros."

"I mean weed." He held up the papers, like *Exhibit A,* then reached across her legs and got the ziplock out of the glove compartment.

"Oh sure. I've tried that too." She rubbed her thigh where he'd brushed it. "I think we should be getting in, though. Seriously. It's my first day and all."

"Relax, will you?" He had to give her credit, she was persistent. "So you're a student, huh."

"Graduated."

"Same difference," Denny said. He spread out a rolling paper on one knee, balanced the bag on the other and began picking through the buds, separating them. "Whatcha study?"

"Poli-sci. Studied. I'm finished." She added, "Actually, first I was a music major, I played piano. I played piano for a long time. I switched at the last minute to poli-sci."

"Poli-sci. Sounds like a disease." She was cute, he decided. There was a softness about her—not fat really, just young, like her edges hadn't settled yet.

"It's short for political science," she said. "It's a popular degree."

21

"What do you do with a degree in poli-sci?"

"Run for office. Ha." It came out more as a burp. "I don't know. Watch people's kids. Cashier at Putt-Putt. Work in bars."

Denny nodded. "Hell. I got that degree." He felt her attention as he deposited the weed onto the paper. Sprinkled it like a taco. He rolled the joint with a few deft twists, then licked the seam to seal it. "Wanna start?"

"No, you."

It tasted good. Like camping. Denny sighed and let it out, watched the smoke curl into blue loops and then fade away. He handed her the joint. She took it between her index and middle finger and clamped it there. Held it like a zeppelin, like it might take off. She brought it to her lips and sucked until the fire glowed. "Wow," she said and smoke fell from her mouth.

"Hey, you didn't inhale it." He liked watching her. There was something Generation X-y about her mouth. It was round, maybe a little lopsided. He took the joint. "Like this. You have to suck it in, all the way, like something sudden." He showed her. "Like a surprise. Like Lena's coming after you," he said, smiling.

She glanced out the window and took the joint. She did it right this time and coughed. "It hurts," she said.

"It hurts so good."

"Yeah."

"That means it's working."

"I don't think I'm high."

"That means you probably are."

"I've never been high before."

He looked at her. Her nose was red from all the rubbing. "Well," he said.

"Are we going back in?" she asked, blowing out hard.

"Relax, will you?"

The windows were fogged up now. She made a fist and pressed the side of it to the pane, then used a finger to top the shape with dots. "A baby foot," she said and giggled. She looked at him, her finger still on the glass, the last toe spreading, getting bigger from her heat. "You have great eyes," she said. "Newscaster eyes."

"Thanks, but they're contacts." He popped one out to show her, then wet it in his mouth and put it back in. "Look natural, huh?" He turned down the vent, leaving them in silence.

"JJ," she said finally.

"Huh?"

"You forgot my name, I think."

"Is that so?"

"Yeah."

"Well I didn't," he lied. "Denny," he said, jutting out a hand.

She giggled. "I've been calling you that all night."

"I knew you were smart." The foot had clouded over. He took a few more hits, offered her some, though he knew she was done, and stubbed it gently in the ashtray. For a dumb moment he thought about giving it to her, like a take-home prize.

"Why do you save all these papers?" She motioned to the stack of *Westwords* on the floor by her feet, then bent down and grabbed one off the top, started flipping through it.

"I don't. I just haven't dumped them. There's a difference."

"Rancid Audio," she read. *"Jam session blasts Bluebird."*

He didn't know why, actually, he still had them. He'd found his apartment a couple weeks ago. It was okay, just north of Denver, in a high-rise called Meadow Acres. Utilities included, steam room, gym. Like a permanent hotel. It was furnished, which was good, because he'd left everything. Which was only fair.

"Dear Diva, My lover fell asleep during sex again. I'm starting to take it personally."

It felt strange, after a shift, going home to unfamiliar things. The furniture was old, plaid with wood trim. There was a lot of it, but for some reason the place still looked empty. Or maybe it just felt unreal. He hadn't told anyone that he and Steph had split up. He hadn't told Lena.

"This is funny. I like the *Westword*. I think I've read this one. Do you ever read the personals? Do you have a girlfriend?"

What Denny wanted was to go inside. He needed the cash. It wouldn't be *so* bad, to throw back a few more, to talk stats with the regulars. He could still watch the game. Things'd calm down the second half and he'd have a little time. Even if he didn't have time, he'd watch. And anyway, what good was it to sit here? Like a loser just sitting here. A crazyman. Denny had a flash then, of his old man, at the kitchen table by the TV, over a yellow legal pad, copying Scripture in crazyman handwriting, the a's and o's like little squares, nothing curving, no mistakes. *If Pop ever gets a job,* he'd said once to his mother, *we should buy a Xerox machine.* And his father had given it to him for that and it'd felt good, actually, because it got his father up and out of that chair. Because for once they weren't all of them just sitting there, waiting.

"Single straight-laced Jewish male seeks same. Naughty schoolgirl seeks dom to fill my every hole." JJ looked off, like she was counting.

Who cared if Lena expected it? He didn't care. And Marna, he thought, it was possible that she would come back, that she was even around here somewhere, chewing her blue gum, holding on to those few minutes of safe, of deciding—*Do I go back in?* There was only power in it if you did, Denny thought. If, eventually, the answer was *yes.*

"I almost forgot," JJ's voice broke in, "where I was. You know." She put the newspaper down. "Hey. Aren't you curious?"

"No."

"No, listen. I was thinking. My name."

"You're high."

"What it stands for. Most people ask what it stands for. Don't you want to know?"

He shrugged. "If you need to tell me. If you have to unload or something."

JJ licked her lips, then touched them with a finger, like she was checking they were still there. "I can't go back in."

"Sure you can."

"Sure I can." She giggled. "But look. Are my eyes red?"

"Yeah. But who cares. So are everyone's."

"They're all stoned?"

"Just relax. It wears off. Christ, you only had two hits."

"I lost track."

Denny flipped on the radio. Found the money show where they told you the end of the world was coming in a few months. People called in about bomb shelters and stocks and gold. They gave you a number where you could turn all your savings into coins.

And what would he say if Steph finally picked up? One day, waking up, he had made the decision. *I can be single again. I can be alone.* You feel a certain way, then get it in your head that there's an answer. That one big change will lead to another. And of course it does— that's the surprise. How a bill becomes a law. How a thought becomes your life.

Denny snapped off the radio and turned to the new girl. "Well," he said, "well, Miss Poli-science-fiction, well, *JJ.*"

She stared back at him, all watery-eyed, her hair in her face, like she was imagining she was beside a pool somewhere.

"Let's go," he said. "Time's up."

"Up? How?"

Denny paused. He tried to think of something to ask her, something she would know the answer to. He couldn't think of what it was.

3.

"*Pitcher of Coors,*" Lena called out again.

Denny poured a pitcher of Bass, started a round for the regulars.

Thanks a fucking lot. As if it was *her* fault he was back there. Meanwhile, the new girl came up and took the Bass pitcher from the mat in both hands, like it was a flower pot. *Christ.* Lena ducked behind the bar and got her own pitcher. As it poured, she waited until Denny glanced her way, then reached above the register and tore down a page of newspaper tacked there—the article about Keith's award. She balled it up and whipped it at Denny, hard. *"Prick."*

"The bartender is a prick," she told 19 when she gave them the pitcher. She tended to her section, falling into the mindlessness of it, taking orders, serving food. She gave wet-naps to 32 for their wings. Freshened their Sprites.

What really made her sick was this: when everything was said and done, Marna would return and it would be like nothing happened. She was down the street doing shots or toking with the alley freaks—it didn't take a genius to figure that out. Her divorce was official—she'd made sure everyone knew it was coming by marking it on the office calendar and crossing off the days, one by one. And, sure, why should something little like a Super Bowl get in the way of Marna's fun? She'd be back, if not in the next hour, then for her next shift, a Lucky hanging from her mouth, her hair unwashed. She'd be buzzed on something, her eyes artificially bright. *Hey guys what's up?* And the regulars would be talking about it to no end—and Colleen behind Marna's back and Keith as a joke, like it was *cute.* And Denny'd most likely let her have it for making him miss his goddamn game. But that would be it. Another entry for Lily's journal. Marna wouldn't be fired. She could torch the place and everyone would say, Oh well, it's *Marna.* Business as usual.

Lena didn't hate her. Everyone thought she did, but she didn't. At least not before tonight she didn't. There was a big thing for a while, when they worked Tuesday nights alone together, where people would come in just to see them argue. Later Lena found out that a couple of the regulars were making bets on who would start something first. And yeah, sure, they bickered—Lena didn't let Marna get away with her usual lazy shit—but it was blown way out of proportion. In fact, Lena had gone over to Marna's a few times for drinks and even had a copy of her apartment key—though that was because Marna kept locking herself out. Her space-cadet husband—*ex*-husband—slept through anything, and before they made the key, Marna kept crashing at Lena's. Would get up in the middle of the night and eat all of Lena's good food.

When Keith came to the bar for drinks, Lena said, "*You* should know where she snuck off to, wanna clue the rest of us in?" He didn't react, just kept moving. You could tease Keith about almost anything, but not about his crush on Marna. Frankly, it was getting hard to take. Like that cartoon where one character is starving and imagines the other as a juicy pork chop. Get a grip, Lena thought, lighting a cigarette.

Touchdown.

"Wipeout!" someone yelled.

Lena watched Denny work, watched the tendons shift in his neck.

He looked up. "Don't you have tables?"

"Yeah, I do, but the funny thing is, it's a little hard for me to take care of my tables without my *drinks*. Is that asking too much? Let me know if it is, really, please do. I'd be happy to take off and pull a Marna on all your asses." She blew out smoke. "Our rookie can take my tables. *She* seems to be getting her drinks." Sure enough, there she was—in the middle of the room holding what was probably that same Bass pitcher, standing still. "Freakin' lost kid at the mall," Lena muttered.

Denny smiled at that. She was pretty sure she caught a smile.

Thirty-four left her an excellent tip. Thirty on an eighty-dollar tab. And they were girls. And they hadn't been drunk. That could mean only one thing: restaurant workers. Lena wished she'd figured it out earlier. She would've comped them a round or two. The Almost Home usually got the staff from the Congo Cafe down the street, known for their big pastel drinks with plastic animals floating inside—and even more for the time a customer choked on a rhino. And there was the gang from Michael's, where you could pay ten bucks, easy, for a crummy martini. Michael's staff was okay, though. Lena had dated one of the bartenders for a while. He was arrogant and had bad breath, but she missed him for a long time after they broke up, maybe still missed him a little, on slow Wednesday nights, when he used to come in.

Tables were no less packed and the kitchen was still hopelessly behind—what else was new—but people weren't ordering much anymore. Check totals were low. The Broncos were killing the Falcons and people were bored. Even Denny, Lena could tell, was bored, though he would never admit it. Well, he wouldn't be bored soon. A group of thirty was coming in. On top of all this. And not even for the game. Singles. They took over the place, table-hopped, and then expected you to remember who they were. Lena hated waiting on them even on slow nights. Lousy tips and loud cologne. Ugly sweaters. It all gave her the feeling of a damp Sunday. Which, actually, it was.

At least the Singles only came in once every couple months—at least they weren't *regular* regulars, who were more than enough as is—who were the reason Lena'd quit taking bar shifts in the first place. On tables, you weren't trapped, forced to take the same blather day in and day out. And the questions. *Hey, Lena, how's Denny and that cute little girlfriend of his?*—right in front of him, just to see if she would rattle. Whoever said that a bartender was like a psychiatrist had it all wrong. Customers didn't want to come in and talk about their problems. They wanted to talk about *your* problems.

When she wasn't delivering food to tables, JJ followed Colleen and tried to catch what she was saying. "Those are tables 1 through 10," Colleen instructed, pointing, "and 11 through 20—that one's 88, no reason, just is. . . ." She showed JJ little tricks, like how to calm people down when they got the wrong order and how to clean off the tops of the steak sauces with one twist of a cocktail napkin.

"Right. Oh, I see. That makes sense." Every so often it occurred to JJ that she wasn't actually absorbing anything. Each new fact engulfed and swept away the one that came before.

It was possible she was still a tiny bit high. Things were definitely different.

She was relieved when Colleen asked Keith to start her on paperwork. A chance to sit down at a desk, drink a soda. The office was just past the last bar stool—the bar stool where she'd sat waiting for Denny. Denny. Denny *looked* like a bartender, JJ thought now, as Keith pulled forms from a file cabinet and told her some helpful hints—Denny looked exactly how she'd always imagined a bartender to be, with deep-set eyes and the kind of dark hair gray could slip into with some degree of character. That's how her mother would put it, JJ realized, *some degree of character.* She stared at the forms and tapped out a sonata on her thigh. It was hard to concentrate. The office was small and hot and the desk was strewn with papers and overfull ashtrays. On the wall, hanging straight in front of JJ, was a calendar open to a topless woman drinking a bottle of beer. The woman's nipples were like huge pink eyes.

"Always use the long spoons for iced tea," Keith was saying.

JJ filled in form after form, feeling more permanent with every line. It occurred to her that she didn't need to write anything down she didn't want to. She could leave stuff out. It wasn't as though the Almost Home Bar and Grill in Denver was going to dig up info on the Cincinnati dog-wash job she'd quit after one week. Or the record-store job, which had required a lot more knowledge than you'd think. Or the nanny job—the nanny job, that too, gone. Easy. Clean slate. JJ pressed the ink into words and numbers. The paper was fresh and smooth with slight waves—you could almost see it coming out of the factory machine, being sliced off.

By the time JJ was down to college work-study and a fictitious stint at an inner-city library, Colleen reappeared and sent her into the kitchen to check on an order of garlic bread.

Lena was there, yelling at the cooks, "Where are my fucking orders? Is every single one of you on crack?" They didn't even look up, just continued burger-flipping and pouring oil and pulling things out of a see-through refrigerator. Their aprons were dirty, their faces wet. A tinny polka from a radio rose and fell beneath the crackle of the grill and the churn of washing dishes. It made JJ want to dance, almost. "It's my ass on the line out there," Lena spat. "My *culó*." She grabbed a few plates of food from a silver counter full of them and was off. Roll of eye, swish of hair.

JJ stared at the counter. Its surface was hot, lit by yellow lights, and it was scattered with stray french fries and onion rings and wilted bits of lettuce.

"Hey," one of the guys called. He waved a spatula. "¿Como estas?"

"Je parle français," she said, in a daze, though she didn't, not since high school. Then came to. "Garlic bread? Colleen's?"

He pointed to a plate straight in front of her. Melted butter, slivers of basil. Her stomach gave a pull.

"Thanks," she said.

"You like?" he asked, almost shyly.

"Garlic bread? Sure."

He waved her off. "Half hour," he said. "Just for you."

"Oh no, but you're busy, and besides, this is my first day—"

"Yeah, yeah. Just don't show the—" and he said something in Spanish that didn't sound very nice, and they both laughed.

JJ hurried off with the plate. She concentrated on the hot not hurting, pretended she was one of those people who walked on lit coals. She tried to remember if she'd fed Norman before she left for work. A guy she'd known in college had given Norman to her. Thank you so much, she'd said and wet her lips in case the guy was about to kiss her. They were alone in his room. She had liked him for a whole semester and thought, Isn't that how it goes, that he would decide to like me back right before I leave? But he didn't like her, as it turned out—not like that—and the frog hadn't been meant as a gift either. *He'd* gotten it as a gift and didn't want it anymore.

Right now, Norman's plastic cube was sitting on her dresser, the only piece of furniture that had come with her boardinghouse room other than the bed. Every morning, she dropped a pellet of food through a tiny hole at the top of the cube. For a while she was giving him two, since it was clearly the highlight of his day—the only time he swam up from the bottom—but the instruction booklet said just one, was very clear about the matter. It also said not to worry about having only one frog per cube. It said, *These frogs do not get lonely.*

College guys, JJ thought. And just *college.* If only she could delete that too. Changing majors, all that indecision. And before, even—no, *especially* before. Everything leading up. Years of piano lessons and music camp and music theory. Certainly that one day, at the end of her junior year, when a professor finally bothered to take her aside and tell her that—*oh by the way*—she didn't have the tiniest chance at a future as a concert pianist.

(Not even in the smaller halls? JJ had asked. Not even with some extra work? You try real hard, the professor had said, touching JJ's arm, leaving a few fingertip dots of chalk dust on her sweater.)

The garlic bread was up and JJ slipped away and ate it in the bathroom. She hid in a stall. Wet toilet paper all over, that sweet dead-flower smell. She sat fully clothed on the closed toilet seat, the plate on her knees. The bread was warm and oily. The best garlic bread she'd ever had. She imagined that any second someone, Lena probably, would slam open the flimsy stall and let her have it. *How dare you.* Or worse, laughter: *You pig.* JJ ate faster, licking the grease off her fingers. And then, still a little high maybe, she imagined Marna walking in, the one who'd disappeared. With her own garlic bread. Surprised at first. JJ had only caught a glimpse of her before—mass of wavy hair, rumpled shirt—so she filled in the blanks. She gave her dark eyes and a beauty mark. A long delicate nose. Maybe a piercing or a small tattoo. A daisy just below her collarbone. No, not a daisy, something more original—a daffodil or snapdragon. Suddenly, she seemed so clear.

4.

If Colleen believed in ghosts, it was only from the corners of her eyes. More and more lately, usually here and usually on game days, when people were packed in so close the air was wet and you could smell much more than you wanted to, she saw him. Just for a second. Not long enough to actually prove anything and always when she was focused on something else—her tickets or her tray or taking an order. But it was him. Unmistakable him. He'd be squashed in at a corner table, too close to the big screen, his hair leeched back in strips over the thinning spots. Both hands on a beer. Even crazier: she sometimes saw herself. And Lily too. It was like a home movie. Lily, a little girl again, scribbling on the back of a paper kids' menu. Her crayon making loops.

Rick had died two years ago, hit by a car. At first it didn't seem possible, and then it didn't seem real. A bad joke. He was crossing the street on his lunch break, paying too much attention to the sandwich he was unwrapping. He stepped right into the line of traffic.

He was there and then he was gone.

It happened the week Lily turned twelve. That afternoon, in fact, when the news had come, Lily'd been planning her party theme, the Garden of Eden, and was on the kitchen floor making flowers out of colored Kleenex. Colleen was in the back yard painting at her easel—or trying to paint. There were two versions in Colleen's memory. In one, the colors weren't right, too thick and bright, and she kept mashing them brown. In the other, though, the picture was working. She captured the back yard not as it was but as it would be when the landscaping was finished. She was filling in the shrubs, giving just enough suggestion of cloud and bird and light.

Afterward, after the funeral and the reception and those first few weeks when Lily stayed home from school and the two of them lay on the living room floor without talking, just watching TV, Colleen looked for that painting. She couldn't imagine what she'd done with it. She checked the house and the back yard, even the bushes. But it was gone—the painting and that patch of time marked by one phone call, the space between event and after.

The driver of the car kept in touch with them for months, called them, Lily especially, until Lily's school psychologist insisted that it was unhealthy, that the man had been seen on school grounds. Lily, she said, was having inappropriate feelings. The psychologist was a pretty woman, one of those soft Southern types, who seemed, with every sentence, exuberant, like she was up for a game of tennis. As Colleen watched her lips move around the words *inappropriate feelings,* she couldn't help but wonder why, clearly given the choice, this woman would want to think about other people's problems all day.

Rick used to take Colleen to the Almost Home all the time, especially during football season, and so once things were settled—and after she quit her job as a respiratory therapist—it seemed natural to get

36

a job there. It seemed more natural than to stop going. Plus, after working in a hospital for ten-odd years, waiting tables seemed fun, a little romantic even. Tons of artists were waiters. Not just actors, but all kinds of artists. Theoretically, she'd have more time to paint.

Maybe, though, it'd been a mistake. He wouldn't go away.

Colleen did her best with damage control. The kitchen was a mess—bus tubs and trash overflowing. Everything felt sticky. Someone had spilled ketchup and it was everywhere, on the bar, smeared on the sides of the garnish tray, on what was left of the clean silverware. Colleen made the effort to get things done and done right, but, even more, she tried not to think about it.

There was a beautiful girl in her section, over at one of the fraternity-sorority tables. She sat in an elegant slouch swirling a Jack and Coke. Her hair was long and dark red and loose and she wore what all the girls were wearing: black boots, low-waisted thrift-store jeans, and an eighty-dollar white t-shirt with a cashmere cardigan looped around the neck. Even though it was freezing outside and you could see the gooseflesh on their arms when they came in, they kept the sweaters there. Like artificial hugs. This girl was more beautiful that the rest. Her skin had a Mediterranean tint and her eyes were sloped and serious, but with a spark. The kind that couldn't be faked. Colleen hated when beautiful girls sat in her section. It was distracting. She wanted to stare at them; she wanted to see how they moved, find out what it was that made them so. As it turned out, the beautiful ones weren't always the prettiest—this girl's chin was too long, her forehead too wide—and it went the other way too. Lena, for instance, was pretty, really pretty. But she wasn't beautiful. When they'd first met and become friends, Colleen had spent a good deal of time wondering why Lena wasn't beautiful, trying to catch her from different sides. And Marna? Maybe. It was hard to define. She was *watchable,* the way she would sit beside the cash register, one foot propped on the sink, the other on the bar itself. She'd laugh, completely at ease, chomping her blue gum, not caring if anyone was looking up her nose or down her blouse—which they probably were. Not caring if she made a scene. Which she did and didn't at the same time. And the thing with watching Marna was, it was never a separate event. You actually felt it, even if she was talking to someone else, not even looking in your direction—it was like she reflected something back, automatically.

Now, Lily was beautiful. Her long-limbed ease. How she moved through space, cutting it at any angle, unafraid of taking up too much of it. And her quick-change expressions, each a surprise. Colleen didn't know where she'd gotten that. One minute she'd be considering you, really looking hard, and the next, in just a twitch of the mouth or chin or eye, it was all different. She'd gathered light, softened or brightened, gone somewhere else and back again. It was like you could peel away layer after layer and still find more. Beauty under beauty. Of course, Colleen was biased. But still.

Colleen wasn't allowed to have Lily at the bar during her shifts anymore—Bill said it was bad for business and probably illegal besides. But then he lightened up a bit, as he always did, and hinted that he wouldn't really care if Lily came in late at night, around last call, when people were too far gone, either literally or figuratively, to complain.

Fourteen going on fifteen was way too old for a babysitter—many girls Lily's age were babysitters themselves. But Lily was a different case. She'd recently discovered boys and recently decided to be aggressive about it. Colleen couldn't leave her alone, not for hours at a time, so on nights Marna was working and couldn't have Lily over her place, Colleen paid one of Lily's twenty-something cousins to keep an eye.

Beth would drop Lily here later. One-thirty or two. It was something to look forward to, anyway. And not just because Colleen wouldn't have to pay Beth any longer, and not just because Colleen plain missed Lily, but also because the visions didn't appear when Lily was around—as if her presence in the present was so powerful it crowded out the past.

Colleen ran down to the break room. She didn't have the time but she did it anyhow, clomped down the stairs carrying table 16's drinks. It was pointless really: if Marna had gone home, she wouldn't pick up. But Colleen dialed the number—what else was there to do? The voice mail came on and Marna's voice played. Then:

Beep.

"Hi, it's Colleen. We were wondering where you were, and you know . . . if you could give us a call. The thing is, we're slammed here, I mean, seriously, Marna, and we're not sure why you walked off and all. If it's something . . . if there's something I can do . . . something . . . you know I'm here for you. . . . Anyway—"

Beep.

"—call us," she finished into air.

She replaced the receiver in its cradle and stood there. Noise and movement thumped above. Nine tables wondered where their waitress was. Food was getting cold, drinks warm—everything meeting in the middle and waiting. Colleen stood still. She had to go back up, but she didn't move. She stayed put and felt the moment stretch out.

It was more of a large closet than an actual break room. You could tell it was meant to store jackets and personal items, but Bill had managed to squeeze in a table, a few broken chairs, and a filthy love seat so familiar they all sat on it anyway. Above the love seat, in purple marker, someone had scrawled: *Drink the water.* The back wall was lined with lockers. Most were empty and the rest had been claimed informally by the wait and bar staff. Colleen hated being down here alone. It made her nervous ever since the time, maybe a year ago, she'd gone through all the lockers. It was past close and everyone else was hanging out upstairs in the almost-dark at table 14, as they often did, hiding from the front doors because it was illegal to be drinking after hours. Colleen had excused herself to fix a contact lens and found herself down here, facing the lockers, then opening them, one by one. Any minute, she'd expected, someone would appear for a jacket or a pack of cigarettes. But no one did, so she rifled through the lockers and took things, slipped them into her pockets and handbag. A crumpled baseball card, some lip balm, a flowered notepad, three coupons for amusement-park discount, a stand-up comedy cassette tape. Just odds and ends, nothing important—or at least she hadn't thought so at the time. She did it for no reason at all, none of it was stuff she wanted. She just did it. A throwback, maybe, to her shoplifting college days. And no one had missed anything until Lena, of course Lena, threw hell because the baseball card had belonged to her grandfather and gave her luck. A lucky baseball card. Go figure. Well, Bill had sat them all down and everyone of course denied it—Colleen herself was so caught up in the uproar that even she grew indignant. How could someone do such a thing? Trust and camaraderie and all. She and Lena went out for beers that night and tried to guess who it might have been.

It still made her nervous to be here. Partly—and Colleen knew this was irrational—she was worried that someone might suspect something, just like how in stores she still found herself being overly clear that she wasn't taking anything, putting things down with crisp, exaggerated gestures.

She opened her own locker and found the vial of lorazepam in her purse, poured the pills into her hand, all of them, a pile of white. You heard all the time about people OD'ing on pills, swallowing whole bottles. How did they get them down? She had enough problems with one or two. Or three, the number she kept in her palm, emptying the rest back in. She choked them down with a few gulps of Cape Cod off her tray—she'd get Lena to pour another—and shuddered. She wasn't a drinker. She liked the idea of drinks—ice, color, garnish—but not the actuality. Not the taste.

Colleen felt her stomach relax. She dialed the number again and listened to the rings, one after the other, imagined them filling Marna's apartment, bouncing off the jumbled furniture, the colored walls. Lily was wanting to do her own bedroom in dark purple now, just like Marna's. Or midnight blue, like Marna's pantry. In Colleen's opinion, Marna's apartment seemed dark and unwelcoming, though at night it did brighten dramatically, the lamps throwing starbursts, changing the bloody reds and murky teals and purples into softer, jewel-toned versions of themselves. Glowing almost, like they were lit from within. If nothing else, the place was *interesting*. All that junk—real junk, not just a manner of speaking—Marna made it work. If Colleen dragged a chair in from the curb, it was just that, a chair from the curb. But with Marna, the same chair was something. It was funky, it fit in with the rest: the spool tables and beaded candle holders, the African mask, the wall she'd covered with the backs of cereal boxes. A zillion lamps. One was shaped like a hula dancer, with hips that moved back and forth. Even that. It all became décor.

For the first time it occurred to Colleen: What if there was a problem? What if Marna was not okay?

But it was *Marna*. Already things were chemically softened. Newly single, crazy, crazy Marna—who'd driven six hours for breakfast at a

Wyoming diner last month because she'd heard they made really good French toast. . . . Lily was still talking about that one, Lily loved that one. She wanted Marna to take her next time. Lily, Colleen thought. Four more hours. Just thinking about her daughter gave Colleen a sense of peace. Unlike Marna, unlike Rick, and unlike anyone else in the whole world, no matter what, Lily was someone who would be there. Colleen had her daughter. It was fact.

Beep.

"Oh," said Colleen, forgetting for a moment what she was doing. "I'm—I'm here," she said into the phone and hung up.

5.

The way Denny saw it, there were two kinds of Broncos fans: the real kind and the idiots. There were the loyal ones—who stuck through the rough times, the lean seasons, the *early '80s*—and the bandwagon phonies who made a big fucking fuss when things were going good, popping up out of nowhere for the playoffs, filling the bars, buying all the gear and shit, the blue-and-orange license-plate frames. *Broncos baby strollers.* Acted like just because they'd moved here last July and had a Denver *zip code* now, that gave them some right, some *entitlement* to the glory pie—and yet when you pressed them, they didn't understand jack about the team. If Denny only had a dollar for every genius who sat at his bar and tried to tell him why it was Atwater and not Elway who should retire, or the *real* reason Elway was or was not going to hang up his cleats—Denny'd heard everything from coke addiction to turf toe. Fuck. *Fuck Elway.* Let him retire. Fuck him. Sure, he was great, a big talent and big star—*media candy*—but the

Broncos were a team, not one lousy guy. They had Terrell and Sharpe, Atwater and Romo. McCaffery. *Takes a lickin' and keeps on tickin'.* As long as they had him at the reins, as long as they had Shanahan—the Mastermind, the Rat, the Svengali of all things offense—the Broncos would be right back in the mix next year. And the year after that and the year after that. In fact, Denny was *hoping* Elway would retire. He was counting on it.

But most of all, he was pissed. Having to watch the game while he worked, it sucked bad.

Especially after last year.

He'd been looking forward to last year's game for months—no, for his whole life—and planned to make a real day of it with Steph, who was also a true fan. It was one of the things Denny loved about her, the way she'd really watch and care about the plays, not act like being a girl was a reason to bow out, to play dumb. Neither of them worked Sundays back then, and they'd considered for a long time what would be the best way to celebrate. They thought about having a party—but then people would be loud, blocking the TV, and someone, Steph pointed out, always got sick. They thought about going to a party, but that would be worse. You didn't have control over the volume that way, or the *channel*—once Denny'd been to a Bowl party where they kept switching during the commercials and forgetting to switch back in time. Christ. But staying home seemed a little lame. So, finally, they decided to go to the Marriott Damon's, where Steph used to work. Everyone liked Steph over there and Denny was still pretty good friends with Barry, one of the managers, who promised them a good table and said he'd maybe sit down with them and buy a few pitchers. What could be better? Denny had figured. Broncos. Big screens. Beer.

(*Steph,* he thought now.)

Not even two weeks before game day, Denny had come home from work—dead-ass tired, feeling like he did now, not in the mood for anything but maybe a bong hit and bed—to find a note from Steph. Two notes. One that she was out with her girlfriends so he was on his own for dinner blah blah blah. And the other. On a napkin: *Your dad, January 25–26.* That's all she'd written. Denny read it twice, three times. He tried to think of things it could mean—anything other than what it said.

Four hours later, he was up waiting in the La-Z-Boy. He'd tried to go to bed, but it was useless, like he'd downed a couple pots of coffee. Did you think I could sleep after getting that note? he asked when she finally opened the door—when, surprised to see him, she gave a high-pitched *oop* and said, Hey cowboy, lookin' to get some?

Note? She dropped her purse by the door and shook off her coat, let it fall on the couch. She kicked off her shoes, then tripped over them. Then tripped over the dog. Giggled. Said, Oh god, you should have seen Cheryl tonight. Do we have anything to eat?

Denny took a deep breath. Very slowly, he said, Why is my father coming to visit the weekend of the Super Bowl?

Oh *that* note. Whatdya mean why? To visit.

Yeah, I got that part.

Well, now I finally get to meet him, right? We can still watch the game. She sat down beside him, on the arm of the La-Z-Boy, and touched his shoulder. Like this was a *moment.* She'd spilled something on her blouse. It formed a pink island over her left boob.

Denny stood up and snapped off the TV. Sure, he told Steph, maybe we'll get scripture at halftime. Sounds like loads of fun.

Is it that big a deal?

Yes, Steph, yes it is.

Okay, she said. But it's your father. What was I supposed to say?

How about no. Or, *No.* Or, Not a good weekend. Or, Super Bowl Sunday, for crying out loud. Or, Broncos. The only day in the whole year that fucking matters. Or, Christ, Steph, don't pick up the phone, let the machine get it, like a normal person.

So call him back. She got up and drifted into the kitchen, like that was the end of that—like *too bad for you*—and got a jar of peanut butter out of the cupboard, started eating it, pulling out big chunks with her thumb and index finger. A glob of it fell and stuck on the island—*you are here,* he thought—but she didn't pick it off. She just kept eating, shoveling it in. Typical. She'd go on these ridiculous diets, vegetable juice and boiled liver and shit, and complain about her thighs, *oh I'm so fat,* and then she'd get a few drinks in her and what would she do but chow down on everything in sight.

That's some great advice, he said. Thank you, Miss Oh-so-sensitive-expert. Thank you, Dr. Dear Abby. And he grabbed the jar from her hand, pulled it away mid-dig, so that she almost stumbled backwards.

Denny didn't call his father back the next morning. Or the morning after that. Or that. Last time Denny'd seen his father was at least five years ago, when his father was still living off his mother's poultry farm, letting her take care of everything, the farm, the bills. The house could go up in flames and his father would be rationing out the words. Please. Help. House. Fire.

His *mother* visiting—now, that would be okay. Denny talked to her on the phone pretty regularly. She liked to call and check in, and a few times a year he made the seven-hour drive back to the farm. She hadn't remarried yet or even done much dating—which surprised Denny. When he first heard that she'd finally kicked out the old man, Denny'd pictured her having some fun, getting into that line-dancing or square-dancing shit, wearing a checkerboard shirt, maybe a hat.

His mother would have been one thing. But his father. As if they'd have anything to say to one another. Plus, Super Bowl or no Super Bowl, now that Denny had moved in with Steph, it wasn't just a matter of his father visiting him. He would be visiting *them.* How could that conversation have gone? What had his father said when Steph answered the phone? Denny tried to push her on it, but she was still sore about the peanut butter. About the way he'd acted.

Sorry, he said. Then again, like he meant it: Sorry.

Sometimes, she said, I don't think I know you, Denny. She had that look going, deliberate and cow-eyed, like something she'd practiced in the mirror.

You know me, he said. How do you not know me?

Well for one, I don't know anything about your father.

My father. My father gives a shit about himself, and Jesus Christ, and—wait, who else? Oh yeah, no one. So, there, now you know.

Two days before his father's arrival, she started cleaning. She dusted the molding, took everything out of the cabinets, reorganized the closets, emptied out the junk drawers. There were piles of papers and garbage everywhere. Don't touch any of it, Steph warned. I have a system. Her head was wrapped in a pair of pantyhose, her hair jutting out in places, sticking to her cheeks in little curls. She was sweating.

Denny said, I don't think he's going to check the refrigerator drip pan.

I just want the place to be clean.

It is clean.

But really clean. Parent-clean.

Listen, Steph, I have some news for you. It's not the *apartment's* cleanliness he's going to be concerned with.

But she kept going around with the Lysol, the dusting cloths. She set up their bedroom for him, put out towels and a matching wash-cloth she'd bought special. Apparently, Denny and her'd be sleeping on the fold-out bed in the front room. She even made a sausage lasa-gna, from a recipe, frying the meat, chopping onions, getting it set to cook, baking it halfway.

This looks good, Denny admitted, poking at the crust along the edge.

She pointed a red-tipped spoon at him. Don't you dare.

Hey. He wrapped his arms around her and kissed her neck, which smelled like soap and garlic. Could you take a chill, baby? Eat a Valium?

It was like the pope was coming or something.

John fucking Elway or something.

The dog skittered around their feet, snuffling, poking its nose up pant legs as Denny did the introductions.

Oh wonderful, Steph kept saying. She touched his father's arm. Look, she said, pointing to the dog. She loves you.

His father made a halfhearted, stiff move to pet the dog and missed, stroked air. Said, We have a Stephanie at our church. Stephanie Saun-ders. Same color hair as you.

How funny, Steph chirped. Isn't that funny, she said to Denny.

For crying out loud, Denny thought. At dinner he wanted to pass her a note. *Quit the production.* She kept chattering. About everything.

The cold. The hot. How the Denver airport is supposed to look like a mountain range, but really it looks like a banana-cream pie.

His father ate quietly, nodding steadily in agreement.

Denny, Steph said, tell your dad about that funny thing that just happened. The truck breaking down.

What funny thing.

You know, when you were stranded and ended up sleeping in some old lookout tower.

Fire tower. That was months ago.

Got lost? his father asked. That's from me, no sense of direction. You got that from me. Can't find my way out of a paper bag.

Steph laughed. You should've seen him, in the morning. With splinters all in his jeans, all the way through. Do you remember all those splinters, Denny? Awful.

I wasn't lost. And it was months ago. And it wasn't that awful. He muttered, You seem to be enjoying it.

Steph studied him for a moment, then turned to his father. You should've seen him, she said again.

His father nodded. So where you working these days, Denny?

Denny paused. Thought, Where are *you* working. His mother was sending checks. She said she wasn't but Denny was pretty sure she was. He said, Same place.

Oh yeah? That's good.

Right. It's a job.

His father paused. Then asked Steph, Mind if I have another helping?

Too much basil, Steph said, beaming, as she passed his father's plate back. I always forget how much is the right amount and then it ends up being too much or so little you can't even tell.

49

Denny got up, went to the kitchen, came back with a beer. He sat down and popped the top. Anyone else want one? Or some shots? Anyone ready for shots?

Steph frowned. Well, she said, glaring at Denny. Anyway.

So about this game, Denny's father said.

It's tomorrow, Denny said, taking a drink. Sunday.

Morning or night?

Steph said, Afternoon.

His father said, Well, that works.

Denny watched him mop his plate with a chunk of bread, watched his face, his dark pores, his short nose, his thin mouth, which, when relaxed, fell loose into a sneer. Now it was in a sort of half smile Denny didn't recognize—like his father was trying them on, new expressions.

In the morning, Steph got up early to cook a fancy breakfast and while she and his father stood in the kitchen polishing off the last of it, discussing Jack Russell terriers, some BS about dog shows, Denny went into the bedroom and closed the door.

His father's flannel pajamas were folded on the pillow, his cracked leather duffel on the floor beside the bed. Denny stood there for a minute. Now the whole room smelled like his father. He slid open the bottom dresser drawer and felt underneath the t-shirts for the wooden box, sat down with it on the bed. He took out his pipe and ziplock of weed and packed a bowl, a good one, then lit it, pushed aside the pajamas and lay back, blew smoke at the ceiling. The pipe was Jamaican, a gift from James, a regular who went to Jamaica every year. He stayed in Negril, the cool part, not the touristy shit in Montego Bay. One of these years Denny was going to go with him. He was invited, James had said, anytime. The pipe was black wood, carved into a man. His mouth was the bowl. It made him look surprised. Every hit, a surprise.

Denny got up and turned on the TV that was beside the bed. It was a shitty set, a little black-and-white number. Denny wanted to move the living room one in here and get a big screen. But Steph refused. She wouldn't throw this one away because it was the first thing she'd bought as an adult. That was so like her, to get sentimental over something like a TV. Piece of crap. The picture was all grainy and it had an on-and-off vertical hold problem—every time something important was showing, it seemed. Like now, the early news was talking about the game. The local sports guy was saying how two weeks' rest prior to the Bowl seemed to favor the Packers because they were more banged up, but his voice kept popping and his face kept traveling up. Denny smacked the side a few times, which only made it worse, so he turned it off. Seven more hours to kickoff.

Steph swung open the door and snapped it shut behind her. I can *smell* it, she hissed. She was still in her bathrobe, but she'd already put on makeup, Denny noticed.

He shrugged, took another hit.

Denny.

He doesn't know the smell. And so what if he does?

You could at least wait until he goes to church.

I'll smoke now. I'll smoke when he's in church. I'll smoke all day if I feel like it.

She said, The door was unlocked, he could've walked right in.

This is my place, not his.

It's *our* place. She gave him the cow look. She said, I'm alone out there.

So stay in here. He blew a line of smoke, made it as long and thin as he could, watched it go fuzzy and dissolve into air.

Denny. I can't just leave him out there.

You're getting along famously.

She fiddled with a dresser pull. You know what? You thought he wouldn't accept or respect me, but I think he does, Denny. And the two of us, you know, as a couple. I think he thinks we're good together, I really do. The dresser pull came off in her hand, and she slipped it into her robe pocket, like a guilty kid.

Denny stared at the ceiling. The paint swirls were like waves. Jamaica, he thought. He'd work some extra shifts and go to Jamaica, maybe walk around the edge of the island, backpack around the whole thing, meet people, smoke some good bud—not the dried shit he was getting from Spencer lately, all seedy. And James wasn't all that bad, he could hang with James—hell, he could hang with anyone in Jamaica, on the beach, with the sun and crazy-blue sky and that bright white sand. An ice bucket of tallboys. Marna was always saying she might come too. Denny watched the paint waves and decided he'd tell James first thing on Monday.

Steph, he said then, we're going to Damon's.

But we can't.

It's the Super Bowl. We made plans and I'm not staying home.

He's your *father*. He's *visiting*.

So, he said, coughing out a hit. So fine. He's welcome to come.

6.

"*I don't know,*" the man said, licking his lips. "What do I feel like?" His bald spot flashed blue, then yellow from the TVs.

"Superburger?" JJ suggested.

"Nope."

"Grilled cheese?" That was what *she* felt like. Right now, with a slice of tomato melted in the middle. And fries. And more of that garlic bread. Things had calmed down a little, enough to notice that she was hungry again. She was surprised to find it was already a quarter to ten.

"Had it for lunch."

"Salad?"

He made a face.

"Well," JJ said, forcing a smile, "I could come back."

"No, no, don't leave, hold on, I'm sure I know."

Table 2 had ordered drinks and JJ needed to enter them into the computer. She'd scribbled them down somewhere so she wouldn't forget. Without turning away from the man—who was tracing a fat finger across the menu, item by item, as if it were a book—JJ flipped through her order pad, read it with peripheral vision. A vodka and apple juice. Could that be right?

"I know what I want," the woman beside the man said. She was wearing blue lipstick and orange face paint. Game spirit, JJ knew, but it was still a little alarming. Especially the mouth, all dark and cracking. The girl with them, presumably their daughter, also wore the face paint—though she'd blended it a bit, so it looked almost fashionable. Both mother and daughter sported pastel turtlenecks and Broncos earrings—dangling minimegaphones. The mother thwapped the menu with the back of her hand. "I know exactly what I want, but it's not here."

The daughter rolled her eyes. "O-kay," she said and turned to JJ. "I'll have a turkey club but no cheese if it's that nasty orange stuff and I only want a little onion and only if it's red."

"Becky, onions give you gas."

"Onions give *you* gas."

"They do give me gas."

JJ chewed the end of her pen. "I could come back. . . ."

"Well, hell, it's a holiday. I'll have one of those sandwiches," the mother said, "only give me wheat bread and extra cheese, and do I want turkey or ham?"

"It's not a *holiday*," Becky said.

"Ham. And to drink, just a club soda with extra lime. Maybe a shot of vodka. A good kind. What's a good kind? Ketel One." She spoke fast. JJ heard, "cuddle one." She wrote down *good shot.*

"I'll have a beer," Becky said and licked her lips.

"A what?"

"A Michelob Light. With a chilled glass."

"Uh, are you old enough?"

"Yeah."

"We're her *parents,*" the woman said.

"Well," said the father, clearing his throat. "I've decided."

JJ waited, pen over paper.

He gave a slow smile. "I've decided I want you to decide. Surprise me," he said and reached up behind JJ—at an angle that probably no one else saw—and patted her ass, gave it a firm rub. "Set me up good," he said.

Things were beginning to slow down. Colleen liked having time to dote on the odds-and-ends people who always chose her section. They weren't so bad. True, they tended to linger, making unusual requests— and true, they weren't the best tippers. But some of them were. Hoff left fifties on full moons and India tipped in home-grown joints when she had them, and the rest were patient. They waited when she was busy. And, unlike at the bar, they didn't expect you to memorize their histories, they didn't quiz you on their stories. There were two kinds of regular customers, Colleen had learned in her couple years working here: the ones who came out for attention, and the ones who—odd as it sounded—came out to avoid it. Colleen understood that, the soli- tude you could sometimes find in a crowd. Lena didn't understand it. She always complained about that second kind of customer. It's like we're *inconveniencing* them by taking their goddamn order, she would say, and made them wait extra long. But Colleen didn't mind. Really, it wasn't so hard. You just needed your little routines, something brief but your own to breeze by with to make them comfortable. There was one guy—Colleen didn't know his name and it was way too late to ask—who sat at the back four-top and made a quacking noise every time he ordered a beer—and, every time, Colleen would shake her head and smile. It was apparently some reference she was supposed to get from an earlier conversation. Or maybe it wasn't a reference, maybe the guy was just quacking.

She brought Fred his popcorn and Tabasco and soda water, she refilled the Corli sisters' teas and told them that no, the game wasn't quite over and yes, kids today were having way too much sex. The hairdressers were fixing to leave, some of them rising now, downing the last of their whatevers and tonics, collecting the little furry lunch boxes they carried as handbags. "Bye, hon," they called to Colleen and she blew them kisses, like they expected.

When she set down India's second half carafe of burgundy, India said, "Join me, why don't you?" She'd nabbed her usual table, 43, the two-top by the front, away from the TVs, and set up her row of candles and porcelain figurines. She even had a miniature crystal ball—though it was just decoration. Colleen had never seen her use it.

"I can't sit now."

"Just for a second," India said.

"We still have a crowd."

"Sit."

Colleen sat. Not a break, just a pause. She propped herself up by her elbows and rubbed her face. Her hands smelled like restaurant. She took a drag off India's cigarette, then watched India take one herself.

"Tastes like mice," India said and closed her eyes, the smoke looping from her lips. She looked thinner than usual, Colleen thought, though that was impossible—she'd just seen her yesterday. Maybe it was all those gypsy scarves. Or maybe it was her hair, tangled, puffed up from underneath, the dye looking recent and too dark. Or maybe India'd just gotten older. It had to happen sometime. In increments.

Leaps through time. Colleen had no idea how old India actually was. It was hard to tell what was *tired* and what was *age*.

"So Marna's gone," India said.

"Apparently."

"Like that, off and gone."

"Yup."

"She doesn't feel gone."

"No." No one ever does, Colleen thought.

"Have a drink," India said. "Please."

Colleen poured a little wine into India's empty water glass and took a swallow. The wine was cheap and vinegary, though better after another sip. There was something romantic, Colleen thought, about red wine, even cheap red wine. The candles helped, flickering and such. They smelled like vanilla. Colleen finger-traced a coin in the table top. The tables were coated with a thick layer of shellac—you could see how it had been poured, like syrup, the edges permanently dripping. Various bits of memorabilia and old junk were frozen beneath its surface, made more important by the display. Random stuff, probably from Bill's home junk drawers: spare change, game stubs, an old college ID card someone had probably forgotten decades ago. The ID had faded, the boy was from another time. Fuzzy hair, orange background.

India took a drink right out of the carafe, held it lightly with her fingertips. "I think I've stopped having dreams," she said. A few drops of wine spilled from her lips. One landed on a purple edge of scarf and beaded there, shivered for a slow moment, like dew on a nature show, only the colors and textures all wrong.

"They'll come back, I'm sure." The Singles were waving for Colleen's attention. She pretended not to see.

"Parsley sage rosemary and thyme," India sang softly.

"I have this dream," Colleen said, picking up a porcelain duck and squeezing it. "All my life, all through my childhood, I had it and I still have it. This house. Big yard, white, two, maybe three stories if you count that small kind of attic. Nothing special, but it always comes in so clear. I can see it now."

"Dreams," India said and yawned.

"And then one day, out of nowhere, this really happened, I took a cross-country trip with a girlfriend, this is years and years ago, before Lily, and on the way, somewhere in Nebraska, I think, I saw it. Right there. We passed it, but I was sure, in that instant, it was the house. The yard, the front door, everything, I swear."

"Yes," India said. "And you told your friend to stop."

"No."

They sat there for a moment.

"They have beautiful barns in Nebraska," India said. She looked tired, as if she might fall asleep, tip right over. She lived in her car, Colleen knew, a little blue Chevy. She never talked about it, but Colleen had seen her once, parked behind Walgreen's, the door open and all kinds of pots and dishes and bedding spilling out. When Colleen waved, India had squinted and pretended she didn't see.

"I ran away once," Colleen said. India's eyes looked soft-focus, her mouth parted. Maybe she *was* sleeping, it was hard to tell. Maybe she was sitting up with her eyes open, just breathing, seeing nothing. "It was only once," Colleen said, "and I came back."

JJ rang in drinks and food. There were a million computer buttons. It didn't help to have Lena breathing down her neck, pointing, sandwiches here, beers right there.

"I got it."

"Then speed up."

"Are you ready to order?" JJ asked table 3.

They stared at her. Two guys with straight, shiny hair and a girl in an army cap and pale blue sunglasses.

"Do you want to *order?*" JJ tried again. Didn't anybody just know what they wanted? Somewhere behind her she heard, "Hey, new waitress!"

"We ate already," said the girl.

"Oh sorry."

"You cleared away our *dishes,*" the girl said, jutting her jaw. She had the kind of bad skin that could pass for ruddiness. "Can you get our real server?"

"Hey, new waitress!" The people calling to her were wearing name tags. They were drunk. They weren't watching the game, they were mostly standing around, getting in the way, laughing loudly, saying things like, "Are we there yet? Are we almost home?" One lady was sitting on the floor, using her chair as a workspace for the necklace she was making out of cherry stems.

Denny refused to give her any more cherries. "On principle alone," he told JJ, grabbing the used glasses and dumping them into the sink. "All that red dye."

"They also want more brandy Alexanders."

"I'm sure they want a lot of things." His cheeks and neck were flushed, which made his eyes look even bluer. He'd be cute, JJ thought, with better posture—though even that wasn't so bad—his slouch was lean and loose, the kind that made men seem taller than they actually were. As if, if they wanted to, they could pull themselves up as far as they liked.

She asked him, "Should I tell them they can't have any more?"

He didn't answer. He was doing a lot of things at once. JJ waited.

Caught herself tapping out "The Entertainer" on the drink mat. She stared at the funny junk behind the bar—a mini–slot machine, a vase with plastic flowers.

Denny squinted at her drink tickets. "Have you ever *been* to a bar before?"

"Pardon?"

"Your orders are fucked up."

She blinked. "Oh."

"All of 'em." He held up the stack, let them fall. "Every single one. Vodka and apple juice? Jesus. And a *seedy* Manhattan?"

"Oh. Huh."

"CC maybe? CC Manhattan? *Canadian Club?*"

"Right," JJ said, feeling her face get tight, "that's it. I don't know what I was thinking. I'm pretty sure that's it."

The people at table 18 left, and JJ tried and failed to clear off their dirty glasses and napkins before the next group sat down. "Boilermakers," they announced and pushed their elbows right into the mess.

JJ scooped up a pile of dollar bills from the center of the table and looked for Colleen, found her sitting with the customer dressed like a witch. "Here," JJ said, handing over the tip.

"Hey, thanks. JJ, are you crying?"

"No."

"We all get flustered. I was just telling my daughter that the other day—Lily, you'll get to meet her. Later she'll be in. The best thing to do, I told Lily, when you're flustered, is to count backwards, it calms you down. Instantly. It's like a drug. I know it sounds too simple to be true."

"I'm not flustered."

"That's what Lily says too." Colleen smiled. "This is India."

"Hi," JJ said. "I'm JJ."

"Parsley, sage, rosemary and thyme," the witch sang.

"How are you doing with the tables?"

"Great," JJ said. "Just fine. I should go get the drinks for 18."

"I'll tell you something," Colleen said, "to make you feel better."

"Remember me to one who lives the-ere."

Colleen said, "Okay, listen, I know this for a fact. Marna's first night waiting tables, right? Not here, like jobs and jobs earlier, in some other state. You know Marna, it's hard to keep track. Anyway, she was carrying a tray of margaritas, a big one, maybe six, eight drinks, and I'm not talking about the glasses we have here, but the ones that really open up at the top. Double, triple drinks really."

"For she-e is a good friend of mine."

Was, JJ thought. *Was* a good friend of mine.

"Anyway—you listen too, India, this is good—so she's carrying the tray and she stops to take an order or set a drink down and she drops 'em."

"No," JJ said.

"Yup." Colleen beamed. "Dumps the whole tray. On a baby."

"No!"

"Yeah. Someone's infant, not even a month old. Ice, booze, glass, everywhere."

"No," JJ breathed.

"True story. The baby wasn't cut or anything, but god, what a mess." She took a cigarette from a green pack lying on the table and lit it with a match. "And Marna's good. I mean, despite the obvious. Taking off and all. But the point is, don't give a thought to getting upset, we all lose it. Sometimes I have to run into the walk-in and count back from ten. Sometimes a hundred."

"I wasn't crying."

Colleen turned to the witch. "Nothing really you can say in a situation like that. *Sorry about your baby? Oops? Can I buy your meal?*"

The witch propped her chin on her palm and stared at JJ. "Do you think," she asked Colleen, "she looks like Marna?"

Colleen shook her head. Smiled. "Not at all." She said, "I remember when Lily was a baby. I know it's a cliché, the it-was-like-yesterday bit? But it's true."

"For she-e is a good friend of mine."

"Was," JJ said.

"What?" The witch squinted.

"*She once was* a good friend of mine. That's how the song goes. *Was.* 'Scarborough Fair.' Simon and Garfunkel."

Nobody spoke for a moment.

Then JJ said, "Really, the baby would be fine."

"The baby?" the witch asked.

JJ said, "With the drinks."

"Oh sure," Colleen said. "Just not okay to drive."

JJ said, "Babies are pretty hardy."

"JJ's a student," Colleen told the witch.

"I was, I graduated." She added, "But I was a nanny most recently." Then regretted bringing it up. Now they'd want her to explain. She got ready to say, *Oh it's a long story.* But it hit JJ that she could make it a victory. It was like the paperwork: she could extract the parts she liked. *The woman I worked for, she had me clean out the washing machine after she used it. And iron napkins! And nightgowns! Can you imagine?—and so I left without saying good-bye.*

All true, and sounded a whole lot better than:

I snuck out in the middle of the night with all my stuff crammed into Hefty bags.

But there weren't any questions. "Yeah," is what the witch said, lighting a cigarette off Colleen's, "a nanny. I can see that."

JJ felt a hand on her shoulder and she jumped.

It was blue-mouth lady, her face paint bleeding tributaries around her lips. "Our food," she said. "Everything. It's all wrong."

7.

Keith knew exactly where Marna was. He'd been trying like hell all night not to think about it. All night he focused on what was in front of him.

Drinks to 5.
Another round lemon drops,
extra cheese on the burger,
med rare, no mustard;
pitcher Bud;
four pitchers Bass.
Change for two twenties down to the nickel.

He kept moving, he ran laps. One long, continuous lap: *computer, tables, wait station, kitchen, menus, drinks, food, checks.* His body found the rhythm and he rode the rush, harnessed the buzz. It was like speed. The real kind, not the shit they sold you in gas stations—the kind that really got you up, the kind that smacked your ass good morning.

Even after they were no longer slammed and people were just waiting for the Broncos to go ahead and finish what they'd started—and Colleen and Lena had slowed down enough for cigarettes and food—Keith didn't break stride.

Keep the outside out, was how he'd explained it earlier to the new girl: Keep your money together, make sure you write everything down. Arrive early. Bar time is ten minutes ahead, so on time is late. He'd given the training speech a million times before. They were the same words, the same order, the same inflections.

Always take something with you when you go into the kitchen.

Always take something out.

Use the long spoons for iced tea.

She did a lot of nodding as she flipped through the Safety First contract, her elbows spread on the desk like she was taking a test. Her curly hair hung like a dark curtain over half her face, tented out where it reached her arms. She had that pale, shadowy look Keith usually associated with his friends' little sisters growing up. When he'd first seen her early that evening—or afternoon, depending on your definition (she'd walked in squinting)—it made her seem eager, even before she spoke.

He told her: The one to never forget is, *Keep the outside out, leave your own crap at the door.* That's the biggie. Focus. He told her: Don't think about the lousy tip you'll get from the asshole with the martinis, don't think about your best friend's dead dog, don't think about your boyfriend—

I don't have a boyfriend, she'd cut in.

Fine, but don't think about him. Thinking'll trip you up, it'll get you every time.

She laughed, though he hadn't meant it to be funny.

What he didn't tell the new girl was this: It was a hell of a lot tougher than it sounded. Pretty much, no matter how hard you tried, the outside came in anyway.

In Marna's presence everything was bearable. She was like good lighting. Things he'd always just done, things that hadn't impressed anyone else meant something to Marna. Like how he read books. Or the award he got for best waiter. Or how he walked everywhere instead of driving. I can't afford a car, he pointed out, but it didn't matter, she got a kick out of that kind of thing.

At midnight her divorce would be final. At midnight—or, okay, knowing Marna, soon thereafter—she and Keith were leaving. She was swinging by to get him and they were going to stop for his things and then maybe for gas—and then not stop again for a long time. They weren't coming back.

Check to table 19;
chick sandwich, no pickles;
chick sandwich, double cheese light mayo.
Forks.

It'd been a long week of lists. He'd never known how much crap he'd accumulated until now. All along, he'd been thinking of himself as a simple-living guy. But the more he took out of the closets and drawers, the more there seemed to be. He gave away his couch to the asshole in the apartment below (who worked nights for UPS and blasted Kenny G in the mornings). He gave his kitchen appliances and vacuum cleaner to the lady next door, most of his books to the Rastafarian at the end of the hall. He sold his LP collection to Planet Spin on Colfax, which just about killed him. But Marna drove a '79 Beetle. There was barely enough room for *him*.

It was an unbelievable collection: everything from Parker to Dylan (including the live concert in Newport just after he'd gone electric, where the crowd starts booing and Dylan turns to the band and screams, *Play fucking louder!*). Denny would kill for that collection—really, it was a crime not to give it to him. The idea, though, was to avoid a fuss. People saying things, getting all serious and embarrassed. Or jokey and embarrassed, which was even worse. The regulars had this tradition where they sprayed you with whipped cream and took pictures and gave out gifts. They did it for the staff and for each other too. When Ready Eddie moved to Maine, everyone chipped in and bought him a fishing rod and a blow-up doll.

No, Marna had it right: a clean break.

That was the plan. The *original* plan was that they'd both work the whole night—make some good cash and slip out together.

But, earlier, when Keith showed up at Marna's before the shift, flowers in hand for her *un*marriage, he found her on her living room floor, sprawled in the middle of boxes and piles of books and clothes, smoking a cigarette and reading cookbooks. Oops, she said. I got distracted. What time is it? Hey, flowers, she said, taking the flowers. She set them in the big living room window, tilted them against the glass.

Keith groaned. You said you'd be ready. Did you pack *anything?*

A few things.

Marna.

You go without me. You guys can handle it. There's always a crisis, she pointed out.

It's Super Bowl, Marna.

Keith, I'm sorry, I really am, I thought I'd be ready. But listen. She stubbed her cigarette into a cereal bowl and rummaged through a box marked *Stuff,* pulled out a Chapstick, rubbed some on her bottom lip. I'll make it up to you. Besides, she said, brightening, Lena loves this kind of thing.

I don't know. This wasn't how Keith had pictured the beginning of their adventure.

It's one of those things, Marna said, it's how packing and unpacking always is. You work and work and nothing looks different until something breaks, and then it suddenly does.

Keith nodded.

It's coming, I can feel it. She told him, You go ahead. She hugged him.

Christ, Marna. *Should've expected as much*—that must have been going through his head on some level. But he wasn't hearing it. He was just feeling Marna's body up and down his own. Hey, congratulations, he said.

Midnight, she said. Thanks for the flowers.

In the end, she agreed to drive in and at least set up, to get things going and make sure there was enough glassware and backup to get them through the rush before slipping away. She wasn't selfish, Keith reasoned. She just saw things different.

Check to table 19;
chick sandwich, no pickles;
chick sandwich, double cheese light mayo.
Two pitchers Bud.

They weren't a couple, you couldn't call it that, not yet. Technically, they weren't sleeping together—though, technically, they had.

Once. Last summer, mid-June.

He'd been lying on his living room floor when she called. Summer was Keith's least-favorite season. Supposedly Denver was a great place in the summer. No humidity, everyone said. One hundred here is like 90 in Florida. But 90 degrees was pretty fucking hot, and when it was hot, Keith sweat. A lot. Zero to drenched in sixty seconds. So he got some good reading done May through August, hid out in the air conditioning, cranked it on high. That day he was picking through *All the King's Men* by Robert Penn Warren. He'd already read it, but it was feeling right. He was slipping into the character of Jack Burden. After a while, he put it face down on his gut and stared up at the ceiling. There was a line he liked, he made a mental note to grab some paper and write it down. Right now, he couldn't move. He had the blinds closed and the curtains drawn and the afternoon was stretching on and on, without lightening or darkening. He felt it come over him then, not a depression exactly, more of a slow, descending weight, pinning him there. For the first time, he noticed that the curtains looked exactly like the curtains his folks had had in their house when he was growing up. He'd never noticed it before—how could that be? All thick and industrial-looking, a sad, yolky yellow. They'd come with the apartment.

And then she called.

Let's hang, she'd said. Let's eat a pizza. She added: Evan's out of town.

Sure, why not, he said. He tried to decide if that second part was a throwaway. Her voice had changed, he thought, a little up and a half pause before. And it was a funny thing for her to say right out, first thing. *Evan's out of town.* Keith had been over there before when Evan was out of town. He'd been over when Evan was in town. He liked the guy okay. Not your ideal husband material—Marna met him at a Dead show when they were both eighteen, and Evan *still* ate whole sheets of acid, still wandered around in long underwear. But he was nice enough. A few times they'd all made dinner together, the three of them at the counter in a row, chopping and slicing like a cooking show, the oil hissing.

Keith showered and changed into a fresh t-shirt and clean-enough shorts and walked outside. It was late day, really pretty actually, the light going soft and muddled in the trees, the wind blowing a little so that even if it wasn't cool, it wasn't bad either.

She picked him up in front of his building and they stopped for bourbon at Liquor-Time Liquor—and both of them tried to pay until they realized that neither of them had brought any cash. So they dug for change in the seats of Marna's Bug. It was hard work, bent over, groping around, and Keith was sopping when they'd found enough. But then Marna was sweating too, her blouse sticking to her skin, forming a dark line between her breasts.

After, they headed to her place, ate leftover Chinese with their fingers while they waited for the pizza. What did they talk about? Lily, Colleen's kid, and how smart she was, how much older she seemed than fourteen. Marna had given her a notebook and Lily took it everywhere. They talked about mountain lions. A four-year-old boy had been mauled earlier that week in Rocky Mountain National Park. They talked about punk music and the Great Lakes and the classes Keith took at DU a few years back, not toward any degree, just for the hell of it. They moved into the living room with the pizza, ate it on the couch. And for a while, that was how the night went: like all the others, light and easy, wonderful in the talking and the not talking. They were so comfortable with each other, they didn't need to fill up spaces anymore. Keith would steal glimpses of Marna, wonder a little, be sure one minute that something was progressing, that something might happen any moment—but then it would close over again, and that was okay too, because it had never been any different.

They finished eating and Marna showed him her latest project, gluing pieces of colored glass to the walls in the bathroom. And it was then that everything changed. One minute they were there, crouched on her bathroom floor, Marna sticking a shard of red glass into white paste, and the next it was all different. There was a silence that grew and expanded and she was looking at him differently—it must have come from her because *he'd* been ready all along. So ready that he was caught off guard. He almost looked away. Right then, he understood why it was that artists fell in love with their models (wasn't that the cliché?). It was because you could look, you had to look. Not just at the mouth or from one eye to the other as someone talked, but a good long stare. When that happened, something gave. Either you changed or they did or both at once.

The bathroom was too small. He hit his head on the bottom of the sink. They moved to the bedroom, which was dark and smelled like earth and animal. They didn't turn on the lights, just stumbled their way to the bed, into the tangle of blankets. Keith tried to slow it down a little (or maybe it was only now, in retrospect, that he tried to slow it down), but they pulled off their clothes and Marna climbed over him, on her knees, her hair swinging down and brushing his chest. She lowered herself, sliding her skin against his, first wonderfully cool, then warmer and warmer, their sweat and their breath and their rhythms combining, so that it was no longer clear where she began and he ended, not that it even mattered.

Drinks to 5.
Another round lemon drops;
pitcher Bud;
four pitchers Bass.
Change for two twenties down to the nickel.

The win, when it finally happened, surprised Keith. Not that the Broncos won, but that they *had* won. The night that would never end was almost over.

Almost.

Keith kept going. He stepped it up. High fives, cheers, calls for fresh booze—he plowed through all of it. *Homestretch.*

The way he'd put it to the new girl was this: It was simple, you had a choice: you could be on top of a rush or under it. Just like a riptide. When it pulled you under, when you fought it, you lost control. Scrambling for tickets, not remembering things. And that was when you were most vulnerable. That was when you'd think about the phone bill or the last time you'd had a good night's sleep or the fact that the girl over at table 54, who keeps tugging at her pantyhose, reminds you of your first crush, who, in turn, reminds you of someone else. . . .

72

You'd think of her. The second her. You'd think of the two of you, far from anyplace like this . . . you're driving, she's hanging her feet out the window. . . . You would skip ahead to it, automatically, and then fight it off again—enjoying that too. Like when you were a kid and you had some prize, a new glove or a comic book, and you'd put it away in a box or a dresser drawer so that you could forget about it. You don't really forget, you just want to, so you can remember.

The backs of Keith's ears throbbed. His teeth felt big in his mouth. He dropped off checks. Punched in drink orders with his thumb. Someone at the bar was wearing purple and it kept catching his eye, hovering in the corner like a blurry grape. Voices were pointed. He tasted yellow on his tongue—a slur of smoke and greasy perfume. Everything was charged; the room itself seemed to vibrate at the edges, just slightly, almost imperceptibly, in a low, metallic hum—like the atoms were getting restless and slowly breaking out.

part two

The left-handed man never comes home.

8.

Colleen sat across from India and organized her checkout. She dug all the tickets and receipts from her apron and straightened them and stacked them in piles along the edge of the table, then added her sales and figured out her tips. India was reading a paperback, holding it up and open, her elbows propped on the table, drinking cup after cup of coffee and cream. "Not to be believed," she murmured. The book was an old romance. It was a soft, faded turquoise, had a picture on its cover of a girl tilted backwards in a man's arms. India brought in a different one almost every night, the covers all pretty much the same, girls tilting and fading.

Three hundred thirty-eight dollars. Not bad, though last year she'd made four fifty. Colleen shuffled her money, faced the bills the same way. She'd give Denny sixty and Lena maybe ten for her share of the bartending and she'd throw the kitchen fifteen or twenty. She was the only one who tipped out the cooks. You weren't technically supposed to, but it made things a whole lot easier.

It was 1:15, a half hour before last call—a half hour before Lily. Only the bar itself was still crowded, and even there things were winding down, everyone paid up, people hovering more than anything else, making halfhearted attempts at complaining and debating—the Broncos, John Elway, the previous year's Senate race, the wrestler-turned-governor—all of it falling away as people left, first in a rush and then one by one, so that the TVs, too loud now, made the most convincing arguments of all, about dish soap and beer and replayed newscasts of the downtown celebrations. Police scattering crowds. One TV was turned to a cooking show, the chef folding something pink into something yellow. Gently, gently, his voice warbled, and Denny reached up and flicked off the volume. He was working up a sweat at the sink, washing the glassware that JJ was collecting for him. She swooped back and forth between the tables in a wild sort of dance. The place was a disaster, of course—a couple overturned chairs, used napkins and dirty plates everywhere—but it was nothing the usual sweep-through wouldn't fix. Glassware then plates then garbage then Windex. Then taking out the garbage and restocking. Every night, the same routine. It was always doable, Colleen reminded herself. It never seemed doable, but it always was, when you broke it down.

Pretty much only the regulars were left now. Lena was sitting down at the bar next to Fran, going through her tickets. Fran and James. Fran and James and *Lena*. What a joke. Lena made a fuss about how annoying and hopeless Fran was, and James, well, god, James. . . . And now look at them, like the best of friends. Lena was drinking Fran's beer. She'd take gulps and then put it back in front of Fran, getting another from Denny when it was empty.

They were back on the topic of Marna.

"I'm thinking Brazil," Fran said. "Seems like Brazil would be a good place to celebrate a divorce. Or Mexico. Isn't she always talking about Mexico?"

"That's me, you idiot," James said. He was Fran's husband. No one knew why. He had wet-looking eyes, and when he laughed or said something he thought was funny, he squinched his eyes and half stuck out his tongue, held it in a thick ball between his teeth. Denver just happened to be the place he'd gotten caught and served time for selling bogus chimney cleanings to old people. That was about ten years ago. Now he lived off Fran, who used to waitress here until she won some legal settlement for a medication she'd been on.

If you didn't know Fran, you might guess she was the artsy natural type. Her hair was wispy and always loose and there was something precise about her features. Made you think it might carry over to the rest of her. You could see her as a teacher or even a scientist. But then she'd open her mouth and talk. Her voice was scratchy. There were dark lines where her teeth met her gums. And then there was James.

"I'll play detective," he was saying now, "but I'd rather play doctor."

"No kidding," said Fran.

Colleen had to admit: it was starting to feel different not having Marna here—almost as if the air had changed density. Though that was absurd. It was only because she was *trying* to feel a difference that she felt one. And anyway, it wasn't like Colleen was even all that close to Marna. Almost close maybe. On the edge of a friendship. Colleen would sometimes feel it tipping.

Marna loved Lily. That, in itself, was enough.

"The happiest people live in Iceland, there was a poll," Fran said.

Marna or no Marna, it didn't seem like Super Bowl Sunday anymore. It seemed like any other night. Last year they'd been packed right up to 2 A.M., when, legally, everyone was supposed to be gone. That was always a pain in the ass, yelling, *Okay, drink up, drink up, you gotta go, you don't gotta go home, but you can't stay here,* and no one listening. You had to practically pry the glasses out of their hands. Like most bars, they set their clocks ahead, but that only helped a little. A lot of customers—the regulars especially—knew about it and used the extra time to linger over drinks, finagle extra shots. If anything, Colleen thought, bar time made the night feel longer.

Colleen folded her tickets and shook through the change in her apron to find a rubber band. She never counted her coins, didn't consider them part of her tips—though some nights, like tonight, there was probably twenty dollars or so jangling around down there. She would toss it later into the giant plastic pretzel jar she kept at home in between her nightstand and clothes hamper. She'd forget about it and then when she'd need it, when some bill was overdue and she'd gone out and spent all her earnings at Pottery Place or on clothes for Lily, she'd remember the change jar and it would be like a gift. "Hey, Lena."

"Hey what. You done? You wanna join us for a drink? We're celebrating divorce. I can't face sidework yet."

"If I start drinking now," Colleen said, "I might not be able to stop. You want to do beer or floor?"

"Floor." Lena turned back to the others.

"Follow me," Colleen called to JJ, who was just about done with the glassware and was stacking it in dangerous formations on the drink mat in front of Denny. "I'll show you beer."

Restocking beer was the worst. No question. First—without getting in the bartender's way—you had to figure out what you needed from the bar coolers, which were hard to see into and were filled with all sorts of other crap: sticky jars of cherries and olives, Bloody Mary and sour mix, the bottles of lemon-flavored iced tea that only Marna liked. Then, after making a list, you had to run downstairs to the beer closet, which was in the basement beside the break room, and fight your way through the cases to find what you were looking for and carry it back up.

"How do you find anything?" JJ asked, peering in. "I mean, in particular."

"Well," Colleen said, propping open the metal door and climbing over a case marked *Amstel Light.* She tossed a few empty boxes past JJ into the hall. "There really isn't a system. You just have to kind of hunt around." Someone many years ago had actually made signs out of strips of plywood and nailed them along the walls. *Bud. Bud Light, Corona,* etc. Most of them had fallen down, though, and the rest were ignored. Cases were everywhere, and even worse, people took partial cases and jammed the extra bottles wherever they could—so it was anyone's guess what you'd come up with if you didn't check the contents of each box. Pilsner with wine coolers. Pub cans with near-beer. *St. Pauli Girl Here* one sign read. It had been twirled around on its single nail so that the red ruler-drawn arrow now pointed up instead of down. The only thing the signs were good for, really, was propping up joints for quick toke breaks.

"Dig in," Colleen told JJ, handing her the list, and began to poke through a case of Icehouse.

"Kind of creepy," JJ said, not moving.

Colleen paused. Felt the closeness of the cement walls. They were ghosted with water marks. The air was dim and greenish—there was no actual light in the closet, you had to rely on the buzzing fluorescence from the hallway. It felt like a cave. JJ was right. It *was* creepy. The beer closet. The whole downstairs. Really, this whole damn place.

Fear was interesting, Colleen thought. Something could be fine, totally innocuous, and then one day, sometimes for no reason, it might change on you. Office buildings. Cops. Bugs. Killing bugs. If she saw one at home, she'd scoop it up in a bit of paper towel and fling it out the door. She tried to remember to gather the pieces later, but at any given time, there would be a slew of soggy white dots covering the front stoop, like after some sorry parade. So many bugs. No matter how careful they were about crumbs. Colleen kept forgetting to spray. That had been one of Rick's chores. He'd kept up with those things—bugs, gutters, raking leaves. He laughed, no doubt, looking down, watching her pinch up little beetles one by one. In the summer at night, she'd turn out the lights before opening the screen and flinging them out, so that the swarms wouldn't zoom inside—though even so, for every one that went out, a few invariably came in.

Cults. Carnivals. Birds. Toilet seats. Toilet lids left up while flushing. She'd seen a show once on the science channel that demonstrated how an invisible cloud of toilet water and waste flew into the air if you left the lid up, flew up in a mushroom burst of shit and piss and covered everything in a four-foot radius. Everything: the sink, washcloths. Toothbrushes. After seeing that show Colleen cut out a white rectangle of paper, wrote *Please shut me,* and taped it to the underside of the lid.

Country roads. The back seat of the car at night. Motels. You never knew what'd be next.

Lily, on the other hand, feared nothing. She was always trying to stand up on roller coasters, crazy stuff like that. If Colleen wasn't careful, Lily would take walks by herself in the middle of the night. She'd walked home from the Almost Home—done it twice back when they lived with Lena and it was possible to walk. She'd gotten grouchy that Colleen was taking too long, chatting with the others, talking "shop," and slipped out and went home. Just like that, at 3 in the morning. "What were you *thinking*," Colleen had hollered the last time, but secretly she was impressed. Sometimes it was a wonder that she herself was able to get from the car to the front door at night.

They sorted through the beer, got what they needed, stacked the cases in the hallway. They worked in silence for a while and Colleen fought all the things she'd like to say. Random things popping into her head and rising in her throat. There was no telling what could come out. My daughter is a genius. My husband is dead. I stole three live lobsters from King Soopers once, snuck them out right under my sweater. *Silence,* Colleen thought as she heaved a couple cases of Bud Light into the hall, silence is a pain in the ass. Even in a moment like this, at work, the most normal time of all, when she didn't even need to make small talk, it was a pain in the ass. Sometimes Colleen could actually feel particles of air swirling around her throat, bringing out all the things she could possibly say. That was the hardest part about being a mother. Not the discipline or the worry. No, it was all the things you wanted to say but couldn't.

"That's the whole list, right? We got it all?" JJ asked. She was filling a box with the last of the Michelob Lights and rolled one between her palms as she leaned over and scanned the list.

"I think so." Three cases of Bud, one of Corona, two six-packs of Red Stripe. PBR. Check. And on and on. Check. Check. Check. "Yup."

"Yow," JJ said. "It's gonna take a million trips to get this upstairs."

"Yup."

"Do you usually do this all by yourself?"

"It seems like hell now, but you'll get used to it."

"Okay. Great," JJ said, not convincingly.

"Uh-oh. Look," Colleen said, keeping a straight face, trying to get a little Lena in her voice, "look what you did." She pointed to the Michelob Light, now label-less, thanks to JJ, who'd peeled it like an apple.

JJ looked down and went pink. "Oops. Sorry."

"You know what that means, don't you?"

"No. Sexual repression?" JJ gave a nervous laugh.

"You have to drink it."

"Really?"

"Sure, house rule, open it up." Colleen grabbed another from the case of them and tore off the label. "Oh shit. I have one too. Defective."

JJ giggled. "But it's warm."

Colleen shrugged. She sat down on a case of Rolling Rock and twisted off the bottle cap. "In England they drink warm beer."

"Oh that's right." JJ opened hers as well, sat down.

"You from around here?" Colleen felt it again. Words bubbling up. She listened to JJ go on about a babysitting job and something about feeding a fish. She enjoyed the ramble. Keep talking, she thought. I can talk too.

"'Despite changes upon changes,'" JJ was saying, quoting from something, "'we are more or less the same.' I think that's really true, don't you? You know, *changed*, but not so different. Though I guess it's not true if you want to be literal about the whole thing. You know."

Colleen nodded. "This will surprise you, but I was a college girl myself."

"It doesn't surprise me," JJ said, but Colleen could tell she was lying.

"I was a respiratory therapist and also got an art degree."

"Wow."

"Well, not that impressive, really," Colleen said, and took a gulp of warm beer. "DCA. Denver College of Art." The beer filled her mouth with a sharp yeasty wash and she swallowed it quickly. "It hasn't really worked out, the art thing, for me."

"Oh. I'm sorry to hear," JJ said.

"Yeah."

"You know, it's funny, I can relate. The thing is—"

"Wait." Colleen held up her hand. There was some thumping above. And shouting. You could hear James's voice, not the words but muffled ups and downs. JJ and Colleen held their breath and listened. More shouting. A pause. Then laughter.

"James," Colleen said, shaking her head. "Don't worry," she told JJ, "we almost never get fights here—though actually, last summer one of the owner's friends brought in brass knuckles and started acting all stupid—but he wasn't being serious. It's a lousy mix, testosterone and alcohol. You'd think someone would have figured that out by now."

JJ said, "They're a funny couple, Fran and James. The way they hate each other."

"I don't think it's hate," Colleen said and thought about it. It was true that half the time Fran and James acted that way—but other times, well, other times, you could be certain it was the other direction. Last year, for instance, for Fran's birthday, James wrote some poems and put them together in a booklet. *Poems. James.* But he can't spell his own name, Lena had said, laughing, when Fran brought them in—you could tell, though, even Lena was impressed. They were crappy poems, of course, *roses are red,* but still. When things went one way or the other, Colleen wondered, which was the way you were supposed to go by? She took another swig. "Anyway," she said.

"Anyway," JJ echoed.

"The teacher just plain hated me. On sight, I think. Like because I had a perm or something, not all natural with stringy hair. Ripped jeans and black turtlenecks."

"Oh right, like the ar-*teest*."

"Right! Like I have to smell bad or something. What is that stuff? Patooi?"

"Patchouli," JJ said.

"Gesundheit," Colleen said and they laughed. "Ugh. Not that I smell good now, mind you." She lifted the back of her hair off her neck, whisked at it with her fingers to circulate air.

"You smell okay," JJ said and sipped her beer. "I played the piano," she said.

It wasn't totally honest that Colleen didn't try to fit in at art school. In truth, she would stand in front of the closet in the morning and pull out the black things first. She became more and more conscious of what she wore. She avoided pastel-colored socks and sweatshirts with leggings—a uniform that suddenly marked her as a *mother*. She began paying attention in malls. Does this look okay? she'd ask Lily before leaving the house. Lily, who at age seven already had an eye for style, would instruct her to untuck or pull back accordingly. Try your navy flats, she'd direct. Go easy on the eyeliner.

Years later, after Rick died, the two of them would play a game at restaurants before their food came. They would do "before-and-afters": one would draw a dumpy, ugly woman, with big fuzzy hair and floppy clothes, and then hand it to the other, who would then take a second piece of paper and put the woman on a diet, sleek down her hair, dress her in clean-lined suits. Finish her with a dazzling smile and sometimes add a handsome guy at her side. It took Colleen a long time to figure out that they were doing *her*. Doing and redoing the tragic housewife. Fix that hair, add a little muscle tone. *Voilà!*

"If a teacher decides she doesn't like you, that's it," JJ told her. "There's not a thing you can do about it."

"Hand me another beer, will you? Thanks. So for the first half of that class—it was called 'Studio Drawing'—we drew straight lines. That was it. Draw two dots and connect them. One-two draw. One-two draw. Three hours in a row, every week, like four, five, six weeks or something. Maybe not that long, but still. Straight lines and then straight lines with no dots and then—oh glory god!—*curved* lines."

"Cheers," JJ said and held up her beer. "To curved lines."

"Exactly. Have an orgasm."

JJ giggled.

"So I got bored and did my own thing. I drew filled-in pears and apples and grapes and the windows and wastebaskets and the teacher's big veiny hands, you know, funned it up a bit. Inflated the teacher's belly, turned it into a parade balloon."

"I like parades," JJ said, nodding.

"For the final project I did this big collage piece I called *Hurricane Heaven* in seven shades of purple with tissue paper and pipe cleaners and glitter and the candy hearts you get at Valentine's Day, and there were unicorn stickers and plastic mini–lava lamps I pulled off key chains. Just about anything you could imagine. It was bullshit, of course, pure cut-and-paste, but maybe the art crept in. I don't know. I wish I knew. Anyway, I won an award for that thing, and the school literary magazine used it for a cover. No joke." She laughed and looked down.

JJ put her beer down and clapped. "That's wonderful," she said. "Hooray! Are you still doing it?"

It *was* wonderful, Colleen remembered. She'd won a blue ribbon—just like in cartoons or 4-H clubs, a silky ribbon with *1st Place* written in gold letters. The teacher wouldn't even look at her in the halls. The dean made her change Colleen's D– to an A. It was *really* wonderful.

But the wonderful only lasted so long. After that, Colleen tried to branch out and dabbled in charcoal and batik and even landscapes in oil, and there were a number of promising starts—she still had them somewhere, packed away. As for the first piece, it had been hanging for a while, first in the house and then in Lena's apartment, but it shed glitter, and Lena's cat would take flying leaps at the things hanging off it.

Plus, it taunted Colleen. Try to top this, it said.

"Well, another time, there *was* this gallery show," Colleen admitted to JJ. "There was something."

She and Lily were still living at Lena's at the time, and some arty friend of Lena's—a horrible man really, smelled like dry cleaning—offered her a chance. He owned a gallery in the city and hung out with hoity-toity people, and you could tell that he found the idea of dating a bartender amusing. This is Lena, my personal barista, he'd tell people. Lena said he had mirrors in his bedroom and that she'd catch him watching himself. Sometimes, she'd told Colleen, he'd asked other women into bed with them. Lena was so blasé about it—she almost made it sound tedious. And maybe it was, who knew?

But so this friend, this gallery owner, had a cancellation and told Colleen that if she could get a portfolio to him to preview by the end of the week, he might be able to swing something. So she covered all of her shifts, cashed in the jar of change—and a chunk of savings besides—and bought new paints and a good easel and brushes made out of animal hair.

The first day, she arranged everything in the living room: put down an oilcloth, lined up the paints, blobbed each one onto her new palate. Pulled her hair back in barrettes. Wore comfy clothes. Waited until Lena was at work, Lily at school. She flipped through the albums and picked out some painting music. Judy Collins, *Both Sides Now.* She stacked all of the dirty breakfast dishes and, feeling productive, emptied ashtrays, then smoked a joint and drank applesauce out of a coffee mug. She turned on a sitcom rerun, *Three's Company*—background noise was good, good—and then sank back into the couch and fell into a dream where Larry tied Jack up to a folding chair and fed him chocolates, one by one.

The next day she woke up early and jogged around the block. Drove to the supermarket after breakfast and chose items that seemed wholesome, packed with nutrients to get her creative juices flowing. Red meat, eggs, spinach. She wheeled slowly through produce and picked out fruit, checked for soft spots and discoloration.

At home she set up her paints and spread out. Went for the abstract, swiped the canvas in broad strokes, then tried for a staccato effect with little dots. Stood back. Disease, she thought, it looks like disease.

She got up and went into the kitchen. She washed the paint off her hands and found a mixing bowl and piled in the fruit she'd bought. She sat down with a pencil and a canvas and followed the curves. She was willing to try anything. She rearranged the fruit. She sliced the fruit and held it up to the light. She ate the fruit. When Lena and Lily came home at night, Colleen said it was going great, that everything was *brewing*.

Wormy apples. Spoiled food. Empty space. Blank canvas. Blank days.

The next day was the day before the portfolio was due. Colleen stayed in bed and called old boyfriends. Two weren't home, one couldn't place her name until she'd repeated it four times, and the last hadn't even been a boyfriend, just a line cook from work she'd gone home with one time, months before, after a party.

"Why don't you come on over," she said to him, taking her best stab at a 1-900 voice, and almost laughed. You have *come to kitchen* eyes, someone had told her once.

Halfway through, she wished he'd just leave. Is it good, is it good, he kept gasping, entirely rhetorical, rocking over her. It was depressing, was what it was. She focused on a splotch on the ceiling, tried to decide whether or not it was a spider.

After, he got up and made a big deal of straightening out the bed and tucking her in and getting them both glasses of orange juice.

"I'm old enough to be your mother, Carlos," she told him.

"I like old women," he said, and sat cross-legged beside her head, on top of the comforter. "Older," he corrected himself and smiled.

"You need to cut your toenails," she told him and watched the spider drop to the night table and land in one of the juices.

She finished the portfolio that night and the next morning. After Carlos left, she dragged out *Hurricane Heaven* and propped it up on the La-Z-Boy for inspiration. She went through every drawer in the apartment and made a pile of glitter and gift wrap and trinkets and anything else she could find. Fake fingernails. Feathers. An empty pack of Lena's birth control. Colleen slapped down paint and paper and dragged charcoal and mashed chewing gum. This is working, she thought, I'm back on a roll, I can do this, I can do this. Just a little pressure, that's all I need. Just a little *enthusiasm.* She slapped materials together and took photos and put them in the best-looking album she was able to find at the all-night drugstore.

Lena showed it to her friend and he said, No.

Candy dishes, Lena told Colleen later and laughed, then straightened her face. He decided on a show of candy dishes. But seriously, Colleen, not all that good, I don't know what Dex was thinking. This guy collects these awful antique candy dishes and glues them into weird formations and finds old hard candy to stick inside.

Very cutting-edge, Colleen said and smiled until it hurt.

She told a version of it to JJ. She left things out, changed things a little. Sometime soon, the gallery owner promised her, I'm very impressed.

"Well," JJ said, yawning and stretching when Colleen had finished the story. "That's a good story." They'd moved from the crates to the floor now, were leaning up against the wall. Colleen didn't have a watch on, but it suddenly felt late. Where was Lily? "That's a really good story. I think you should keep trying."

"Thanks."

"I like collages," JJ said. "I really do."

"I like peanut butter," Colleen said absently and sighed.

9.

The summer Lena was eight, three farmhouses down the road were robbed in one day. Whoever did it only took things that were outside—some irrigation equipment, a trailer hitch, a three-wheeler—but Lena's mother was worried that if someone was crazy enough to haul off a tiller dead-smack in the middle of the afternoon, who knew what else they'd do? She went out the very next day and got a dog. Lena was allowed to pick out the collar and name him. He was big and sleek and black so Lena named him Bear. Her father built a doghouse and hammered a stake into the ground to tie him to. It just about killed Lena to see Bear stuck like that, spending his life in the same muddy circle, so she'd untie him in the afternoon before her father came home, then again after supper for the night. She yanked the stake and hid it. She pointed out the obvious: a dog on a rope wasn't much good for protection.

Lena would take long walks with Bear up the dirt road behind their house, by Jensen's cornfields and the junkyard and Greystone Dairy; she walked hard and fast to clear her mind. She'd imagine that the two of them were walking away. Once Bear dove into a tangle of brush and came out with what Lena thought was a stick until she grabbed it from his mouth. It was the splintered-off leg of a large bird—dull gray, the talons intact and curled. Another time, Bear led her to a cow skeleton, the bones jumbled, sifting out of order, a few clumps of animal left here and there, spots of red and fur.

That's how it was in Lyle, Indiana, the middle of nowhere—*Bum Fuck, Egypt,* Lena called it, even back then, even to her grandparents—it was muggy, buggy, there were no other teenagers for miles, and everywhere you turned, death flickered. Possums and raccoon smeared along the edge of the road. Cats. Birds. Snakes. Out in BFE you didn't need high school biology to understand the life cycle.

And yet Lena wasn't prepared for the morning she walked out for the mail—half asleep and only in her nightshirt, nearly tripped by the scutter and dash of Bear around her legs—and watched, as if it were one fluid motion, the dog leap into the road and get flattened by a Jeep Cherokee. There was blood everywhere, spreading, a splash of cherry-colored paint.

Her mother got another dog. And then another. After Bear there was a long line of dogs, of strays picked up from the pound or found collarless on their property. Big, small, lean, hairy. To Lena, they all blended into one animal. One after the other, they would take off too far and either get run over or else just disappear. Fall, Lena's mother became fond of saying, into someone else's life.

Bear was the only good part about growing up there, Lena'd told Denny a while back, about a month ago. The last time they'd hooked up, that's how long it'd been. They were at Denny's—at *Stephanie's*—lying naked on top of the sheets, sharing a bottle of purple Gatorade. They'd just made love. Lena told Denny, It sounds dumb, but it just wouldn't be right.

Denny nodded. It's easy to get close to a dog.

I could never feel that same way again.

Sure, he said. It was one of the things she loved most about him: he understood. He'd grown up in Nebraska instead of Indiana, but when you got out to where all you saw were fields and fields and, oh look, more fucking fields, it was pretty much the same. He reached for his cigarettes and winced. He had two broken ribs. They didn't know it yet, or weren't positive yet if the ribs were bruised or broken and how many. He'd done it that day going snowboarding for the first time. Afterwards, he didn't call Stephanie at her work. He called Lena, told her to come by. No point in going to the hospital, they agreed. There wasn't much you could do about broken ribs. Also, Denny didn't have health insurance. Just about no one Lena knew had health insurance.

Lena lit his cigarette for him and asked, You have any dogs growing up?

Sure. And some cats. And a goat. And my father.

Lena laughed. She ran her hand lightly over his arm, then his leg, along the tautness of his hamstring. She said, You know, I might just have a thing for country-boys-turned-snowboarders.

I don't snowboard. That's the problem. He shifted and grimaced.

I'll be gentle. She took the empty bottle from him and found a place for it on his nightstand—and noticed something. Hey, she said. It was a copy of Keith's Best Server photograph, clipped from the paper—not the article, just the picture. You saved it. She held it up. It was of Keith, of course, with his banana grin—smudged, so it looked

95

like he was missing a tooth—but, also, in the back, were Denny and Lena. They were horsing around, Denny's arm circling her neck and the two of them cracking up. They weren't in focus, but it was the first thing your eye went to.

Sure, he said. Keith's award.

Oh please. That's not why you saved it. She held it up and laughed. That's not why you *trimmed the edges with scissors.*

He shrugged.

She said, You have to admit, it's a good picture of us.

It's fine.

Admit it. She bit him lightly on his bare shoulder, held her mouth there.

Hey.

Admit it or I'll bite, she said into his skin, tasting him.

You're already biting.

I'll really bite. She gave a low growl, tried not to laugh. It felt good, it was tempting, the tension of his flesh against her teeth.

Yeah, okay, okay, sure, it's a good picture. It's actually a fucking great picture—I'm strangling you. I should have finished the job.

She clenched down then let go.

Ow. Denny rolled into her, laughing, rubbing his shoulder, clutching his side. It was a good, hard bite that would leave marks—but it wasn't as hard as it could have been. It was odd to know you could do it: actually sink in.

She watched him now as she finished up with her tables and sat down for a drink with Fran. A month, she thought. He'd wiped down the bar and was emptying the garnish trays into glasses. He tore off a neat square of plastic wrap and smoothed it over a pint of limes.

96

They understood each other. They just did. Even if neither of them would admit it out loud, even if the excitement came in waves and they acted one way to each other one day and another the next—and even if it had been an entire month—they both knew it was true: more than anyone else—Marna, Keith, *Steph*—when it came to getting Denny, when it came to really knowing, Lena was the only one.

Victory. Broncos win again. Denny rinsed garnish trays and watched another replay. Elway taking a knee and the clock ticking down to zero. Then the trophy presentation and the moment of hush and Terry Bradshaw asking Elway about retirement and Elway saying, well, he didn't know yet.

So there you go.

When the win happened, everyone whooping it up, Denny shouted *yes* with the rest of them, shot a soapy fist into the air. But the truth was, it just didn't feel like a win. There you had it, Denny thought, another night ruined by the Almost Home.

And he'd gone and let it happen. Practically asked for it.

Sure, there were all sorts of other things he could blame it on. The hysteria over Elway. The fact they'd cinched the win in the first half. Or maybe it just was *too* big a deal and it hadn't registered yet. Or maybe it would never register—hell, maybe the rush had simply lost its rush. Probably, Denny thought, it'd always been this way and this time he was just sober enough to notice.

Or probably, he thought, it was last year.

Damon's was packed. They had to squeeze through the mob, and Denny was suddenly sure his father would change his mind. Fine.

97

Excellent. Denny could call him a cab. But the old man didn't turn around. The friction of the crowd half dragged off his jacket, but he kept going, followed Denny and Steph to the table—which, sure enough, was right up front. The best table in the house.

About time you got here, Barry said, his hands full of dirty glassware. There was a glaze of sweat across his face and goatee. Could've sold these seats. Hi, Steph.

Hi, Barry.

We're here, Denny said. Barry was waiting for an introduction, he could tell, but he didn't have the energy.

I'd try to join you, Barry said, but Lizbet twisted her ankle and can't work. You'll be lucky if we don't call you back on, he said to Steph.

It was an old joke and she gave the old laugh, bigger than necessary. Sure, sure, she said, pointing to Denny. Over his dead body.

Their waitress came by, some new lady Denny didn't recognize, her short skirt showing a map of spider veins. Pitcher of Bud, Denny said. His father got a club soda. The pregame show was wrapping up. Good. Right now, Denny could do without all the blather. He didn't need others telling him what to think, reminding him of the odds, how it was impossible, this win. The beer tasted good. Denny drank down a glass and refilled it. See, he told his father, a lot of people think being a fan is only about where they live. It's not.

His father nodded.

Just because you move, that doesn't mean nothing. It's about loyalty. It's about choosing and sticking. It's about knowing the players and the stats and really watching, you know. Paying attention. Asking the right questions.

I'm from Baltimore, Steph told his father. But I'm like Denny—I've been die-hard Broncos for years. Before I moved here.

His father nodded. He was being a sport, Denny had to admit. It occurred to him then to feel a little bad, even, that he'd been *expecting* it to be a disaster, his father coming out to visit.

Terrell was running mock wind sprints and stretching his hamstrings. Shanahan paced the field—the Mastermind, looking for cheese. Then the commercials, which even Denny thought were pretty good this year. Louie the Lizard trying to kill off the Budweiser frogs. A Tabasco-sucking mosquito. Barry brought two plates of mushroom poppers and the three of them dipped the poppers in ranch, polished off both plates and then a medium pizza and a basket of wings.

This is a running game, Denny explained. That's the only way they can ever do it. Pure running. Power.

Davis was really throwing himself into it. His dive for a first down had set things rolling. He was unstoppable—that is, until the end of the first quarter, when he got slammed at the thirty-yard line.

The crowd groaned.

Jesus fucking Christ, Denny said.

Denny, Steph hissed.

Oh. Sorry. Denny poured himself another beer and watched Brett Favre throw a dud pass. Ha. Favre had this golden-boy image, but Denny had heard more than once that he was a speed freak, maybe even hit his wife. At halftime, the cheerleaders ran out and did their thing. There was a tribute to Motown. Announcers came on and said it wasn't looking good for Davis, that he had a concussion and that it wasn't looking good for the Broncos. Not one lineman over three hundred, one goon announcer was saying—like that was news, like that wasn't the most obvious thing ever.

Out of nowhere, Steph reached over and touched his father's arm. I'm so glad you made this visit, she said. We're really glad—right, Denny? She was loopy by now on Cape Cods, had been doing dumb things with the limes, stacking them, pretending they were talking to each other.

Right, Denny said. He lit a cigarette. Sure, he said. And as he said it, he realized he might actually mean it. Watching the game with his father, filling him in—the old guy listening—it was turning into a not-so-bad time.

It lasted for about three, maybe four minutes, that feeling.

And then his father cleared his throat. He said, I have some news. I'm moving back home.

Steph gasped. *Terrific.*

Denny set down his beer. What?

His father cranked out one of his newfangled smiles. We're getting back together.

Getting back together. Who?

Whatdya mean, who? Your mother and me.

Denny stared at him. Shook his head. Said, I just talked to her. She didn't say nothing.

I know.

She would've said something.

She wanted me to say something. That's why I'm here.

Ah, Denny said. He picked up his beer. Set it down. Well.

I think it's terrific, Steph said.

We got that the first time, Steph. Denny turned back to the game. The second half had started. He tried to clear his head. He focused on the screen. The Broncos received. Terrell snapped up his chin strap and jogged onto the field. Just as Denny'd predicted.

His mother. Taking the old guy back. Square one. Skip to my Lou. Denny downed his beer in three long gulps. The waitress brought another pitcher and Denny filled his glass. He drank that too, fast. He filled it again, then filled Steph's empty highball and his father's club soda glass, poured the beer right in, fizzed it up. Water into wine, he said. Let's toast. To my father. To Mom and Pop. To family reunions.

Steph kicked him under the table.

A vein in his father's forehead flicked into view. He said, Maybe I should go. But of course he just sat there.

The waitress passed the table and Denny tapped her arm. Hey, he said. C'mere.

Whatcha need? She was maybe forty-five or so, with fake eyelashes. You could tell because one set was coming off a little, sliding off her real lashes like a leggy bug.

What's your name again?

Valerie, she said.

Do you have a second, Valerie?

Not really.

Denny, Steph said.

He was acting, he knew, like an idiot customer, some dumb prick. He took her arm. Valerie, I could use a favor. My name is Denny. This is Steph and this here is Pop.

Denny, Steph said.

His father looked down at his lap, as if something were there. Instructions. A Bible.

Valerie shifted her weight and glanced over her shoulder. You could tell she was new, too afraid to pull back her arm and walk away. Listen, she said weakly, whatcha need?

On the screens, Terrell charged the goal line. He met a wall of green and yellow, then plunged to the other side, into the end zone. The bar echoed with the whir of cheering. Somewhere in the background *"We will rock you"* played.

What I need, Valerie . . .

He was drunk. He was an asshole. He didn't care. He felt his buzz—the accumulated buzz from this morning, from this afternoon, from as far back as he could remember—hum up through his body, rise through his neck and push against his skull. He pulled the waitress closer. He told her, What I need is a date. Maybe, if I can be truthful, Valerie, I need more than a date. Something to cheer me up. My girl and my dad here seem to have hit it off, you see. And now he's got another one at home, can you believe it? My dad's more irresistible than you might think. So I need something, you understand? For myself. Valerie, I have a proposal. How would you like to sit on my face?

10.

Keith never minded doing garbage, but tonight he was enjoying it. He'd served his last drink (an Alabama slammer to Spencer, who was now half asleep on a Single's shoulder). He'd printed his last totals, done his last checkout. Out in the dark back corner of the parking lot, for one final time, he heaved bag after bag of trash and bottles into the dumpsters. Trash in the big, already overfull blue dumpster, recycling in the smaller black one (though, from what he'd heard, it all went to the same place anyway). It felt good to stretch, to have room. To be throwing something heavy. He liked, in particular, the reverb of breaking bottles, the way each crash traveled back.

A couple cars drove by, one fast, the other slow. Marna was never on time. Midnight had come and gone. *I can explain* would be her first words.

The last bag landed with a satisfying pop and sent wet napkins and half-eaten food cascading. Keith wiped his hands on his jeans and

sloshed back through the swamp of dark water and dissolving cardboard that separated the dumpsters from the rest of the lot. His boots
were thick-soled and waterproof; he enjoyed their impenetrability.
Right after he'd landed this job, Marna had introduced herself and
congratulated him, then told him that if he was smart, he'd get good
footwear. Something you can stand in all night, she told him. Her face
had a smattering of pale freckles that reminded Keith of light hitting
water. Her lower lip was dry and split in the middle and she kept licking it. She couldn't help it, you could tell, her tongue kept going to it.
She said, And then there's the matter of protection. She nodded to his
Converse high-tops, the soles peeling in the front.

Protection?

Yeah.

Do you get, he asked, much trouble at the Almost Home Bar and
Grill? Then grinned: he didn't want her thinking he was *worried*.

Well, she said, grinning back, last night Hammer didn't quite
make it to the bathroom.

Keith supposed he did need a good pair of boots. He drove to the
nearest mall, where he walked around the stores testing different
brands, clomping stiffly down the aisles. It had been a long time, he
realized, since he'd bought anything for himself that couldn't be eaten
or read or drunk or rinsed down the drain. He lived a spare life, as best
he could, but he knew the sorts of things you should splurge on. Paper
towels. Liquor. And now boots.

And a lucky thing too, because Keith's second week on the job,
Bo Tamowitz went and knocked the slicer off the prep table, sent
it sailing right onto Keith's right foot. How bony, DT-ruined Bo
had been able to *move* the slicer—a nifty contraption of blades and
stainless steel about the size of a small car engine—let alone get it
airborne, would always be a mystery to Keith, but he did, and if it

weren't for his steel-toed WorkMaster 27s, Keith would have been hobbling around for more than just a couple days. Something else he could thank Marna for.

Another car. He watched the headlights appear and get brighter. A sedan. Then a pickup. It was like being a little kid, waiting for your mother after Little League. You knew she'd show up, but the time before she did was almost unbearable. The other kids would leave and there you were, holding your mitt, staring at the road, positioning for the clearest, longest view possible. She'd only be minutes late, but in those minutes there was no way of knowing for certain it wouldn't stretch forever.

He unlocked the back door and went in and was about to slam it behind him when Colleen's kid appeared and slipped her slim frame and gigantic backpack through the closing doorway.

"Eek," she said and stumbled past him into the narrow hallway. She always did that, showed up out of nowhere. Scared the hell out of Keith a couple times.

"Oh look," he said, "a parking-lot weasel. I thought we got all those."

"Not this one." She leaned sideways, her pale, straight hair fanning down like a broom, and released herself from the pack, slid it off her shoulders and let it thud to the ground.

"How's your cousin Beth?" he asked her. "How's life? Reading any good books?" He liked Lily. He didn't usually like kids, but he liked Lily. You didn't find many kids like her—who would look you in the eye and really talk. Really have something to say.

Lily snorted at the mention of her cousin. "She's selling these bottles of liquid minerals now. You pour it in your orange juice and it looks like squid ink. And it *tastes* like squid ink. She gets people to buy it by calculating how long they can expect to live without it." Lily unzipped her backpack and poked around inside. "I hope you had a better night, Big Keith."

"I'm thinking I may have."

"Busy, huh. Good money?" She began pulling things out. A sneaker, a pot of lip gloss. The spiral notebook Marna gave her. A jar with something yellow inside. A sneaker. "Oh good." She held up a plastic bottle shaped like champagne. It was filled with white jelly beans. "Look. The black ones were labeled for divorce, but this seemed more appropriate, you know? Also, honestly, who likes black jelly beans?"

He laughed. Then felt bad. "Marna's not here, Lily."

She frowned. "But it's Sunday."

He nodded. "She was here. She took off."

"But we're going to *celebrate*. We have plans."

"When did you make them?"

"Forever ago. Weeks." She stood there, staring at him.

"Oh." What was he supposed to say—*She forgot?* For a second he considered telling the truth—not just because he felt bad for Lily but also because if he would tell anyone, he'd tell Lily. But all he said was, "She'll come back, she's my ride."

Lily narrowed her eyes. "Are you sure?"

"Yup," he said. And suddenly it washed over him—they were leaving Denver. He and Marna were leaving Colorado. He'd lived here all his life. In all of it—the preparation and the divorce and the last night of work and *Marna*—he'd somehow lost that part.

"I don't believe you," Lily said and sighed loudly. She restuffed her pack and zipped it, stood up and brushed off her jeans. She heaved the backpack over one shoulder and headed off through the kitchen to the bar. "Who's bartending?" she called but kept walking, fast, like a waitress late for a shift.

Moments after she'd disappeared, James and Fran appeared, pushed through the kitchen doors. Mutt and Mutt.

"I checked on your last table," Fran said, twirling. "They're fine. I refilled their waters and told them not to stay all fucking night."

"Great, Fran. Thanks."

She headed to the walk-in. "I told Denny I'd get him stuff for the bar." Fran's favorite thing was to run errands. I like to feel useful, she'd say. (*She likes to feel used*, was how Marna put it.) When anyone would suggest she ought to just pick up some shifts, she'd point out that it was only fun when it was optional.

James opened the prep table and began taking things out.

"Help yourself," Keith said, but he didn't care.

"It's not my fault service sucks around here." James plunged a hand into a jar of pickles, the hair on his wrist waving like paramecia in the brine.

Keith had seen plenty of Jameses in his time and not just at the bar. There were men like him all over, at every job he'd ever worked, in construction, in telemarketing: hard, greasy little guys who had that certain kind of jaunty meanness that, for whatever reason, came off as charisma to some people.

Fran reappeared with cans of whipped cream.

"Hey, cool, whippets," James said.

Keith groaned. "Please don't." As often as not, when someone ordered a daiquiri or dessert, the cream came out in a runny drip.

Fran said, "Personally, I don't need to hear my brain cells popping to get a thrill."

"Well, I do," James muttered and followed her back into the bar.

The night they made love, Marna wrapped herself in a sheet and went into the kitchen, came back with sliced apples and Cheetos and iced tea. Hey, she said, what does Pennsylvania make you think of?

Pennsylvania?

Just what comes to mind, you know, whatever washes over you. She said, Pennsylvania. Hmmm. Kind of faded? Makes me think of a day-old horoscope.

You moving?

At some point, Marna said. Then: What about Massachusetts? That apple-picking smell.

Sure, he said. I've never been.

Me neither.

Moving all the time—seems like it would be exhausting.

It's not. If you take breaks.

It sounds like an endless shift, Keith said. You know that dream—your section keeps filling up with more and more tables?

Marna laughed. Oh god, she said. The tables keep appearing and wanting things.

And somehow the sun's in your eyes as you try to take orders, but your pen runs out and anyway, they keep materializing, the customers, wailing for sides of mayo, their palms out. . . . They were both laughing. Keith took a drink of tea. She'd only brought one glass, they were sharing it. He said, It's exactly like one of those Greek myths—a curse that never ends. You keep thinking it's going to, that you're about to reach your goal, but you never do.

I took a class in myths once, Marna said. She wiped her mouth with the back of her hand. I really got into it.

He wanted to kiss her neck again, pull her in closer, but she was still eating. He thought about how it had been, just a little while ago—and then before that, when they'd first gotten up and come into the bedroom, when he knew and she knew and he knew that she knew.

Marna said, You know which one I like? The one where the man gets older and older but doesn't die. That one used to freak me out.

Or Prometheus and his liver, Keith agreed. Or Athena in Zeus's skull. Whenever I get a headache, I think of that part where she bursts out. And then there's the great story where she weaves the tapestry and turns the other woman into a spider.

Or Persephone, Marna said and sighed and flopped backwards into the pillows. Oh, Persephone. Daughter of the moon, living in the underworld with the god of death, who saves her. And that watermelon she ate, making a godawful juicy mess.

Watermelon? He lay down beside her.

Sure.

He smiled. Pomegranate, right? And she was the daughter of the *harvest,* taken *against* her will. What did you get in that class? He buried his face between her shoulder and the bed and breathed the air around her skin.

She yawned. Pomegranate. Pomeranian. Poop. It was, she said, scrunching her forehead, then relaxing and smiling, it was like this . . . she'd eaten the whole damn watermelon and for every seed she spat . . . for every seed she got to stay another year away.

The cooks were gone. The kitchen smelled of ammonia and grease. If you looked closely, even now, with the floor still glossy with mop water and the stainless-steel equipment wiped and gleaming, you could see that the floor buckled darkly in places, near the grill and under the sinks. The pots and pans, stowed in jangled heaps on the lowest shelves, were dented and burnt. Dry-goods shelves were scattered with corn-meal, the overhanging oven hoods fuzzy with grime.

And yet it was possible *not* to look closely. In fact, with the heat lamps off and only a minimum of overhead light bearing down, the kitchen offered the distinct illusion of calm and clean.

It was the last time he would stand here.

He got a half-dozen sub rolls out of the cooler and brought them over to the prep table, reopened the lid. He split the rolls with his hands and piled on meat and cheeses and vegetables. He found Bo's stash of Mars Bars behind the pickles and took a few, then grabbed some oranges for Marna. Then a lemon and a handful of butter pats for the hell of it. You never knew what you'd want on the road.

11.

Lily kept a running tally of all the guys who wanted to fuck her. The latest version went like this:

Randall Dean
Lance (bagger at Save-a-Lot)
Mr. Davis
Rochelle's two brat brothers, Brent and Tyler, and possibly their father
The bus driver
Denny

Denny had only recently been added, and Lily wondered why she hadn't noticed before. He looked up at her now as she sat down on a stool. Gave a little smile. Came over. He was wearing his black Neil Young concert t-shirt, the words on it worn into dashes and polka dots.

"Hey there, L-pad," he said. "Good to see you."

"Right back atcha." She licked her upper lip. "You stick around just to see me?"

"Sure thing."

"Yeah, right. Who do you like more—me or Marna?"

"Always you."

Who do you like more, Lily asked silently, *me or Lena?* Bitch. Hag. Makeup whore. She said, "So Marna took off."

"Yup."

"She's not coming back."

"Dunno."

"She's not. I can tell. It sucks." She sighed. "I guess she divorced us all, huh." She looked away. Then smiled. "Not that I'm not happy to see you, of course, Denny."

"Of course."

She leaned in. "How 'bout a drink? My mom's downstairs."

"How 'bout some ID, Lily?" He scooped ice into a pint glass and filled it with Sprite, then popped in a straw and plunked it down in front of her.

"Very funny."

"A drink," he said, "is a good idea."

There was such a difference, thought Lily, with older men. She watched Denny stretch down to pull a bottle of beer from the cooler, then click off the top with the opener and slug back a gulp. Maybe he'd talk and maybe he wouldn't. Nothing like the guys—the *kids*—Lily knew from school. They were all talk. All jumpy nerves. Lily stirred the Sprite. Take Randall Dean, for instance. Randall Dean, Randall Dean. Randall Dean in high school now, point guard for junior varsity, always bouncing around—and not just on the court either. On the sidewalk, just walking down the street, he'd be hopping all over, never staying calm. Even when you could tell he was trying to be cool, it was all there, the *trying*. The jitter beneath his skin. Which was nice skin, in any case—Rochelle thought Lily was crazy to stop seeing him. Nice eyes, bright white teeth. Tall, which was always good. For a while, before her mother nailed her window shut, Lily would sneak out at night and meet him at the corner, where he'd be waiting in his Pinto with a six-pack or a bottle of something sweet, which Lily preferred. They'd drive out by the reservoir and climb into the back seat and try to chat a little before getting on to business, pulling things down, sliding things up. It was really an ordeal, all that positioning and repositioning. Are you sure you're doing this right? Lily had asked him the fourth and last time they'd gone at it, the closest they'd come to actually doing It. It was obviously the wrong question because he'd shot up and climbed back behind the wheel and tire-squealed it out of there before Lily had a chance to even get her pants back up.

Not that it stopped him from calling. Not that it stopped him from going on and on about basketball or his buddy, Zeke, who fell rock climbing a few years back, fell eighty feet and died. Randall talked so fast, Lily would be out of breath at the conversation's end.

Come meet me out, he'd plead before hanging up, a hint of moan in his voice.

Maybe soon, she'd say, her stomach a little funny. Quit being so anxious, she wanted to say. Just take a goddamn *chill*.

And then there was Stephen Lawrence, whom Lily had asked to the Sadie Hawkins dance. It was a whim really, she didn't know why she did it. She didn't even want to go to the dance all that much. Stephen sat by her in Honors English, was always working out geometric proofs for the math team he was on. He wasn't so bad, though, really, if you got past the combed-back hair. He had smoky, sad-looking eyes. There was even something sexy about the pressed oxfords and slacks he wore, made Lily want to wrinkle them up. She had a thing for the unexpected. In the drifty time of almost-sleep late at night, or in the morning before she was totally up, she'd guide her dreams and work in all sorts of formal and proper men, in oxfords, in suits and ties, men anonymous and unknowing, walking down the aisles of hardware stores or in businessmen meetings, and in those dreams she would go right up to them, not saying a thing, and stick her hand right down their pants, just like that, reach right in and take hold where it counted. But of course it had never happened—certainly not with Stephen Lawrence, pressed pants or no pressed pants. Can't do it, he said mournfully a few days after she'd invited him to the dance. I asked my mom and she said no. No prob, Lily said, shrugging it off, it was just as friends anyway. And she pretended not to notice at the dance—with stupid Thad Riser, who kissed like a dying fish—when Stephen showed up with Mindy Salsburg, the kind of girl any mother would approve of, braids so tight you thought her eyes would pop out.

When Lily thought about him, though, late at night, Stephen, or Randall for that matter, or the bagger at Save-a-Lot, when she talked about boys at sleepovers with Rochelle in the other twin bed, it was more exciting. I love thinking about those arms, Lily would say, and those hands going down down down, and both girls would giggle in the dark and Lily would wonder if Rochelle was touching herself too. They talked about how it would go, how his hand would first slide up her shirt—it felt cold to even think of it, gave Lily a jolt—and then snake down her pants. Slow, not grabby, like it had been with Randall. Lily rewrote it the right way. She'd be wearing her best panties, the ones her mother didn't know she had. And he would notice. His hands would ease them down, the fingers reaching below the lacy material. . . . It was hard to picture Randall's or Stephen's or Lance's face in all of this, and really, truthfully, it wasn't any one of them at all, covering her mouth with his, opening her mouth with his, moving down. Down down down. It wasn't even a faceless, pressed businessman. It was Mr. Davis.

How embarrassing to admit it even to herself.

Mr. Davis taught shop at Thorton Middle School. Bland, portly, unnoticeable. A close-clipped beard and mustache. Wore light-blue polo shirts and coveralls every day, wet sweat moons under the arms, and had a quiet, low way of talking, like if you weren't listening that was your problem. And people did listen. That was the crazy part, though not nearly as crazy as the day Lily realized she was hopelessly in love with him. She didn't even like shop all that much until that day. And then suddenly, it was all different, his voice was echoing down her throat and she'd go hot when he looked over or called on her and she was taking her work home and doing it before supper and would stay after class for extra help with the spice-rack project, watching how he set a nail, his thick fingers working deftly around a flash of silver.

So when Rochelle and Lily talked about blow jobs, it was Mr. Davis and not Randall whom Lily was really imagining. Neither girl had ever given a blow job—weren't even quite sure if there was or was not actual blowing involved, they had heard both—but a lot of kids said they'd done it and Jennie Maslow had done it for sure, and there had even been an incident last semester in Ms. Roth's fourth-period Algebra where Maryanne Lucciano blew Jet Phillips right smack in the middle of class. Possibly on a dare, or just because Maryanne was that way—it depended on who you talked to. But it was real. It really happened. Ms. Roth turned around to do some work on the board and Maryanne skittered right over and squatted under the desk and went to it. It took Ms. Roth a full few minutes to realize it and then—Lily could just imagine it—the look on her face! Lily would have given anything to have seen that. She thought about it often during class, any class, but especially in shop, which was her very last class of the day and gave her something to look forward to. More and more, Lily found herself thinking about Mr. Davis on top of her, moving over her, holding on, going to work. What would he do, she'd wonder as she watched him point to an overhead diagram or work the jigsaw, his goggles moist and foggy over his clear green eyes, if right then in class she slid over and kneeled down and unzipped. Exposed him right there, in the light of day with everyone watching, and took him in her mouth, slid it in.

I think I'm a nymphomaniac, she confided to Rochelle.

Me too, Rochelle agreed. They spent hours poring through the dirty magazines they'd found in Rochelle's attic. Would you do that? That? How about that? *Of course* was always Lily's answer. It's all good, she'd say. One time, when Lily's mom was at work and Rochelle and Lily were over at Marna's place—and Marna had run down the street to get food—the two girls read Marna's *Joy of Sex* book. It turned out to be less fun than it sounded. None of the pencil drawings was as sexy as they'd expected, lots of body hair, and the guy looked more like a girl. There was even a picture with the guy-girl tongue-kissing a woman's furry armpit. I don't think, Rochelle said, you have to do that kind of thing.

Well, no wonder, Lily said, grabbing up the book and flipping to the copyright, it's way out of date. Those things go in and out of style, you know.

In and out and in and out, Rochelle shrieked, flopping back on the bed and almost spilling her very-berry smoothie on Marna's rainbow silk duvet.

Lily began getting all sorts of images in her head, all sorts of guys moving over her, guys she didn't even want to see like that. The hunch-backed crossing guard and Roland, the hall monitor. A couple of times it wasn't only guys either. Mrs. Zemecca, Rochelle's mom, standing in front of the girls, giving them glasses of juice, and then suddenly her blouse would peel away in Lily's mind, and her big white boobs would be right there, soft and jiggly in Lily's face. *Awful, awful.* Needless to say, there were many things Lily couldn't tell Rochelle.

Oh that Randall, is what she did say.

But now Denny was an interesting development.

"How's school?" he asked. He was wiping down the bar, making circles with a dish rag.

"How's work?" she shot back.

"Right, right," he said. "Good point."

"I can't talk about school without a drink."

"You do have a drink."

"C'mon, Denny." She watched him pull back the last of his beer and toss it in the bin. "You're teasing me," she huffed and spun around on her stool. He had a girlfriend, Stephanie, but from what Lily had gathered, it wasn't a very good relationship.

"One," he said and glanced over to where Lena and Fran were squawking it up. "Just one." And, like Lily knew he would, he got a mug so no one would see and poured a shot. It was green. Watermelon liqueur.

"That stuff?" she complained. "Not even forty proof. I might as well breathe cough-syrup vapors." She took it, though. She liked the taste of liqueurs, and if she wanted to, she could always sneak back later, when they were all at the corner table drunk and blathering, and free-sample some Goldschläger. Now that was good stuff. Eighty proof and with real flakes of gold, which Lily picked off her tongue and saved in napkins. At home she had a thimble almost half full of gold. She was going to melt it down when she had enough, maybe make some earrings or turn it in for cash.

"Now, don't tell your mother," Denny said, which is what he always said.

Don't tell your mother. The words echoed wickedly now. Denny pulling down her pants, Denny licking down her belly. Denny. Lily stuck the tip of her tongue into the drink, then rubbed it on the roof of her mouth, watched him wring the bar rag, suds up the sink. Older men and younger women—it was the oldest story in the book. Humbert Humbert wasn't done in by some middle-aged biddy.

Sometimes Lily would stare at herself, naked, in front of her bedroom mirror, turning at various angles or lying down. She wasn't bad-looking. She'd avoided that second round of baby fat that had done in so many of her friends. Her breasts were nice, maybe not as big as they could be, but she had plenty of time. She struck poses she'd seen in the dirty magazines. Legs together, bent over. Her hands over her breasts, but barely covering, her mouth wet and pursed, her hair falling in her face a little. She tried to see all of it as he would see it—the *he* a bit muddled, perhaps, and changing. Mr. Davis's hands. Denny's jaw.

"So tell me?" Denny broke in.

"Tell you what?"

"About school, kiddo. Wasn't that the deal?"

"Oh," she said. "Aced a history quiz without studying. Read three library books, lost two textbooks. Fucked one shop teacher."

"What?"

"Oh it's nothing. That sort of thing happens all the time, you know." She watched Denny's face. It was hard to tell with him, how something registered. She rounded her shoulders a little, leaned her elbows on the bar to give him a hint of cleavage. "Last year Mr. Apopolis left his wife for a student he'd been screwing since she was in his ninth grade history class, which, if you ask me, wasn't so stupid if you saw his wife."

"How terrible," Denny said, but he cracked a smile—proof he was on to her.

"No, see, it's not really, and besides, girls aren't so young when they're, you know, young these days."

"I guess that's true."

"Oh it's absolutely true." She paused. Drank half the shot. "Yum. Hey, can I bum a smoke?"

He laughed. "You don't smoke."

She shrugged. "Maybe. Maybe not. Anyway. I could give you all sorts of examples—"

Someone came up behind her and wrapped a moist hand over her eyes. "Well, *fine,* Lily, don't even come over and say hi."

"Ugh, Lena, you're sweaty, get off." Lily ducked out of her grip.

"Well. Hello to you too." Lena flounced her hair and then climbed up onto her knees on a stool and leaned over to the taps to refill her beer, giving the world a full fanny shot and splashing beer everywhere. "Whatcha up to, girl? You hear about Marna?"

"Nothing. Yes," Lily muttered and took a sip of shot. If I close my eyes you'll be gone. She'd tried that one so many times. The year she and her mother lived with Lena was the longest year of Lily's life. If I count to one thousand backwards and forwards, you'll disappear. Zap. I'll even eat a bug. Chew a caterpillar. Zap. Zap.

"Denny, isn't it incredible?" Lena asked and tried to cup Lily's chin in her hand. "What happened to the little girl? I remember—"

"You're drunk," Denny said and winked at Lily.

"God," Lena blathered on, "maxi pads. Training bras. Training bras!" She raised her glass of beer. "Your mom and I, Lily, we were wondering for so long when you would need one. *If* you would need one."

Fuckyoufuckyoufuckyou. "Funny," Lily said brightly, pausing for a moment to finish off her shot and slurp down the rest of her Sprite. "That's funny because Denny and I here were just wondering the same about you."

She hopped off the bar stool and headed across the room.

India was hunched over a book. *Wind in Summer.* "Earth to India."

"India to Earth," India muttered and turned a page.

Lily sat down and scooted the chair close to the table. "India, I need you to do my fortune. Only you can't charge me because I'm broke."

"I'm busy. Come back later."

"It is later."

"Not by my watch."

"Can I have a smoke?"

"No you can't—" India lowered her book and scanned the table. "Okay, very funny. Give them back."

"What?"

"Where are my cigs, Lily?"

"What cigs? I don't even know what cigs are. I'm a minor. And shouldn't you know, if you're a psychic, where your cigs are anyway?"

"Lily."

"Oh hell, here." She tossed them back on the table. "But seriously, can you answer some questions, India, please? Pretty please?" She pushed up a sleeve and slid her hand across the table.

"I don't administer vaccinations."

"I just have a couple questions, India."

"Okay. Okay, okay." She put the book down. "And I have some advice for you."

"Fine, but I have questions." From the corner of her eye, Lily saw Denny and Lena talking, leaning into each other. "Specific questions."

"And I," India said, closing her eyes, "have specific advice."

12.

"*This is what* we call debriefing," Keith told JJ, lifting a shot from a tray of them and placing it on the table in front of her.

"Oh," she said. "What is it?"

"T'killya." He distributed the rest to the others, plunked each one down in a circle. Everyone was gathered around table 14, which was tucked in the corner near the dartboards. JJ was pleased with herself for remembering the table numbers, and even more for remembering so many names. Except for the last old man at the bar—whom Denny was, at that very moment, helping out the door, causing a big white dog to pop up from the walkway and do a little dance—JJ knew the name of everyone left.

"Can we at least wait until *after* she's finished her sidework to get the new girl drunk?" Lena asked, dropping another handful of forks onto the pile of silverware JJ was rolling inside napkins.

Keith shook his head. "Unavoidable," he said.

Next to Fran was James and then, when she wasn't jumping up to do things, Lena. You could tell Fran and James had been together for a long time. They had that sharp kind of banter going back and forth that no one else paid attention to. A few tables away, Colleen's daughter, Lily, was talking to the witch, nodding to whatever she was saying.

"Drinks," Fran said, holding up her shot in one hand, her mixed drink in the other, "the elixir of forgetting."

"Forgetting?" Lena scoffed. "Forgetting what? You weren't working."

"I'm helping. I helped. And now I'm helping you forget." She turned to JJ. "Aren't I, Gigi."

"JJ," Colleen said.

"Sure," JJ said. "I can't remember a thing."

"Don't blame that on Fran," Lena said.

"Supposedly, you know," Colleen said, "we only use ten percent of our brains."

"Some less than others," Fran said, looking at James, who was lighting matches and shaking them out. He tore off a corner of napkin and touched it to a flame. It ignited, lifted into the air for a second, then was gone.

"And you know what my theory is?" Colleen asked. "You know what I think?"

Lena reached over and patted Colleen on the arm. "We're just glad, sweetie, that you do."

Another thing that pleased JJ was this: despite having drunk three beers, she was functioning fine. Better than fine. She felt strong. After running around all night—actual running, actual sprinting—and after she'd reached a point where she was positive her head couldn't hold one more detail or her arms one more tray—in fact, she'd dropped one

full of glasses right smack in the middle of all the tables, causing everyone in the place to stop talking and clap—after all that, she still helped
stock beer, clear away dishes, and sweep the floor. She'd learned to cal-
culate sales and tip-outs, made sure to thank every one of the kitchen
workers—learned to say *pretty* in Spanish—and was now, with Colleen, rolling the knives and forks into napkins, piling them into baskets.
And drinking. And drinking. And yet JJ wasn't tired. Or, if she was,
she was *over*tired, the kind of tired that gives you more energy, not less.

"I need a lime," Fran complained.

"No, you don't," Keith said. "It's good tequila."

"A good lime, then?"

"Nope."

"You're kidding."

"Nope."

"I think," Colleen said, sipping at hers, "tequila tastes like
Band-Aids."

"Okay," Lena said, slapping one hand on the table and raising her
shot with the other. "Let's do it. One, two, three."

They all drank their shots. JJ tried to get all of hers down, but her
throat closed up. She coughed and, doing her best to keep the liquid
in, grabbed a chunk of napkins from the stack she was working from,
pressed them to her mouth.

"You're making the new girl sick," Fran said. She picked up a butter knife from Colleen's pile and looked at her reflection in the blade,
tilted it back and forth.

"It went down the wrong way," JJ said.

"Is there a right way?" Keith asked.

"Yes," Lena said.

"I like tequila," JJ said. Sometimes it was just a matter of deciding,
she thought.

And then it occurred to her: if she'd known to begin with how tough it was to be a waitress, she might never have tried. And yet here it was: the night was over. She'd survived. According to Colleen, rolling silverware was the last thing on the list for the two of them to do. It wasn't as simple as it looked. The silverware was still a little damp from being washed, and so the trick was to wrap it up before the napkin dissolved. Roll fold roll. Colleen and JJ each had their own piles of napkins and silverware. Every so often Fran would reach in and do one "for old times' sake." She had a bad habit, JJ noticed, of dropping cigarette ash right where she was rolling. Lena, meanwhile, was still restocking the stuff on tables, going around with a tray of condiments, filling the sugar and Sweet-and-Low caddies, wiping off the salt and pepper shakers. She was doing it gradually. She'd sit and drink and then get up and do a few tables and then take a break. At one point, she gathered a bunch of candles and lit them on table 14, in the middle of everyone's drinks and ashtrays. They were the kind of candles you saw at Italian restaurants, nestled in dimpled red plastic bulbs. *Happy birthday, Mr. President,* Lena sang as she lit them with a lighter. The small patches of light opened up their corner of the dark dining room, spread a haze of calm. With the lights lowered and the TVs off, there was a stillness that JJ could never have imagined just a few hours before. Not silence exactly—across the room you could hear Denny doing things in the office, shutting drawers, jangling change, and there was the talking, of course—but the noise seemed contained in pockets, flickering like the candles. What echoed was the quiet.

Keith collected the shot glasses. JJ's was still half full. "Better luck next time," he told her.

"Hey, Denny," Lena yelled in the direction of the office. "Join us." When she didn't hear anything back, she lit a cigarette and turned to JJ. "Your rolls are all wrong."

"Oh Lena, they're fine," Colleen said.

JJ looked down at the one she was in the middle of doing. Roll fold roll. Was it fold roll roll? She thought about the joint Denny had made. It seemed so long ago now.

"No, they're not fine, Colleen. And yours are wrong too."

"I've always rolled them this way."

"I know. Look. They fall apart." Lena lifted one up a couple inches off the table and let it drop. Sure enough, the napkin sprang open. The fork bounced away, chimed against the floor.

"Yipes," Colleen muttered and went after it.

"What am I doing wrong?" JJ asked.

"Watch." Lena lifted an open napkin from JJ's stack and laid it down, then plucked up a fork and knife, and in a flash of movement—too fast for JJ to understand the order—she had a tight bundle.

"She is the best," Fran said. "Strong wrists."

"Top that," Lena called to Keith.

"Keith won an award," Colleen told JJ. "Best Server in Denver."

"Ask Keith why he doesn't do roll-ups," Lena said smugly.

"Why don't you do roll-ups?" JJ called.

"Because I have a hairy ass."

Fran and Lena shrieked. "Too much information," Lena said.

"Oops, sorry," he said with mock horror, "what was the question? I got confused."

"Nothing wrong with a hairy ass," James said.

"The reason," Lena told JJ, "that he doesn't do roll-ups is that his are worse than yours."

"It's true," Keith said, coming over. "I'm not all that good of a waitress."

"Exactly," Lena said. "Finally."

"That can't be," JJ said, "if you won an award."

"I have nice legs," Keith said. "It's my saving grace."

James raised his bottle. "To nice legs."

"You don't have nice legs," Lena told Keith.

"Nice abs?"

"Ha."

"Well, fuck, I don't know what it is then."

"I think you're good," JJ said. "I saw you working."

Keith turned to her. "Thank you," he said.

He wasn't ugly, she thought. Not at all, once you got to know him. He looked like he could be in a rock band, maybe, the way his head was shaved and he wore his jeans low and baggy—and he had this wholehearted kind of smile that was always a surprise. You didn't expect to see it, for some reason, on his face. You expected something meaner. It embarrassed JJ a little, seeing him grin like that, at her, all for her, and she looked away. "You're very welcome," she said.

127

13.

"*Oh no.*" *Lily* rolled her eyes. "I've heard this."

"You haven't heard it."

"It's about the Ethiopian chick who makes blankets."

"Quilts."

"Yeah, quilts. Can't you just give me my fortune?" Lily sat back, sighed. India tended to tell the same stories over and over. Though, in all fairness, it wasn't as though Lily had anything better to do. Denny was in the office counting money, and Lena and Lily's mother and a bunch of their friends were at the corner table blabbing it up. This was always the longest part of the night, when Lily had to wait while her mother finished up and then lingered over her free drinks, saying, Just a minute, just a minute, like Lily was a dog wanting a walk. Plus, if Lily wasn't careful, Lena would recruit her to do waitress work, glopping together ketchups or filling salt and pepper shakers. When she'd been little it'd been fun, but now it was just boring work. Don't you want to be helpful? Lena was always asking. No. If she wouldn't—in a million, trillion years—do it for money, why would she want to do it for free?

India took a drink of coffee and restarted the story. It wasn't a bad story, Lily remembered. It was about a girl who has a hard life and then discovers that she has the magical ability to make quilts that solve problems for people.

Across the room, Lena let out a sudden showy laugh to something someone had said. No one laughed for real like that. And no one *normal* laughed for fake like that. As if she could read Lily's mind, Lena glanced over, so Lily snapped her attention back to India, who was warbling on about Abeo and her mean grandmother. India had a good voice, low and thick. People who spent a lot of time in bars, Lily had noticed, often had good voices. Which made sense. What else could you do in a bar other than talk? Except drink and smoke, but probably those helped too. Denny had a wonderful voice. Confident, even, and clear. And Keith's was booming. Marna's was like see-through fabric, like one of India's scarves, light but strong. Lena's, though, sucked. Not just her laugh. Her words came out harsh and high when she got excited, which for some reason made Lily think of a rusty cheese grater.

"Cripes, Lily, are you listening?"

"Yes."

"Oh yeah, what did I just say?"

"Abeo was eight years old when she sewed her first magic quilt and it was really really beautiful, though at the time she didn't know it was magic."

"She was seven." India tapped a china zebra on the table, like, *Ha, I caught you.* She had a whole bagful of junk that she'd spread out on the table. Lily liked to carry stuff too, even unusual stuff, but India lugged around so much more. One time when India went to use the bathroom, Lily peeked into her bag and saw a family-sized box of instant potatoes.

"Okay, okay," Lily said. "Go on." The next part, where the girl discovers she has magic powers, was Lily's favorite.

India pinched the bridge of her nose and looked down at her coffee cup. There were two red marks from the pinching. "I just realized," she said. "How late it feels."

"India."

"I'm gonna finish." India yawned. "I could use some wine. Get me wine and I'll continue." She reached down into her bag and pulled out a few dollars. "Tell your mother one more red."

"Okay." Lily sighed and rose and started over to the table. Her mother and Big Keith and the new waitress were facing the other direction. Fran was drinking a shot. Lena was lighting candles. Lily hesitated. She glanced back at India, who was staring into her coffee cup. What the hell, Lily thought. She tucked the money into her back pocket and shuffled over behind the bar.

It was spotless, everything wiped down, smelling of Windex. The fruit bar was put away, the sink was scrubbed, the metal shaking cups were shining on their shelf. Nothing was left out—though you still had a *sense* of him. Lily could feel it: a hover of *Denny.* Every object he'd touched was buzzing on some low level. And there *was* one thing left, she spotted it: a cigarette butt on the floor. It had fallen into one of the circles cut out of the rubber mat. She could tell it was his because it was only half smoked. She crouched down and picked it up, touched the tip of her tongue to the mouth end and imagined their spit molecules joining. Take me away, she thought, sending mental waves back to the office, we'll go to a faraway country and run around naked. She thought about lighting the half cigarette with a match from one of the books on the bar, sitting down right there on the mat and smoking it, but India was waiting and it was only a matter of time before someone would come back for a drink. So she stood up and stuck it into her pocket with the money, then climbed onto the bar to get a wine glass. There were only three and they were all spotty and had faint blotches of lipstick. Not Denny's fault, probably from the shift before. Lily grabbed one of the glasses and rubbed it with her thumb. She looked for the red wine, found it and uncorked it, poured it into the glass. Fran glanced over and waved. Lily froze. She waited for her mother or Lena to turn around, but they didn't. For a second Lily thought about pouring herself one as well, but recorked the wine and slipped back to India's table, trying not to spill it.

"That's a good pour," India said.

"We can share," Lily said and took a sip. It was sour, nothing like the strawberry Boones Farm Randall sometimes gave her.

"It'll stunt your growth." India removed the wine from her hand.

"I'm already tall." The sip had warmed her, spread into her chest, made her think of the commercial for stomachache medicine with a see-through version of a person so you could watch the medicine seeping in, going to work. "How old were you, India, when you started drinking?"

But before India could answer, Lena butted in to clean out the ashtray India was using. She was gathering them from tables, emptying them into a plastic bucket. She took her time dumping theirs, making a big production of it, setting down her bucket, acting like India's animals and candles were in the way, confusing her. "Are we fortune-telling?" she asked, all fake brightness. Cheese grater.

"No," Lily and India said together.

Lily said, "Lena, India's in the middle of telling me something. Could you go ask my mom to hurry up, that I'll be ready to go in a few minutes? Please?"

As usual, Lena ignored what Lily wanted. She set down the tray of ashtrays on the next table and sat, joined them. Reached into her apron and dug out a pack of cigarettes, took out two, handed one to India. "Is it the one about blankets?"

"Quilts," they both said.

Lena lit her cigarette and then India's, like Denny liked to light his, with the match still attached, then shook the whole book and dropped it on the table. "What a shitty night," she said, sighing. "Lousy Marna." She blew out smoke and looked at it, really watched it, like anything that came out of her had to be special.

Lily said, "Keep going, India."

Lena said, "Hey, I have an idea, maybe she could join the circus and be the girl who rides the elephant. Or kills the tightrope walker. You need a little action to keep it interesting."

Out of the corner of her eye, Lily saw Denny come out from the office and join the others. Lena couldn't see him, she was facing the wrong way. Lily tried to get Denny's attention without making it obvious. While India got to the magical messages that appeared and told people what to do, Lily sent her own messages in mental waves to Denny: *Look here, look here. Love Lily. Lena is evil. Lena has big knees.*

But Lena was the one who turned and Lily saw her face change when she saw him. It was like something was poured in from the top, it made her expression go rubbery. "Ladies," Lena said, mashing out her cigarette, "excuse me. I already know how it turns out," and she stood, scooping up the bucket and tray. She kissed Lily on the head and walked off.

Lily imagined that the kiss left a drop of acid. It spread, melting her hair, leaving her skin scarred and shiny. "Can you tell me *her* fortune?" she asked India, watching Lena slink over to Denny, get behind him and rub his shoulders. "How she falls in a hole somewhere and never comes out?"

"You want me to continue or not? And would you quit drinking my wine? You're gonna get sick."

"Go on."

"Okay. Here's the thing. Abeo starts wanting more answers. So she closes her eyes and thinks real hard and waits for a quilt to start forming in her fingers. *Expects* something. Fast. Now. Any second, any second. But nothing happens. It doesn't work. So what does she do? She forces the needle, forces the designs and words. And these quilts are just as pretty as the other ones, but their messages make no sense. *Ripe raisins lose love. The left-handed man never comes home. Three chickens at dawn drown music to madness. Five buttons for real, six to steal.* But Abeo pays attention. That's the thing. She takes them seriously, she's afraid not to. She stops eating raisins and listening to music. It just so happened that she'd been planning to marry a man who was left-handed, so she lies and tells him that she's fallen out of love and moves to a different village."

Denny was both-handed. He'd shown Lily once how he could write with either one. He told her that he was born left-handed but his dad made him use his right and now he was glad because he was comfortable either way. He showed her how the handwriting was almost exactly the same, just at different slants.

India swirled the last bit of wine that was left in her glass. Lily waited for her to keep going, but she didn't. "And then what?" Lily asked.

"That's it."

"What do you mean, that's it?"

"That's it."

"India! That can't be it. I remember the story and in the end she meets an American man who flies and fixes planes and they fall in love and have babies and buy a farm in Wisconsin and she's famous."

India frowned. "No, that's not this story. Go ask Lena if you want a different one. I don't know what happened to Abeo. It's a true story, not a fairy tale. She probably took her own bad advice and fell off a cliff."

"Well, that sucks." Lily picked up the wine and finished it. She wondered if India's teeth were fake. They were very white and straight. Either they were really nice or fake. "Now my fortune?" she asked and pushed her hand across the table. Denny was laughing at something. Maybe he had forgotten about Lily altogether and was, right now, imagining sex with Lena, imagining pulling down Lena's underwear . . . it was too awful to think about.

India didn't take her hand. "You have many things to come."

"Can you please be a little more specific? Come on, take my hand."

"Specific? Didn't you hear a single thing I said?" Still, India did take her hand and ran her thumb over the palm, like she was trying to get the creases out. "You," she said sharply, "have many things to come."

"Oh cripes. That's easy," Lily grumbled. "I could say that."

"So? Save me the trouble then."

"Come on, India, tell me things. Can you tell me anything about who likes me at my school? Does Denny love Lena?"

"That's none of your business."

"What if it is, maybe a little?"

"Why do I even bother, Lily?"

Lily sighed. "What's it like, India?"

"I told you—"

"No, not that." She felt a little silly thinking it, much less saying it, but she did anyway—who could she ask if not India?—she lowered her voice and said, "Love. What's it like? You can tell me that."

India looked away, blinked. "Well, sure."

"Because I know all the things it's supposed to be, how you're supposed to see it, and I think I know, you know, about feeling it, but it's hard to be sure of the truth, to be sure that you're, well, feeling it right."

"The truth is," India said.

Lily leaned forward. India had a funny smell, kind of like old fruit, but in a way, it wasn't so bad on her. Lily was used to it, thought, *India* instead of *old fruit* or *old laundry*.

"It's the saddest thing," India said and possibly shifted her teeth, just a little. "It can ruin a life if you're not careful."

14.

Not long before he died, as an early gift for her twelfth birthday, Lily's father gave her a coin. He'd found it overseas when he was a merchant marine, picked it up off the ground beside a fish vendor in an outdoor market. It was old and brassy, with a snake on one side and a Japanese letter on the other, and it felt heavier than it looked. When it'd first caught his eye, her father told her, he thought it was a fish scale and almost didn't bend down to double-check. But it was just one of those good-luck things. He pocketed the coin and then, for the hell of it, took out his billfold and bought a fish— even though he didn't usually cook his own meals, and even though (and this was Lily's favorite part) he didn't *like* the taste of fish. He picked a fat flounder still wet from the sea and brought it back to the base, where he cooked it over a fire, turned it into an excellent dinner.

But the coin was lost now. And the desk from his study. Gone. Chair. Gone. Clothing, pipes, model cars, gone, gone, gone.

Here's what was left: two ticket stubs from a Broncos game, a paperback on backcountry survival tips, and a photograph. Lily kept it all in her backpack. The photo was taken when Lily was seven. It showed her on her bicycle for the first time without training wheels. Her father looked angry, but he wasn't, he was just nervous. He was watching her wobble away and then pick up speed down the hill.

Lily spent a whole afternoon looking for the coin. It was the Fourth of July, not quite a year after her father died. While her mother and her mother's new coworkers moved everything out of the house and onto the front lawn, Lily crawled around the perimeter of her bedroom. Or what used to be her bedroom—nothing was left, only the carpet. A stretch of faded blue. The afternoon sun coming through the curtainless windows was making her drowsy. They'd opened every window in the house, but the air felt heavy anyway—thick with funny smells that Lily couldn't remember noticing before. Sweat and metal and mildew. It was as though without any furniture to pin it down, everything had been released and was stirring up. Years and years of who knew what.

Bad memories, probably, Lily thought. She flopped onto her back and closed her eyes and tried to *feel* where the coin might be. *Corner of the closet* popped into her mind, but she jumped up to check and found nothing. Just a Smarties candy wrapper and a hunk of dust that looked like dryer lint.

Fourth of July used to be Lily's favorite holiday. She loved everything about it: the fireworks, the barbecue, the smell of summer and suntan oil. Firecrackers. Even the name, *Independence Day,* was exciting. Lily liked to think you could apply it personally, not just nationally, and planned someday to take a hot-air balloon ride across the country to celebrate.

But it was hardly independent to move from your own house into the apartment of your mother's coworker. That was what they were doing that year—instead of grilling sweet-and-sour pork and eating melon on the back porch, they were packing almost everything they owned into boxes that Lily's mother brought home from her new job. Books into *Southern Comfort* and *Bel Aire Triple Sec.* Records in *Armando's Superior Paper Products.* Summer clothes in *Iceberg Lettuce,* winter in *E-Z Butter Substitute.* Instead of lighting sparklers, they were dragging out lamps and digging through closets. Instead of roasting marshmallows, they were setting aside their most essential items—only what would fit into eight boxes, a milk crate, and a trunk.

Lily and her mother were going to have to share a room.

It's only temporary, her mother pointed out. You get your own bed, of course. It could be fun, she said. Like an extended sleepover.

She'd broken the news only a few weeks before, while Lily was sitting at the kitchen table worrying about a homework assignment she'd forgotten to do. She was pouring cereal into a bowl and her mother was scribbling a fork through a pan of egg. Then, out of nowhere:

We've lost the house.

Lily put down the milk. What?

It's not ours anymore, it belongs to the bank. I've been wanting to tell you.

Just like that. Like, *We need more light bulbs.* Or, *Lucille down the street got a new puppy and named it Mac.*

Well, Lily said, get it back.

I can't. That's why the bank has it. We can't afford it.

Which bank? It was a dumb question and an even dumber thought: Lily saw the tellers in their purple suits and their scarves and name tags and bowls of candy, moving in. Setting up velvet rope lines in the den. Taking dibs on her bedroom. Get it *back,* she told her mother. Don't just stand there, go down there and get it back.

This isn't easy for me either, you know, her mother said. If you think it is, well you're wrong. But look, we both know it's not the end of the world. We have options. We'll get another house at some point. She licked the fork absently, then made a face. Oh yuck, she said, salmonella. She wiped her tongue on a paper towel. Look, Lily, don't be mad. I'm sorry. You know that, right?

Yes.

Can I ask you a question? You know I love you.

Yes.

You still love me, right? Her face had gone soft, like pudding.

Outside, like any other morning, the early bus stopped with a huff and a whine and then took off again. In her head, Lily tried on all the things to say:

Dad wouldn't let this happen.

What about that new stereo, all those shoes? How much did you spend on the air purifier?

People work these things out—why, *just for once,* can't you?

But all she said was, Yes.

If I were a coin, where would I be?
Anywhere but here.

Lily's bedroom walls looked like photographic negatives, bright white squares of clean—not framed photos and pictures but their opposites. Their place-keepers, like the walls were willing to save the spaces. She rescanned the edges of the room—she was sure she'd seen it, just yesterday—then went downstairs for something to drink, tiptoed past the dining room, where the others were trying to move the china cabinet. I know we got it *in,* she heard her mother say.

The kitchen cupboards were open and empty, the strawberry shelf paper curled at the edges. Lily opened the refrigerator and was met with a blast of warm, rotten air. They'd left a few things inside, some rock-hard hot-dog rolls, a head of lettuce, and a bottle of grape juice, which Lily now pulled out. She unscrewed the lid and sniffed. Her friend, Rochelle, swore that juice turned alcoholic if you left it long enough. Lily wondered how long. She tipped some of it into her mouth and swallowed, fought to keep it down. Maybe Rochelle was right, it tasted horrible. Lily rescrewed the lid and put the juice back into the fridge. She cupped her palms under the kitchen faucet and drank, then wiped them on her shorts and touched behind her right ear, dug her nail into the patch of skin she used for that very purpose. A small scab she kept opening and reopening. She'd been working on it on and off for months. Sometimes it seemed like everything she felt went right to that spot.

Lena, Lily thought. Lizard, leper, leprechaun, Lena. Lily met her for the first time a few weeks ago. Well, hi there, Lena had cooed, bending down, putting her hands on the fronts of her legs, like Lily was three instead of almost thirteen. She reeked of drugstore perfume.

Lazy lousy loud loser Lena.

Lily and her mother been managing just fine. They'd worked out their own way of doing things since her father had died. She was old enough to take care of herself. Was free to hang out with Rochelle or lie in the hammock and read books. Her mother was even making friends at her job, wasn't staying home, lying in bed quite so much anymore. They ate what and whenever they wanted. They used paper plates and Styrofoam cups.

So what was the point, Lily wanted to know, in messing it up?

Tell me the plan, Big Keith said, setting down his end of the couch. How're we getting all this stuff into storage? There was a wet mark on the fabric where his hand had been. This is not, he told Lily, fat-people weather.

Oh hell, Lily's mother said. She was wearing what she'd been wearing all three days they'd been sorting and packing: a pair of pleated tan shorts and a too-short grubby white t-shirt with ladybug appliqués, meant for a teenager. She picked at a ladybug and stared at their belongings jumbled across the lawn—as if noticing for the first time that they were there, like an accident—oops—everything out in the open for anyone to look at: dressers, dishes, a toilet plunger, a laundry basket of bras and underwear. To Lily's horror, her mother's bare mattress, propped up against the front porch, showcased a gigantic stain.

There's just so much, her mother complained. I was thinking that maybe it could fit in your pickup, Denny, but I guess I should have rented a truck. Shit. I guess I should have thought of that.

Lily rolled her eyes. I *guess*. Already two people had stopped by and tried to buy things.

Wait. I have a better idea.

Yeah? Denny lit a cigarette with a match, which he shook out and dropped on the lawn. *Fwoosh,* Lily thought, imagining the front yard exploding into flames.

Lily's mother wiped the corners of her mouth with her thumb and index. She got a funny, faraway look on her face, said, Storage is expensive, isn't it? Maybe we should drive it to your grandmother's, Lily, or let someone borrow it, or, actually—she paused. I could give it away.

Lily said, What?

If anyone would want this stuff. Which I doubt.

I could use another dresser, Marna said, swishing her long crepe-papery skirt across the lawn. Marna was not petite, maybe even a little big-boned, but beside Big Keith—whose heavy black boots had been thunking through the emptier and emptier house—she looked ready to blow away. Lily watched her run a hand over the top of her parents' bureau and wished that she would.

Oak, Keith said.

Is it? And hey, I like that chair. You sure you don't need this stuff, Colleen?

Lily's head hurt. Maybe it was the juice. Maybe Rochelle was wrong and it turned into poison, not wine. Lily faced her mother and said, very carefully, We should ask Grandma to hold it for us. That was a good idea.

Think about it, Lily, it'll be a fresh, clean start this way.

Oh look, Marna said, a vacuum cleaner.

I don't *want* a fresh start. But it was too late. Already, Lily could tell, her mother's mind was made up. Already she was able to see what would happen: her mother's coworkers swooping in like buzzards, more of them, an entire restaurant of them. Then a Goodwill truck, scooping up remains.

Listen, Lily, I'll buy you all new stuff. When we get things settled and can move into our own place again, I swear. Nice stuff, not this crap we got from Grandma Rand. Look. It's falling apart. She grabbed a post on Lily's headboard and wiggled it. See? Crap. She said it brightly, like this was bound to be a good time, like losing everything would maybe be fun.

Lily stared back at the house. Even from the outside it looked empty. The others had left, their vehicles tied down, overfull, and Lily and her mother stood motionless, like two more leftover items.

Exactly. This is it, Lily's mother said, though Lily hadn't said a word.

Don't you dare cry, she told her mother silently. This wasn't my idea.

And when her mother wanted to snap a photo—*Go there and wave*—Lily refused, walked to the car instead, the back of her ear throbbing, and strapped herself in, pretended, when they drove away, that she wasn't looking sideways. That she wasn't memorizing everything inside and out, the way it had been: her room, the back yard with the old swing set, the long hallway closet, the den, her father's chair. The coin, glinting like a fish scale, nestled somewhere, in some corner, where Lily would never find it.

It was a tall, thin duplex painted snot-green. They climbed the left set of steps, the side Lena rented, and knocked, heard back a singsong *Welcome home,* found Lena in a yellow kitchen, dressed in cutoff jeans and a bikini top, poking blueberries onto a sheet cake in rows.

Look, she said, it's a flag. For a July Fourth party, Lily! I wanted to keep it a surprise. Do I look domestic?

No, Lily said.

Her mother said, Isn't that wonderful? Look, Lily, the blueberries are stars. To Lena, she said, Fourth of July is Lily's favorite holiday.

I may have outdone myself, Lena said. She licked frosting off her fingers and followed them outside to help carry stuff in.

Lena's apartment was tidy and full of matching furniture. On the wall were pictures of vases with flowers and trees with flowers and birds with frothy wings and tails that *looked* like flowers. They were all hung too high, making it seem as though they were floating toward the ceiling.

Isn't it a relief, her mother whispered to her as Lena led them through the mint-colored living room, up a narrow flight of stairs to the spare bedroom. Don't you just feel the calm? The serenity?

It's okay, Lily answered in her regular voice.

Lena had taped a computer-printed sign above the doorway. *Home sweet home.* The room was square and smelled like mothballs. There were twin beds, a throw rug, one night table, one window, and a closet. It was half the size of Lily's old bedroom.

It's lucky we like each other, her mother said.

Lucky, Lily thought. Another damn L-word.

When the three of them had finished dragging everything up—it didn't take very long—Lily's mother frowned. What did I do with my purse? she asked. She moved the trunk and checked behind her giant art-school collage. Didn't I just have it?

Maybe you gave it away, Lily said.

It'll turn up, Lena said. Let's look around downstairs. Come have a drink, Colleen. People'll be here soon. I can get you something to wear. Lily, sweetie, you settle in and unpack.

I'll be downstairs, honey, her mother said. She smiled and kissed Lily on the forehead, like someone else's mother, not hers.

Lily closed the door, locked it, and stood still, listened to the voices trail off. She tried to imagine the room feeling familiar. The window faced an empty lot next door, where one lone tree leaned over a scatter of dirt and weeds. A plastic grocery bag was caught in the branches; it inflated and deflated in the wind—looked, Lily thought, like it was trying to breathe.

She pushed the beds, one and then the other, in opposite directions against the walls, then separated her things from her mother's and dragged them to the bed by the window, took inventory. Clothing, shoes, boots, a folder of papers from school, twenty-six books, a bag of office supplies, a backpack filled with special things: a music box, a chicken neck in a jar (a gift from Rochelle that Lily hid from her mother), ticket stubs from the Broncos game her father had taken her to, a now-empty velvet pouch she'd used for the coin, and an envelope of pictures she liked, that she'd torn out of her mother's magazines, ads showing athletes running and jumping, caught midair so it looked like they were flying. Also, there was a pillow case of stuff she'd managed to grab at the last second, just random things, some refrigerator magnets, an old calendar, the living room clock. Junk. The wrong things. Already, Lily could sense important stuff missing. For instance, she didn't remember seeing the clay handprints she'd made for her parents in kindergarten. It was like running away from a fire. She'd taken the teapot and left the cat.

Lily sat on the floor beside the books. They were her favorites, the ones she liked to read over and over. Some from a long time ago, from when she was little. They were still good. A few Judy Blumes, *Alice in Wonderland*, *The Hobbit*. Others she'd discovered more recently. *The Catcher in the Rye* had been a gift from her father (though it didn't fully count because it was also from her mother). Lily especially liked the stories where terrible things happened to good characters. In *The House of Sixty Fathers,* which she'd read four times, a boy, separated from his parents during a war, got so hungry he ate grass. In *Island of the Blue Dolphins,* a girl found herself stranded and had to figure out what to do. Sometimes Lily would just read her father's backcountry survival guide. There was something comforting about knowing what to do. Eat bumpy berries, not smooth (with the marked exception of a white Alaskan berry). Focus on water. Don't be afraid to eat bugs. Lily had written one of her father's favorite jokes in the margin: *If you're lost in the jungle, watch what the monkey eats . . . and eat the monkey.* Lily could tune out anything by reading. Half her last winter vacation had been spent by the heat vent in her room, where she'd lie wrapped in an afghan with a book and a few packages of Ho-Hos and imagine what it would be like to eat bugs and grass. She'd read and read. One minute it would be light outside, the next dark.

By the time she went downstairs, the rooms were filled with people.

There you are, Lena said. She'd brushed out her hair and painted her lips bright pink. C'mere, you, she said, clamping an arm around Lily, steering her through the crowd. . . . And this is Fran and Denny and Dexter . . . everyone, this is my new roommate!

I've met these people, Lily said, but it didn't seem to matter.

They ended up in the kitchen by a folding table, where Lena had set out a bowl of ice and bottles of liquor and soda and paper napkins printed with stars. Lily's mother was sitting beside the table, wearing a short skirt that made the tops of her legs stick out funny, like they were made of raw dough. She was drinking a blue drink out of a cup that read, *Kiss me I'm horny.* How's our room? she asked.

How about a Shirley Temple, Lily? Lena asked.

Lily shrugged and watched Lena pour ginger ale and red syrup into a plastic tumbler. Out the window, she noticed a ladder propped against the house. What's that for? she asked.

That's for later, Lena said. For watching fireworks.

I'm going up now, Lily told her mother.

Later, Lena said.

Lily said, Okay—but the first chance she got, while Lena was slicing the cake, laughing at her own jokes—her mother still sitting there, laughing along—Lily slipped out the front door.

She climbed slowly, then faster, past the kitchen window, scrambled up to the top rung, and pulled herself onto the roof, which was hot and smelled like tar, its roughness scraping her bare legs. It was angled just enough to keep her flat against its surface as she scooted farther up—where, to her dismay, she found someone already there, sitting against the chimney, smoking a cigarette, her fuzzy hair tied up in a knot, her long white skirt tucked close around her legs.

Lily wanted to turn around and go back down, but Marna had already caught sight of her.

Make yourself at home, she said.

Home. It was starting to lose meaning. Lily crossed her legs and leaned back on her hands, looked off at the patchwork of treetops and pavement and roofs. It felt cooler up here, the breeze moving uninterrupted.

Have some. Marna reached down and passed her something silver. It was a bottle, small and flat. Not too much, Marna said. It's strong.

Lily unscrewed the top and sniffed. When she was little, her father used to give her tastes of his beer, which she never liked very much but always wanted to like—the foam on top looked so creamy. But this didn't smell like beer, or like rotting grape juice either. It was sharper. It smelled like old-lady perfume. Lily put the bottle to her mouth and tilted it back, touched a dab to her tongue. It burned. She tilted it again and this time let more out, enough to swallow, which she did quickly and coughed. Uh, she said, without meaning to. Her eyes watered. It *tasted* like old-lady perfume.

Marna smiled and took back the bottle, drank from it. It's kind of an acquired taste, she said.

It's interesting. Lily's chest felt warm. It wasn't a bad feeling. Down below on the ground, a few kids walked through the empty lot. There was some whizzing and popping and Lily saw that they were setting things off, lighting them and running, sending sparks and red dust into the air.

We'll get to see the show later. Marna motioned to the sky, which was empty, going hazy with orange twilight, the color of Broncos tickets. She said, We have the best seats in the house. And I brought sparklers, but they're downstairs. We'll light them later.

Sparklers are kind of boring. And it's not the same to see fireworks from far away, Lily said, remembering the summer her father brought some home for her—secretly, so her mother wouldn't know, the two of them going way out back after dark, behind the woods, behind the little lake. Lily loved the danger, how it felt to hold a paper rocket in your hand, heavy and light at the same time. She loved watching the time run out, waiting until the very last possible second. A few years ago, Venus Ellis, who was a grade above Lily and very popular, lost one-and-a-half fingers from a zipping mary. Someone had given it to her at a party, handed it over and lit it, and Venus panicked. Froze right up—just stood there, holding the thing, until: *bang*. Lily hadn't been there, but she heard about it from Rochelle, and then tried, that fall, to sit by Venus at lunch and get her to talk about it. What was it like, she wanted to know, that moment, right before it went off? But Venus wouldn't say, just picked crust off her sandwich with her good hand, the firecracker one tucked in her lap, until her friends told Lily to go away.

Marna gave her the silver bottle again and this time she took a little more, closing her eyes with the sting. Thank you, she said. Her whole body felt warm.

So, Marna said, taking a puff from a cigarette, you're all moved in?

It's just temporary.

Well, that's good, right? A short adventure?

Lily snorted.

Adventure, Marna said, that's not the right word, is it.

No, Lily said. She wished she had some water. The alcohol made her mouth dry. The stars were coming out. Lily stared at one until she realized it was moving. A plane. A bead of man-made light creeping across the sky. The only time planes seemed fast was in movies.

Marna said, I think this will be a good year.

It should be for someone, Lily said. Statistically.

Marna laughed. Well, aren't you cynical for just fifteen.

I'm not fifteen, I'm thirteen.

Just thirteen? Marna put her hand over her mouth. I feel terrible, giving you drinks. Fifteen was bad enough. Really? Only *thir*teen?

Well, in a couple of weeks I'll be thirteen. She shrugged. I drink, she said.

If you do poorly in math class next year, I guess it'll be my fault. Brain cells and all.

I'm good at math.

Right, Marna said, I'm not surprised. She handed down the bottle. In that case, I suppose a little more won't hurt. And it's a special occasion after all. Independence Day. Your birthday. Mine. Mine's next month.

Lily drank another sip and found a star that didn't move. The dark was coming on quickly.

It's great, isn't it, Marna said. I love looking out like this, everything shrunk down to size. Like you could just hop your way across the city.

Lily asked, How old will you be?

Twenty-eight. She rubbed out her cigarette against the roof and lit another. I'll invite you to my party. I'm thinking about buying presents for my guests, kind of a reverse party.

I bet a lot of people will come to that party.

One year I threw a costume party and two different people came as the Loch Ness Monster. Without planning it. What are the odds of that?

I had a birthday once where three people got me the same gift.

What was the gift?

This one kind of doll, Lily said, a little embarrassed. You could cut her hair and it would grow back.

Very cool, Marna said. That's an excellent idea. She pursed her lips and blew a line of smoke. She said, People tend to buy me snow globes. I had to start collecting them.

Those things with plastic dandruff?

It makes you wonder, doesn't it, what people think of you?

Lily laughed.

But I guess it could be worse, right? Than snow globes and cool dolls. It could be socks. Or those little smelly soaps that come wrapped up in gift sets.

I bought my mother those kind of soaps for her last birthday, Lily said. She said it for no reason at all, it wasn't even true. They hadn't even celebrated birthdays last year.

Oh, Marna said, I'm sorry I said that, then.

No, it's okay, don't worry about it. I don't like them, but she does. Out of the corner of her eye, Lily watched Marna smoke her cigarette, head tilted to the side. She seemed so calm. It came off her like heat. You could take or draw or paint her picture and you probably couldn't capture how calm she was. Lily asked her, What did you do with all of the stuff?

All of what stuff?

Our stuff.

Oh. Well, I got the dresser, the blue lamp, the blue bowl, and a chair. And the pineapple serving tray. I was excited about that. Did Denny end up taking the vacuum?

Yes.

I know Keith got the records. I put the lamp in my bedroom, the bowl in the living room, and the chair and the dresser aren't settled yet. Maybe you could come over and help me figure it out.

Lily looked away. The lamp will probably catch on fire, she said. My mom patched up the cord, which you aren't supposed to do.

That's true, you're not.

The chair was my father's.

Oh. Marna paused. Shit. Lily, I'm sorry, I knew that. Another pause. Or I didn't know about the chair, just about your father.

Lily shrugged.

Lily, it's still yours. I'm serious, I'll just keep it for you. Or I could bring it over. I'm sure there's room for one chair.

Lily regretted bringing it up. It doesn't matter, she said.

I should have known, Marna said.

It's just a stupid chair. Lily picked up a loose pebble of tar and tossed it over the side, half hoped to hear one of the kids from before say, *Ow*. But the lot was empty. They'd left a while ago.

She and Marna both drank a little more and Lily lay back and faced the darkening sky. It seemed to swirl. Her arms felt long and hollow.

Marna lit another cigarette. Mmm, she said, inhaling. Smells good, huh? It's not a regular cigarette. It's a clove.

Lily didn't answer.

They're horrible, Marna said. They practically rip your lungs out. Otherwise I'd give you one. Lily could barely see her face. What she saw was the white skirt. And the cigarette, tracing red lines in the dark.

Give me one, Lily said. I don't care.

Well, I care.

Okay, Lily said. If you want. She scratched behind her ear, gave it a good hard dig, then turned over onto her hands and knees and scooted closer to the edge of the roof, imagined falling off. A street lamp out front clicked on, just then—and for a second, before her eyes had time to adjust, the garbage that was strewn across the side lot looked almost pretty, kind of festive, blurred into little blotches like balloons. But then Lily blinked and the soda bottles and napkins and fast-food bags went back to being soda bottles and napkins and fast-food bags. Closer to the house, she spotted something beige and rounded and familiar. Her mother's purse. It was sitting in the tall weeds beside the front steps, waiting to be noticed. Lily aimed a pebble at it and missed. Aimed again, missed.

This makes me *nervous,* Lena complained. The others were helping her, pulling her up by her wrists, Denny on one, Big Keith on the other.

You're doing great, Denny said.

It's your roof, Lily pointed out.

That's right, and if I fall, I'm taking you all down with me. She got up, then stumbled back into a sitting position. She untied and retied her bikini top and finger-combed her hair. Most of the party had moved up here and was spread out. Marna was still at the top, Fran and a couple others were near the ladder, swinging their feet over the roof's edge, singing, off-key, *Bye, bye, Miss American Pie,* eating peanuts out of a paper bag and spitting the shells. Denny was with his girlfriend, Stephanie, who reminded Lily of a pixie with her short, choppy hair. She was the palest person Lily had ever met. And people said *she* was pale. James had his eyes closed, was listening to a Walkman. The light from the street lamp made them all look yellowy-green. Lena's boyfriend came up, holding a plastic pitcher, a stack of cups tucked under one arm. Margaritas, he said sullenly, hopping up beside Lena, sloshing a little on his leather pants.

Aren't you hot? Lily asked.

Hands off, Lena said, he's mine.

It was all-the-way night now, but heat still hung in the air. Millions of little bugs swarmed in patches, like gusts, and Lily swatted them away. When no one was looking, she'd been taking drinks from a bottle that the others brought up and had now forgotten, had discarded as empty. If you tilted it, there was still a good fat corner left.

Any minute, someone said—and sure enough, not long after, the first bright burst appeared in the sky with a whoosh.

Lily thought of her mother in the kitchen—she was still, Lily was sure, sitting there, drinking. People were probably trying to get her to chat, to talk about the move, and Lily could picture how her mother would respond, in that slow, syrupy way that she had when she was sitting and drinking and thinking.

A blast of blue, then white, then lime green, each of them shooting up and arcing out, exploding into an umbrella of light. But so far away, Lily thought, so different from the ones her father sent flying for her that night in the field behind their back yard.

They passed around another bottle and pitcher. No one was paying much attention now to where the drinks were going, to what Lily was given, and she took sips and felt her torso stretch longer and looser. She lay back under the flashing bursts and felt her whole body flatten, spread thinner and thinner, until she was like Marna: light and papery. She could catch a breeze and float away.

After the show, after the end, where all the leftover fireworks were sent off at once, one after the other, all the colors whizzing together in patterns that had, by then, gotten predictable, certain colors taking certain shapes—after it was all over, everyone climbed back down, slowly, feeling below for every rung, coaxing each other. And sure enough, inside, Lily's mother was where Lily had left her, though her drink was pink now, not blue, and she was playing cards, a spread of them perched in her hand like a fancy Chinese fan.

Hi, Lily, honey.

Someone was handing out more cards.

Right here, Lena said. Deal me in. She sat down beside Lily's mother and drummed the table with her open palms. Everyone? Watch out.

I'm in too, Lena's boyfriend said. He was standing in front of the open refrigerator eating cold fried chicken with his hands, pulling strings of it off the bone and dropping them into his mouth.

Lily felt a pang of nausea. The room tipped one way and then the other.

Wonderful, her mother said. Cards for Lena, cards for Dexter.

If it had been *Lily* and not Lena's boyfriend shoveling in the food, touching everything with greasy fingers, her mother would have freaked. She would have whipped out the antibacterial spray and paper towels and explained what was really happening microscopically, on an invisible level. Just because you can't see it, she would say, doesn't mean it's not there.

I want to go home is what Lily wanted to say now but realized, at the same time, the problem with that request. Her head felt heavy, her mouth sticky. Someone somewhere was taking pictures, the flash flashing. Please stop eating, she wanted to tell Lena's boyfriend, who was chewing on a wing, feeding his frown. Maybe she did tell him that. Someone said something.

I believe it's bedtime, Lena said then.

I don't have a bedtime.

It's not a bad idea, her mother said. It's late. How late is it? she asked Lena.

Late.

It's late, her mother repeated. It looked like her bright pink lipstick—Lena's lipstick—was doing the talking. Moving her lips for her. Awful pink.

I want to go back, Lily said.

Back where?

To the house. I left things.

Left things what?

All sorts of things.

Lena broke in, That reminds me, and flounced off.

The room seemed to buzz, the camera flash pulsed. *Smile,* someone yelled.

You're drunk, Lily told her mother, and just then it started coming back: more and more of the stuff they'd forgotten. The back issues of

Life magazine. The Father's Day cuff links. Photo albums. *Photo albums.* Lily tried to remember if she'd seen them in the cedar trunk—maybe the blue album, but that was the baby one. All Lily and her mother. Her father was missing. He was holding the camera.

I might just be, her mother said. Drunk. And I deserve it. She smiled, then grimaced at her cards. Pulled one out and slapped it down on the table. I'm good at this, the lipstick said.

We need to go back, Lily said. Now.

We'll go back. Okay, honey. Give me a minute. Remind me in the morning.

Look! Lena reappeared and held something out.

The coin. Her father's gold coin. Lily's throat closed and opened again.

Oh Lily, her mother said. Weren't you looking for that?

Lena said, I found it on the stairs, it must've fallen out of your stuff. It's from one of those dragon and adventure games—please tell me you don't play those things, Lily, oh god. Lena laughed.

It's not from a game, Lily said. It's from Japan.

Maybe it's *made* in Japan, but it's a playing piece. See? You can see the seam from where they poured it into the mold. She held it out.

Lily didn't take it. It wasn't the right coin. She didn't need to see it.

Don't you want it?

Her mother said, Lily, say thank you.

It was her mother's fault. She'd switched it. She'd done something with the real one, spent it, threw it away, saved it for herself.

You don't look good, Lena told Lily. You're not going to be sick, are you? You haven't been drinking, have you?

I'm perfectly awake, Lily muttered and poured herself a glass of tap water, then ran upstairs to the bathroom to throw up.

She sat by the toilet, sank back into the fuzzy bath mat. I can stay here forever, she thought, closing her eyes. They can bring me food and books. She curled up, right there on the mat, and picked behind her ear. It was already crusting over. It always amazed her how fast it healed. She peeled off the new scab—the pain felt good, a thin, high note—then went deeper, dug into the raw wet beneath, the soft red that went all the way down.

She woke sometime later, confused, then remembering, her head hurting, her ear stinging. She sat up, then went into the bedroom, which was dark and empty. She shuffled through her backpack for her watch. One-eighteen. It was quiet below. She crept downstairs slowly and edged toward the kitchen, where she could see her mother, asleep, sloppily, her head on the table, her arms stretched out. Lena was washing silverware at the sink. Everyone else was gone. Empty cups were scattered everywhere, along with napkins and the little-kid party hats Big Keith had passed around. Lily stepped in something sticky that grabbed at the soles of her bare feet. There was a tumbler of beer left on an end table near the kitchen doorway, and the smell of it hurt Lily's stomach. Next to it were the sparklers. They were unopened. They'd been forgotten. And beside them, its zipper open like a gaping mouth, was her mother's purse. Maybe the kids in the lot had gone through it, Lily thought. Stolen things. She reached inside for the wallet. No, it was all there. A twenty and some ones. And receipts, lots and lots of receipts, money wasted on all sorts of useless junk that was now gone. She flipped through the credit cards and photos—Lily in first grade, in second grade, in fourth, with all that metal in her mouth—to the very last one. It was the Polaroid, folded in half so it would fit in the sleeve, of Lily on the lawn on her bike and her father watching her ride away.

She put the picture in her pocket and replaced the wallet, then picked up the sparklers and took out a few, looked around for something to light them with.

Hey, Lily, why are you up?

Lily froze, peeked into the kitchen.

Lena turned off the water. What's wrong with your ear? Are you bleeding?

Her mother stirred and grunted. Huh?

I'm fine. I just need a lighter, Lily said, spotting one on the counter. She snatched it up and was about to turn around and leave when Lena grabbed her arm.

What do you need a lighter for?

Sparklers, she said, pulling away.

Lily's mother rubbed her eyes. Lily? There was a lemon pit stuck to her cheek from the table. Lily?

What.

You gotta know, her mother said, yawning, I feel bad when things are going wrong. Lily. You know?

Lena suddenly pretended to not pay attention. She got a garbage bag and began stuffing things in.

Lily said, Yes.

Can I ask you a question? You know I love you.

Yes.

And you still love me?

Lily flicked the lighter a few times, then touched it to the tip of a sparkler. It hissed and spat yellow.

Oh, her mother gasped, turning to Lena, is that okay?

Outside! Lena yelled.

158

It's *okay*, Lily snapped. Sparklers aren't *anything*. They're *harmless*.

Outside! Lena screamed, giving her a quick shove out the door, which was just fine with Lily.

It was cool now, a little chilly even. Lily paused, faced the empty lot, the sparkler spraying light into dark. There was a scatter of bottle rockets and cherry bombs on the ground, used up. Tomorrow they'd be even less than that—just bits of colored paper, soaked with dew.

Still holding the lit sparkler, Lily climbed the ladder, maneuvered herself up with one hand and the other elbow onto the roof, where she shimmied to the very top, by the chimney, where Marna had been. She sat back. Looked up. The sky above was dark and silent, though off in the distance, beyond her old neighborhood, Lily could see faraway fireworks, little bright blooms against the horizon. Red, yellow, blue, barely there. It was as though the celebration had struck, like a storm, and had now moved on, drifted elsewhere.

It was like her father: getting farther and farther away.

Lily lit another sparkler and closed her eyes. She felt the flecks of fire, listened to the crackle. Happy, happy, she thought. Laughing lazy loopy Lily. She stayed very still, barely breathing even, and pretended that the sparkler was a firecracker. A popper or a silver fang. She grasped it lightly between her thumb and index finger, held it out, imagined that any second it might go off.

15.

She'd fed him. She hadn't fed him. She'd fed him. It was possible to accept either scenario. JJ thought of Norman, sitting on his pebbles, staring through his plastic walls—at what? her scatter of makeup on the dresser beside him, her unmade bed, the door—how far could small aquatic frogs see?

"So who's ready for some real fun?" Lena asked. She'd filled two pitchers with beer and set them on the table, handed out fresh glasses to everyone, went around the circle: Fran, James, Denny, Colleen, and then Keith. When Lena reached JJ, she asked, "Don't you have a curfew?" and JJ, before she thought to stop herself, answered, "No."

"Let the girl stay and drink," Fran said. "Let her see what we do after hours."

"Do we *do* anything?" asked Keith.

"The best hours are the after hours," Fran said.

It hadn't occurred to JJ that she shouldn't stay—that she wasn't automatically invited—and a quick heat of embarrassment began to rise. But she didn't move. She sipped her tequila shot and let Keith fill her beer glass.

"We're playing a game," Lena announced, spreading napkins in the center of the table in an overlapping circle, like a platter of cold cuts.

"Let's play quarters." Keith dug into his pockets. "Who has some? I changed mine in. Hey, Denny," he called over to the bar, where Denny had been doing something at the register. Now he closed the drawer and came out from behind the bar, walked over slowly. They all watched him. Everything was like a show, JJ thought—though, actually, at the table, *they* were the ones who were spotlit.

"I gave the loose ones to Lily," Denny said. He motioned in the direction of the Centipede game, where Lily was zipping and zapping, leaning over it in a hostile sort of way.

"Forget about quarters," Lena said. "Denny, you're just in time."

"You got your checkout? I need it."

"Just a minute. Relax. Have a beer. You deserve it. You haven't stopped moving since you got here. You're worse than Keith."

Denny paused. Sat down.

James said, "I know a game we could play."

"Strip poker," Fran said. "Or Mother May I! Marna's version!"

Lena seemed to consider it.

JJ's chest tightened. She didn't know what Mother May I was— *any* version—but apparently it was even worse than strip poker. Just the thought of having to take off clothes. She tried to remember what kind of underwear she had on.

"I'll play strip poker," Lily called over.

"No you won't," Colleen called back.

"No," Lena said. "This is a new game. This is a game I learned back in Indiana at a place called Nick's. Where they really know how to play a game. None of that pussy quarters shit. Hold on."

They all waited as she trotted off behind the bar and came back with a plastic bucket full of beer. *Hal's Slaw,* it said on the side. Lena carried the bucket in both hands and set it down on the napkins, tucked even more around its bottom. "This'll do." She grabbed a pitcher and went to pour beer into Denny's glass, the only one still empty, but he put his hand over the top.

"Not playing," he said. "Not drinking. I'm leaving after this cigarette."

"No, you're not," Lena said. "You're not leaving yet. You haven't done the final checkout. And you don't get *my* checkout until you play a round. Weren't you at the meeting? There's no 'wussing out early' in '*team.*'" She grinned, then pulled the glass out from under his hand and filled it. "Besides, if you play right you won't have to drink." She told everyone, "It's called Sink the Bismarck." She dropped a small glass into the bucket so that it floated, mouth up. "This is the Bismarck. We all go around and pour a little beer into it from our glasses, and the idea is not to sink it, but to fill it just enough to make it sink for the next person. If you sink it, you drink it."

"That's easy," James said.

"Very easy," Lena said.

"So basically, it's a backwash game," Keith said, getting up with his beer and going to the front door, looking out.

"Oh ick," Colleen said.

"What's a Bismarck?" asked Fran.

"That's a Bismarck," JJ said and pointed to the glass.

"It's really a buffalo, right?" Fran said. "Or maybe a place?"

"That's *Denmark,* you idiot," James said and laughed.

"Okay, okay," Fran said, "no fighting, let's do it. I'm ready. I'm first." She stood up and poured beer into the floating glass.

"Wait," Lena said. "Let's make it more interesting."

"Run," Denny muttered.

"For every round, we're going to pick a topic and everyone has to say their answer as they pour. Like, bad things you've done to other people. Or," she looked at JJ and smiled, "crazy places you've had sex. That's the first topic. The craziest place you've done it. Okay, go ahead, JJ."

They all looked at JJ.

"Lena," Denny said and groaned.

"You, sir, had better start thinking. You're up soon. But if you need help remembering . . ."

"Why don't you go first then, Lena," Keith said.

"Okay. I will." She tipped some beer into the highball. "Laundromat."

"Laundromat," Fran squealed, "open or closed?"

"Open," Lena said. "Very open for business." She looked over to Denny, who didn't look back.

What, JJ thought, would she say when it was her turn?

"I'll be next," James said. He rubbed his hands. "Let's see . . ."

"You can pass," Fran said. "No one wants to hear your answer."

James stood up. "Hmmm."

"No thinking," Lena said. "If you take too long, you forfeit."

"There's just so many," he said, pouring his beer, "but I'm going with airplane. Airplane. Mile-high club, baby!" He swiveled his hips.

"Oh gross," Colleen said. "I don't even want to *pee* in an airplane bathroom."

"Who said anything about a bathroom?" He slapped the table and sank the Bismarck. "Yes!"

"You're not supposed to *want* to sink it," Lena said.

"That's a total lie," Fran said. "You never did anything on an airplane except fall asleep and drool."

"How would you know what I do? Huh? How would you know?"

"You have to drink it," Lena said.

He reached into the bucket and fished for the glass.

"Oh *ick*," Colleen said.

"What? They're clean." He pulled out the Bismarck and drank it like a shot, licked his fingers, then refloated the glass.

"Alcohol is antiseptic," JJ told Colleen.

"But still."

Barn? JJ thought. Was that believable? *Swimming pool?*

"Your turn, Fran," Lena said. "And JJ's next."

"That's not going in the circle," Keith pointed out.

"It's my game, I get to pick the order."

I have to leave, JJ imagined herself saying. Now. Something important. I forgot. But she didn't say anything. She felt glued to her chair. The building could catch fire, things could start falling around her, and here she'd be.

"Okay." Fran giggled. "Remember when there used to be pool tables in here?" She turned to James. "This is before you, so don't you even say anything."

"That doesn't count," Lena said. "We've all done that."

"It counts," Denny said.

"No, it doesn't count, we cancel each other out. That's like saying 'in bed' or 'in the car.' It all cancels out."

"That's bullshit," Keith said. "It absolutely counts. And it depends on what kind of car."

"Fine," Lena said and smiled, "it counts. And now it's JJ's turn."

JJ stood up, her knees feeling heavy. "Do I pour first or say first?"

"It doesn't matter," Lena and Fran said at the same time.

She poured. Tipped the glass, let it dribble into the Bismarck. "Shower," she said, going red.

"What? I couldn't hear her," James complained.

"Shower. In the shower." It wasn't the best answer, she knew, but it wasn't a total lie. There had been a party at the Boulder hostel, before she'd found the nanny job, where she'd met a guy named Justin. He was a couple years younger than her and from Santa Cruz, California. He had that half-bleached-out hair you saw on boys who spent a lot of time at the beach. They sat in the hallway of the hostel by the bathroom and talked until it was late and everyone else had either passed out or gone to bed. They talked about the president and processed food and the Peace Corps—which Justin claimed was a scam, that really it was just as capitalist and screwed up as anything else. Totally, JJ had murmured. She didn't agree with a thing he said, but she liked to watch him talk. He had slightly pouty lips, like a girl.

After they'd talked for a while, Justin stood up and said that it was too goddamn hot—which it was—and he peeled off his shirt. I'm taking a shower, he said, and removed his pants. He wasn't wearing any underwear and JJ tried not to look. And she tried not to look like she was trying not to look. Wanna join me? he'd asked and walked into the bathroom, turned on one of the showers, got in behind the thick green curtain. I don't know, she said. He said, You can wear a bathing suit or something if you're shy—and before she could really think about it, before she had time to realize that he wasn't serious about putting something on, that it had been a *joke,* she ran back to her room and found the sexiest thing she owned, a tap set, made out of silk. She'd never worn it. It was soft pink—*dream,* the catalog had called the color. She slipped it on in her room and hurried back, climbed in. They kissed. His mouth was icy. He put his arms around her. It was all wrong, though. Someone came into the bathroom to pee and JJ almost slipped trying to be quiet, her arms flying out to steady herself, her legs at awkward angles. Her belly jiggling. It's okay, she told herself. Love is awkward, this is totally natural. But when she went to continue the kiss, Justin started laughing and JJ looked down to see that the dye from her tap suit had bled; there was pink everywhere, a river of dream.

JJ sat back down and waited for the comments, waited to hear how stupid her place was. But no one said anything. No one was even looking at her. They were looking at James.

"Well, well, what do we got here," he said. He was bent over, going through something on the floor, someone's bag. He pulled out a plastic bottle of all-white jelly beans. "Jelly beans," he announced.

"Hey," Lily yelled from the video game. She shouted over her shoulder, "Quit it, James. That's my backpack. Don't open those."

He poured a few in his hand and popped them into his mouth, chewed.

Keith said, "Christ, James."

James shrugged put back the bottle, poked around. "What the hell you got in here, Lily?"

Lily yelled, "Quit it, James, I mean it!"

Fran said, *"James."*

Colleen grabbed the backpack away from him. She waited for Lily to turn back to her game, then looked inside, pulled out a canning jar and held it up to the candlelight. There was something orange and lumpy at the bottom. "Oh god," Colleen said. "She keeps the weirdest things. Oh god, it's growing mold." She tiptoed to a nearby trash can and dropped it in.

Marna's comforter smelled like horses. After they made love, Keith stayed in bed and listened to her pad around the kitchen, opening things, closing things, the slight smack-smack of her bare feet against the linoleum.

What were you like in high school? he asked as they ate. He wanted to know things.

In high school? She laughed and took a drink of tea. I was a cheerleader. Did welcoming committee. Knitting club.

You were a cheerleader?

No. She smiled. Keith, I can see *you* in high school.

Was I a cheerleader?

I can see how you carried your Trapper Keeper, how you were excited about the work you'd done the night before—but you wouldn't talk much in class.

I talked, Keith said.

So I'm wrong?

Probably not. He lay back. Normally he'd be a little grossed out by a place like this. The bedding needed washing. Evan's dirty dishes everywhere. For a scrawny little guy, Evan produced a lot of dirty dishes. But tonight nothing was bothering Keith, nothing could be bad. He was in Marna's bedroom with Marna.

They got to talking about places they'd never been. Michigan sounded hard, the way the letters crunched together. Oregon was worn out. Delaware sad, but in a good way. Marna liked Inspiration, Idaho, and French Lick (and neighboring Gnawbone), Indiana, and they both found something sympathetic about the Dakotas. Keith wanted to turn on the hula-girl lamp beside the bed to see Marna's face better, but he was naked and didn't necessarily want her to see *him* better. He looked out at the Denver lights and beyond, to the dark on dark of the mountains. It was hard to tell if he could really see them or if he just knew they were there and filled them in, automatically.

Marna asked, When's the last time you went on a good road trip? You know, like cross-country.

Never.

She sat up. You've never been on a road trip? Really?

I've been around Colorado. And cripes, I've *been* to other states. What's that thing called? *Big metal bird? Aero-plane?*

She laughed. You've never just packed up your car and drove off?

I don't have a car.

Oh right.

But I'm up for it. He paused. Let's do it, he said.

Sure, it'd be fun.

No, I mean now. He sat up beside her. He wanted to pull her to him. Her sheet had slipped and the moonlight touched on her collarbone, lit her skin.

But she said: Now? She smiled. I'll let you know.

It was a good idea. He could already see the two of them out there, on the road, stopping only for gas and when they felt like it. Staying in motels with weedy lawns—or camping. The two of them in a tent. Keith got a flash of it, the twilight-colored air inside the tent. He told Marna, C'mon—we'll pack everything up or sell it or, hell, put everything we own in a pile and burn it, and it would be like we were never even here. You know? No evidence. No one can miss us if we never existed. No sidework for the imaginary.

She was laughing. She said, Oh but there'd be *something*. I've always thought that when you disappear—that when you take off or escape or die, you should leave something behind. You know? Like in science fiction when they travel back in time and drop just a speck, some little gift about the future. She smiled. Even in the half light he could see it. She moved the empty tea glass to the night table and wriggled down under the covers and sighed. She murmured: Don't you think?

"Colorado Springs," Keith announced and poured his beer. It sank, he drank.

"How is *that* crazy?" Lena asked.

"No one has sex in Colorado Springs," Keith said. "You know. Uptight bright-white right."

"It counts," Denny said. "It counts twice."

Fran giggled. "Do you think religious people ever whisper, *Fuck me?* Maybe just once, by mistake? You know, only in the deliberate act of procreation."

Of course what Keith *wanted* to say was this: *In Marna's bedroom.* He fought the urge to bring up her name, in any context, just to say it. Instead, he waited for it to come up naturally, which it did—and went away and came up again.

"How about the time Marna made Potato Phil eat that girl's burger?"

"I thought it was a BLT."

"I thought it was my dick."

"Shut *up,* James."

"So the girl was bugging Marna—oh I remember, the girl complained that her drink was weak—keep in mind that this is *Marna,* who can't pour a weak Roy Rogers, right?—and then she started talking on a cell phone, right at the bar, real loud and squawky, and so Marna says to Phil, just like this, Hey, Phil, I'll pay off your back tab if you go over and eat that perfectly good Superburger that's getting cold."

"And did he?"

"Fuck yeah. But get this, first he says, I hate pickles, and so *Marna* says, Give me the pickles, I love pickles, and he does and they eat it together. Right in front of the girl, who's just shit-shocked. Just stands there. They even use her napkin."

"I saw Marna dunk a pickle into hot chocolate once."

"You ever had one of Marna's mudslides? It's the same ingredients, but I can't get mine to taste that good."

They all nodded.

"This is like a wake," Colleen said.

"I should go," JJ said, beside Keith. "I should get home."

"Relax, enjoy yourself, you earned it," he told her, patting her shoulder, getting up. He had to keep checking. Front and back doors both—she might not take 2nd, she might go an alternate route, right to the parking lot. She could be waiting, there was no way to tell. This place was a goddamn tomb. The windows and doors were dark glass—you had to get up close to see anything.

They were leaving Denver.

Keith fought it now: the smallest pang of regret. He could've made more of an effort to do things. Sure, when he was little he did the rounds with his parents, visited the attractions, stood at Four Corners, in all four states at once. Drove to the top of Trail Ridge Road. Went into the gift shop, saw the tourists bumping around, giddy on too little air. But it wasn't the same.

He was no longer a waiter. He felt himself sliding out of that skin.

A good Janis Joplin song came on as he crossed the dining room, heading for the back door. Colleen turned up the music and swayed a little by the bar, smiled at him as he passed. "This reminds me of Marna," she said.

16.

It was Denny's turn and Lena watched him stand up and concentrate on his pour in that careful, inner-lit way that he had. Watching him made it all come back to Lena at once: the Denny she used to
know—all the time, not just every few weeks. Or months. Denny from
a couple years ago, grinning at her when she came up for her first order
of drinks. Denny asking, Hey, when you working next? Beating her in
a game of after-work darts, fetching the darts after every turn. Handing
them over, that first time, he'd squeezed her palm.

And she'd hardly cared. Back then, it was just something else
happening.

Look, we don't have to do this, she'd told him in his truck, her face
in his neck.

Oh yeah we do, he'd breathed.

That was the problem with good memories: they were remind-
ers of what no longer existed, what you didn't *realize* existed at the

time—and they materialized not as *Colleen* would have her think, as
hazy photographs, but as lousy disappointments.

"Now your crazy place, Denny, you're not exempt," Fran said.

Lena murmured, "Fire tower," and raised her left eyebrow, but he
didn't look at her.

He shook his head. "I don't kiss and tell."

James said, "Denny, my man, we are not talking kissing."

Fran said, "There can be *some* kissing."

He still didn't look at Lena. Just grinned at all of them and sat
down.

Well, fuck him. "Coward," she muttered.

Feeling a quick tug of vertigo—she was, admittedly, a little
drunk—Lena put down her glass and settled back in her chair. Slowly.
Smiling. *Never reveal anything,* Lena overheard her father tell her
mother once when Lena was very young. Probably he had been refer-
ring to something specific—finances, a business transaction, maybe
just a poker game—but the phrase had stayed with Lena as if it had
been spoken in a larger sense. If she had a personal motto—which, of
course, she didn't—that would be it: *Don't reveal a thing.*

The best medicine for getting over a man was another man. Anyone knew that. And with not just a little satisfaction, Lena was able to
look back and trace her own recoveries. One after the other. She'd had
a certain thing for restaurant managers for a while and then deejays and
then—who knew—the construction contractors who'd frequent the
Almost Home during the summer months for beer and pork sandwiches, all sweaty and foul-mouthed. There were all kinds of men.
Some doctors. A defense attorney. Lena liked a guy who could make a
good argument. There'd been Ben, the hot-dog franchise king, and
Dave, who—well, she'd never figured out what the hell he did, though
he always carried a big wad of bills. There was Dex, the gallery owner,

who had an oversized Adam's apple. The biggest, in fact, Lena had ever seen. Sometimes it distracted her out of an orgasm, the way it would jump up and down as he moaned. Still, she stuck with him longer than the others—nearly two years. He was mysterious and fun, would call her up at the last minute and swoop her off to some out-of-the-way place, some cliff or weird ethnic restaurant that didn't give you silverware. They'd fuck on the way there, on the way back, someplace in between. He wasn't the type to bring her things or call her every night, but that was fine with Lena. Nothing was more irritating than a guy who tried too hard.

Of course, there were a few things about Dex she could have done without. The Adam's apple for one. The threesomes for another. He was big into group sex, was always suggesting Lena lure her friends to his gallery, which was connected to his apartment. A convenient stairwell and couple lines of coke away. Since she flat-out refused to fuck her friends, he settled happily for complete strangers, giddy little bimbos he'd find at bars. Or cliffs—or weird ethnic restaurants. At first, actually, it had been kind of thrilling, the girl-on-girl fantasy thing. Lena'd even get things rolling every once in a while—that was how Dex liked it, seeing her surprise some girl with a tongue kiss, or, even better, a sliding hand on the thigh. A few times she and Dex actually tied the girl's hands and ankles to the bedposts and took turns teasing her—slapping her, for instance, with a plastic spatula.

Like any routine, it got old quick.

We're right out of some cheesy porno, she told him, not even a good one. The girls he chose were always so young and had such obviously fake tits. She wanted to know, What's that supposed to mean, that you always want a version of *that?*

Don't think so much, he'd said—and certainly *he* didn't, the way he went at them.

Hey, look, don't let me get in the way, she snapped on more than one occasion, jumping up and leaving the room. She'd fix herself a drink in the kitchen and put on music, loud, so she couldn't hear them.

Can you at least not kiss them on the lips? she asked him one night after the girl—this one was a college kid who'd actually mentioned her *schoolwork* right in the middle of things—had left and he was pulling off the sheets, which Lena insisted he do immediately after every "party."

Which lips? he'd asked, smirking. Please be specific.

Fuck you, Dex, she'd answered, more out of habit than anything else.

Denny never would have said *which lips*.

"Let's get something to eat," she told Colleen beside her. "I want to get drunk, really drunk, and I don't want to get sick."

"Okay, good," Colleen said. "But it's almost my turn."

"I'll take your turn," James said. "Bring me a sandwich."

"Yes! Bring us food, Lena," Fran said.

Lena and Colleen went back into the kitchen and fried up some poppers and chicken fingers. Unless she was doing the cooking herself, Lena wouldn't eat a thing from this kitchen. Not after the time Denny said he saw one of the kitchen tools mess with her burger. He wouldn't say who it was or what they did, no matter how much she yelled and threatened him. And not knowing, of course, made it so much worse. She'd never done much herself, beyond the ten-second dropped-it rule—and just once spitting in a drink. Which the asshole deserved. She'd seen plenty, though. A girl she'd worked with at Fourth Street used to slip Visine in drinks if the tips weren't good enough. A drop or two of Visine and you'd be in the bathroom all night. Even worse, one time at Chuck's Pizza, a shift manager had been so angry at a customer that he'd done something to her order that required a full ten minutes in the other room.

But still, even if you overlooked that kind of thing, restaurant line cooks were the dirtiest fuckers on the planet. Always reaching into their mouths, picking their teeth. Scratching. Take Bo Tamowitz. Just looking at him was a good diet.

And what killed Lena was that the others didn't care. All of them ordered food, ate it without a second thought. More than once Lena had even caught Colleen eating leftovers off a customer's plate. *Colleen,* who made such a big stink about germs and freaked out if the milk was out of the refrigerator for more than two seconds. That's how Colleen was, she'd have all those goddamn rules and then, for no logical reason at all, would just break them.

Lena shook the basket in the bubbling oil. The appetizers were done when they floated, but she liked them extra crispy. "Did I ever tell you," she asked Colleen, "about the dead cow I found?"

"No."

"When I was a kid, with my dog, we found this cow." She shook the basket a few more times, then lifted it out of the oil and dumped the poppers and fingers onto a plate.

"Is this going to make me not want to eat?"

"No," Lena lied. There were some things she enjoyed telling Colleen. She couldn't help it. "I'm talking barely a cow, mostly bones, a little skin. Dried blood. Maybe some guts, kind of shriveled into long, stringy—"

"*Lena.*"

"But that wasn't even the worst." She paused. "You wouldn't last a day in the country, Colleen."

176

"I wouldn't," Colleen said. She stuck a popper in her mouth and chewed. "Go on."

"So two days later, I hear my mom talking to one of the neighbors and find out that when the cow died—do you want to hear this?"

"Yes."

"The cow was giving birth and something went wrong and the calf died and the mother went paralyzed. Just froze up, with no one around to know. It could have been days, maybe weeks, just lying there, not being able to move—can you *imagine?*—just lying there and staring out, until buzzards came. Parasites ate her. Alive." She lifted a chicken finger from the basket and dipped it in barbeque sauce. "Not a thing she could do but let it happen."

"Lena, why do you tell me this stuff?"

Lena shrugged, ate the finger. "By the way," she said, washing it down with Colleen's beer, "I'm ending it with Denny."

She had no regrets. She'd done her share of crazy things. The three-somes, a little role-playing, one-night stands. Lots of girls were worried about words like *slut* and *easy,* and then—Christ—called themselves *feminists.* Lena enjoyed her body. She had nothing to be ashamed of, wasn't going to let anyone dictate how she should feel, what she should do. If she wanted to do something, she would do it. If she wanted to fuck someone, well then, she would fuck them. She'd never had a problem with that.

And the guys, in Lena's experience, never had a problem with it either.

Periodically, Lena took stock. She was not unattractive, not dumb. Not so old. She had a great ass—every guy she'd been with had told her so—and sometimes people asked if she had ever modeled. Thirty was not so old. It wasn't like she'd been married and divorced a million times. She was almost married once, to a venture capitalist. She could've been rich if she had married him, could've quit working and gardened or interior decorated or whatever the hell she wanted to do. But two weeks before the wedding, she fucked his best man and then fessed up.

How did you explain that to the minister? Colleen had asked when she heard about it.

The *minister*. Not, what did you do about all the presents people had sent, or the dress you'd bought yourself, or, gee, what about the rest of your whole fucking life now that you've fucked it up, but *What did you tell the minister?* Colleen always asked the wrong questions. After Lena went to Las Vegas with the Grandby rugby team—having only waited on them once—Colleen met her at the airport and asked if she'd caught any good shows. When Lena flew to St. Louis to meet a married lover, Colleen asked about the *arch*.

How should I know? Lena had answered. I never left the hotel room.

As for Denny, Colleen's advice from the beginning had been to spend time with *Stephanie*.

You might like her, Colleen said in that motherly way she had—ironic considering the kind of mother she was. She said, Maybe you'll see the whole picture. Get things under control.

Now Colleen asked, "Do you think Stephanie knows about you two?"

"Does it *matter*?"

Colleen looked away. Her feelings were easily hurt. "I like Denny," she said.

"Well, goody. You might be in luck. There might be an opening."

"I didn't mean it that way."

"Well, I mean it," Lena said, crumpling a napkin and shooting it into the trash can. "I swear, Colleen. I'm giving him an ultimatum, either move out and get rid of her or forget about me."

Colleen nodded. "Sure. That's fair."

Lena sighed. "I need to think of other things," she said. "He's driving me crazy."

The man in St. Louis was a friend of a friend. They met at a dinner party a couple months before he left Denver. Lena watched him from a few seats down. He wasn't the usual sort of guy she went for; he was on the short side and old side, but he had this half-mumbled way of speaking that made everything funnier and more important than it might otherwise be. She watched him joke with their friends; he traced shapes on the table or in the air while he talked. She watched him whisper to his wife, touch her hair.

They met for drinks. One time and then another and another, always early in the evening so he could make it home by an acceptable hour. They would go out or Lena would fix Irish coffees and they'd sit in her living room on the couch. It was her favorite possession, her butter-blond leather couch she'd spent three years getting out of layaway—the whole time imagining exactly this: the lights dimmed to low, herself and a lover sprawled, drinking elegant drinks. Or *starting* to drink. Usually they let them go cold. He'd be wearing his suit—even on days he had time to change, she wouldn't let him. It was like unwrapping a present, opening to softer and softer fabrics and then skin. Lena loved how his cock felt hot and unfamiliar on her tongue. Even after the first time, that initial moment seemed so accidental. She'd pause and look up at him, like, oh wow, how did *you* get *here?* Go ahead and stay a while.

179

Lena was fine with it, however, when he got the job promotion and had to move to St. Louis. It was starting to bug her, just a little, the way he was always *early* for their dates, and she'd recently noticed that he had this habit of humming and rocking on his toes whenever they waited for a traffic light or elevator. St. Louis, she decided, would be far enough away to keep things interesting. They could still meet up, just less often, maybe once a year like that old movie. Alan Alda. A cottage.

She waited a few months or so and then found herself thinking about him again—the low gravel of his voice, the way he'd scratch her back after they made love—so she called him up and said she'd be in the area. It just so happens, she said. She bought herself a plane ticket and a knockout black dress and booked a room in the best downtown St. Louis hotel. Their plan was for her to page him when she arrived, then he'd slip out and call her from a corner pub. They'd have a few drinks, catch up, enjoy each other's company, etc. *Etc.*

Only, when she did page him—after she'd arrived and checked in and bathed and moisturized and tweezed and dressed—he never called back.

"The thing with Denny," Colleen was saying—she could never just leave something be—"is I always think there's more going on than it seems. You know, underneath the surface."

"Of course there is," Lena snapped. She dropped more poppers into the fryer, watched them bubble up. "He's not James."

"Oh god, that's a good thing. Can you imagine?"

"Fran's an idiot," Lena said. "What do you think of the new girl?" she asked.

"I like her."

"She's an idiot too. She has a crush on Denny."

"She's just young, Lena."

"No, *Lily* is young."

Colleen got that moony look on her face she got whenever you mentioned her daughter. For some reason that look drove Lena up a wall. "Lily *is* young," Colleen said.

And needs a talking to, Lena thought. Someone ought to do something.

Last week Lena saw a police chase on the news. She watched for a good twenty minutes before, finally, she had to leave for work—she'd planned on leaving early to nab the good section but ended up sitting at the foot of her bed, keys in hand, watching the TV. The guy zipped in and out the side streets of west Denver, a whole fleet of cops following him. He knew what he was doing, he timed each light just right so he didn't have to stop. He dodged cars, swerved pedestrians. But not all that fast. He had the window down, his hand on the roof or else out straight, fingers open in the wind. At one point he even smoked a cigarette. A real wack job, the newscaster had said. But to Lena it made perfect sense. He knew, after all, that he'd be caught. His gas would run out or they would figure out a way to cut him off. And then he'd be fucked. He knew that. In the meantime, why the hell *not* take a breather? It was a nice day, Lena remembered. A warm afternoon.

Her other motto, if she had one: *Remain free.*

"We didn't make enough for everyone," Colleen pointed out as Lena picked up the plate of appetizers, only a handful left now, to carry back in.

"It's not kindergarten."

"I know," Colleen said, sighing, hopping down from the counter where she'd been sitting. "Don't you wish it was?"

Lena was able to recognize certain things about Denny. For instance, his silences—and his step-by-step way of doing things, plodding along, never willing to jump ahead. When push came to shove, he wasn't her type. He dressed like a sulky teenager in his denim and black t-shirts, and he walked funny, his torso stiff, all the movement coming from his legs. He listened to A.M. radio. He *worked in a bar.* A couple times she'd watched him sleep, his mouth open a little, lips sticking together in the corners, and wondered if this was what she wanted.

But it was Denny. She looked over at him now, drinking his drink, flipping a matchbook through his fingers—and all she saw, past, present, future, was *Denny.*

Twice Steph had called him a coward. The first was after last year's Super Bowl. The second time was a couple weeks ago. They'd just woken up and were watching the news and he hadn't even planned on saying anything, but the words formed in his mouth and it was just as easy to let them out as not. He said, It's over. I can't do this anymore. I'm sorry.

Steph stayed quiet for a long time. Then she got up and put on her robe and brushed her teeth, used the toilet. She made a pot of coffee, enough for both of them, as usual. He watched all of this, pulled on his sweats and followed her into the kitchen and smoked a cigarette. He liked to watch her in the morning. It was his favorite time to watch her, before she put on all the makeup and her skin was fresh-looking and ruddy and her hair all wild. For a few minutes he let himself imagine that he hadn't actually said anything, or that she hadn't heard him. But after the coffee finished brewing, she poured two mugs and mixed the sugar and milk and slammed them down on the kitchen table and in a low, steady voice he didn't recognize said, I hope you don't think I'm surprised.

He didn't answer.

Right, she said, keep your mouth shut. Don't say anything. She muttered, Strong silent type.

He stirred his coffee.

You don't do anything, she said. No, really, Denny. You don't. You don't take chances. You think you do but you don't. She looked at him, unflinching, her robe askew, her face raw and beautiful.

The others were laughing at something Lena had said, Denny didn't know what it was. He wasn't listening. He took a drink of beer. It hit him: it wasn't too late. It was one thing to make an effort, it was another thing to make something happen. Anyone could dial a phone, shit. Leave messages. No, he had to see her face to face—he could do that, he could put his tail between his legs, he could say whatever he needed to say. He'd drive straight to the apartment, go up to the door, and say—what? One thing in a million might be the right thing to say.

Denny lit a cigarette. This wasn't something to rush into. He didn't want to get there too early, for one thing. Steph didn't work Mondays, so she'd be out late. She'd be out with her girlfriends at Tonic for an after-hours victory party—and he pictured himself showing up before she got back. The place dark and locked. What then? He'd be standing outside his own apartment. He still had a key.

Would he go in? Sit down in the kitchen, open a can of something, feed the dog?

He would stay for one more beer. Finish the books. Wind down. Get his thoughts together. *It wasn't too late,* that's what mattered. This was the night. It was Super Bowl. Broncos had won. For good or bad, she was thinking about him too.

17.

Beside JJ, Keith stood up and cleared his throat. "Listen up," he said. "I've worked here a long time, and we've been through a hell of a lot, and I know you guys pretty well, and so it is with the utmost reverence and respect that I offer this." He pulled something out of his back pocket and tossed it on the table. It was a plastic baggie rolled into a narrow dark strip. "Hey, kids," he said, "wanna get high?"

They all laughed. Keith frowned and took a bow. JJ clapped. If she wasn't positive he'd been joking around with the speech, she'd almost think that his eyes had gotten teary, just a little, just for a second.

"Hallelujah," James said. "I was hoping someone would have some."

"Keith," Lena snapped, pointing her chin at Lily, who had come back to the table and was sitting beside Fran, drinking a soda.

"Oh sorry," Keith said. "I didn't mean *kids* kids."

"Go play one more game," Colleen told Lily.

"I already played one more game."

"Play another."

"I'm sick of Centipede. I get my name up every time."

"Just one more, honey, please? Or do your homework. Don't you have any homework from Friday?"

Lily stood up. "Let me get this straight. You want me to go over there and pretend I don't know you're smoking pot?"

"Lily."

"I am not saying a thing," Lena said.

"Because I know you're smoking pot. I'm not an idiot. And you want to know something? I don't *care* if you smoke pot."

"Lily," Colleen said, not looking at her. She plucked out a strand of hair and wrapped it around her little finger, squeezing off a circle at the tip.

"Let the kid smoke some pot," James said and Fran kicked him.

"We'll go soon," Colleen said. Her fingertip was red, like a berry.

"I am not saying a thing."

"And I appreciate that," Lily told Lena. To her mother she said, *"One more,"* and stalked back to the video game.

"Hey, sorry," Keith told Colleen.

"Don't be sorry." She picked off the tourniquet with her teeth. Color flooded back through her finger.

"I should've thought first. Before I just pulled it out."

"Yeah, you and me both, buddy," James said and slapped the table. Everyone ignored him.

"Do you have rolling papers?" Colleen asked.

Denny does, JJ thought. She shifted in her seat to see if he was smiling too, but he was looking in the other direction, at the witch, who was curled over, her head on her folded arms. JJ had forgotten about her.

"No papers. Pipe." Keith held up a corduroy pouch, unzipped it and slid out the pipe. It was small and rounded, made of dark, murky glass.

Denny asked, "What's with India?"

"Sleeping," Colleen said.

"Hey, India," Fran called. "Come smoke."

"Let her sleep."

"Well, then you can deal with her when we have to leave, Colleen," Lena said. "I'm not going back over there. She smells."

"What if she's not asleep?" Fran asked.

"She's asleep," Colleen said.

"How can she sleep after all that coffee?"

"When I was up writing term papers," Keith said, pressing bits of the pot into the pipe, "I'd drink a whole case of Diet Mountain Dew and still fall asleep."

"Wow," Fran said. "That's a lot of chemicals."

"Nothing wrong with chemicals," James said.

"Term papers," Lena said, frowning, creasing the bridge of her nose. A vertical line appeared or disappeared depending on her expression. "Keith, when were you in college?"

"Just a few classes for the hell of it."

"I hate papers," JJ said. "Hated papers." She added, "Except this one I did on doppelgängers. I worked hard on it. The professor was good."

"Was it one paper or two?" Keith asked, smiling, and JJ laughed. He handed the pipe to Colleen, then got up and went to the front door.

"What if she's dead? What if she's not sleeping but dead?"

"Would you quit it, Fran," Lena said.

"She's sleeping," Colleen said, blowing smoke. "If you knew India, you'd know she was sleeping. When was the last time any one of you had a conversation with her?"

187

"Here. Watch." Lena twisted around. "Hey, India."

"Oh come on, Lena, leave her be."

"Hey, India, old girl."

India didn't stir.

"You know," Lena said. "If she's dead—"

"She's not dead."

"But if she is." Lena took the pipe and lit it and sucked in the smoke. "If she is dead, on that very remote chance—because god, does she look healthy—we'll have to drag her into the alley."

"What?" Fran yelped.

Keith said, "That's sick, Lena. You're cold."

"Well, what would the alternative be? Have the cops find her here? Like it was our fault or something? I don't want to be here all night talking to cops."

"Fuck no," James said.

"Can we please not talk about this?" Colleen asked. "Hey, India," she hissed.

No movement.

"I mean," Lena said, "what would be the point in getting into trouble if she was already dead anyway?"

"It's true," Denny said, and his saying it made it so. There was a silence.

"I am not dead." India lifted her head and shook out her hair.

"Oh good," Fran said. "Then come tell our fortunes."

India stood up and sat back down again. It was hard to see her. She was beyond the candles' glow.

"She doesn't tell fortunes," Lena said. "She just talks."

"How would you know?" Colleen asked.

"Hey, can we go already?" Lily called from the video game. "Denny will take me, won't you?"

188

"Sure."

"That's ridiculous," Lena said to Lily. "You're all the way in the other direction. Denny'd be driving all night."

Colleen said, "We're *going*, Lily, *soon*."

"When exactly is soon?"

"We should all go," Fran said, sighing.

Lena turned to JJ. "Why are you doing that?"

"What?"

"Drumming your fingers like that. Quit it, will you? It's weird. It makes me nervous."

JJ dropped her hands in her lap. She'd also been working the pedal with her left foot. Beside her, Fran was smoking the pipe and so it would be her turn next. How did it work again? Was it the same as with the joint? Denny had given her a hint that had been really helpful. She tried to remember what it was.

This isn't, JJ thought, very relaxing. All these things you had to think about.

"Here," Fran said, passing the pipe and the lighter.

JJ took it, a little afraid she might drop it. It was heavy for its size. She brought it to her mouth and tried to light the pot at the same time.

"Oh god," Lena said. "It's not a *cock*. Don't stick it *in*."

The others laughed. JJ mumbled, "I know."

"There's a carb," Denny warned and JJ nodded like she knew what he meant. Carb? Carbohydrate? She tried not to giggle and stared down her nose at the pipe's swirly glass. She heard a chair screech back and then Denny was beside her, lighting the lighter and showing her how to do it.

"Like this," he said, holding her finger over a small hole on the bowl of the pipe.

189

In front of the others, it was a little like having him cut her steak. But he felt good beside her, warm and in charge. And it worked. She coughed out a blast of gray-blue smoke. "Delicious," she said and everyone laughed. Someone clapped, Colleen probably. JJ's head felt big and puffy and then tight.

Denny was smiling at her. "You're a pro," he said. He took the pipe and smoked from it, then handed it to Fran. Then grabbed his beer and headed to the office.

"I read somewhere," Colleen said, "that we only use ten percent of our brains."

"You said that already," Lena said.

"But I was thinking. What if we only use ten percent of our lives?"

Lily came back to the table. "Game over."

"Lily, I'm hurrying. Really."

"Hurrying what? It's *3:15*. You do remember that this is Sunday and tomorrow is Monday and I have school on Mondays?"

"You can take tomorrow off. We can have a mother-daughter day. We never do that."

"I don't want tomorrow off." Lily bent down to her backpack, zipped it open. She rummaged inside, first slowly, then faster, pulling out a couple of folders and a sneaker. "Where is it," she said.

"Where's what?" Colleen asked.

"My stuff. The jar. The photo."

"What photo?"

"*What* photo?" Lena echoed.

"None of your business," Lily told her. She turned to her mother. "Give it back. It was right here. Right in the pocket at the top. I want it now."

"Don't speak to me like that, Lily. I don't know what you're talking about."

"Where is it? Did you put it in your purse?" She reached for the purse, but Colleen held it away.

"I told you, I don't have it."

Lily crouched down and shoved her things back into the backpack, zipped it. She called, "Denny, I want to go home."

"*Lily,*" Lena said, "will you take a freaking chill? Jesus."

"*It's none of your business!*" Lily grabbed up the pack and slung it over her shoulder. "I'm going home," she announced and turned and headed for the kitchen doors.

Lena said, "I'm going after her."

"Oh Lena, would you?" Colleen asked. She rubbed her face in her hands, then looked up, her mouth a little open, like she'd started to say something but was too tired to get it out.

18.

"I'm going after her," Lily heard Lena say behind her and so she picked up as much speed as she could without running. She refused to run. She banged into the kitchen and headed to the back door, the door to outside, the door to freedom—and would have made it if Lena hadn't sprinted ahead at the last second, throwing herself in front of the door. *"Ha."* Lily tried to scoot under her arms, but Lena slid down to block her there too.

Lily stepped back. "Fine," she said. "I'm an expert on waiting."

"Take a seat." Lena pointed her chin to a folding chair beside the sinks. She was out of breath. "Lily. Go sit. Now. I'm not kidding."

"I'm just going home, Lena."

"Well you can't just walk out the door, it's the middle of night! Maybe you forgot, but you're a *kid.*"

Maybe you forgot I'm not *your* kid, Lily thought. She said: "Most people want kids to stay *out* of bars."

"Lily, we need to talk. We haven't talked since you and your mom moved out."

Thank god.

"You know you can come to me? Right? About anything?"

"Sure," Lily said. She stared at her sneaker toe. In health class last week, she'd decorated it, drawn a picture of a flower. It'd smeared so now it looked like the flower was moving, sprinting off.

"When I was your age I had a favorite aunt, my Aunt Rhea, who I always talked to. She was really cool, lived in this condo that used to be part of an old church." Lena removed her hand from the doorway to scratch her forehead, then whipped it back in place. "Sometimes it isn't easy to talk to your parents, you know. Your mother."

Lily shrugged.

"Come on, sit down. Please? For me?"

She didn't move.

"I'm only trying to help you."

One, two, three. Lily counted the acne scars on Lena's face. She wore makeup to cover them, but you could always tell, especially at the end of the night under the kitchen lights. Dark splotches under the orange. Four, five, six.

"*Fine,* we don't have to talk. Fine. I don't have the patience for this kind of . . ."

She kept talking. Lily thought hard and imagined Lena's stringy hair transforming into worms, into octopus legs, coiling around her neck and sliding along her chin and her mouth, snapping off her witch lips, one, snap, two.

". . . someone has to be responsible. Someone has to *really care.*" Finally, Lena dropped her arms from the door frame and, without missing a beat, Lily lunged for the knob. But for a bag of bones, Lena was pretty fast. She snapped back into place and blocked Lily's hand with her knee.

"You're not my mother," Lily said. "I know you think you are."

"I had to put up with your shit for a whole year, Lily, and now you're going to listen to me because I actually care about you, *unlike* your mother."

Lily wanted to hurt her. It was a sudden, delicious feeling. She wanted to grab something heavy and bash it over Lena's head. But of course she didn't. She took a breath. She said, "You know what Denny told me, Lena? I almost forgot. You know what he was saying to me when I first came in and was at the bar and you asked what we were talking about? He was telling me about *Steph,* how they might get *married.* And I said, 'Oh that's good because we all love Steph.'"

All the real color drained from Lena's face. "Very cute, Lily."

"You can make a fool of yourself," Lily said, "if you want. I don't care."

In one swoop, Lena came away from the door and smacked her across the cheek, hard. Lily's ears rang. She grabbed her backpack and took off back through the kitchen, down the basement stairs, to the door of the extra bathroom, where she hopped up and felt along the door frame for the paper clip and jammed it into the lock. She jiggled it around until there was a click and the door opened, then leapt in and slammed the door, locked it, breathing hard, not even moving to put down her backpack or turn on the light. Just stood there in total darkness. She could feel the heat of Lena's hand on her face.

She waited for the sound of high heels on the stairs—or maybe the others had heard and Denny would be the one to come down, to see if she was okay.

More likely, though, it'd be her mother.

But no one came. Lily stood still in the pitch darkness. She could feel the smallness of the space, the walls around her pressing in. It was the kind of feeling that could make her panic, if she let it. If she wanted it to.

It had been a while since she'd been down here. She used to come here all the time to get away when her mother was taking too long—which she almost always was—would hide down here with a book and sit against the locked door reading or, after Marna had given her the notebook, writing. Not like a *diary,* which was what everyone assumed—as if Lily would be stupid enough to write down anything that mattered—but just things. Lists. People she wanted to meet. The guys who wanted to fuck her. Things not to do if you're stuck above treeline in a thunderstorm. And some artwork. Little doodles. She'd sit and daydream on paper. It was a little like talking to Marna, actually. But then her mother figured out where Lily was going and flipped out. And yeah, it was kind of gross—to be sitting on a bathroom floor—but it was just *dirt.*

Although who knew what Lily'd find now when she turned on the light. Dead bodies. Rats. A gaping hole to hell.

Or maybe Marna. Hiding out too.

Lily didn't move. She could hear people above, footsteps, voices. Fran laughing. The dark felt thick, Lily let it fill her up, enter through her nose and mouth and ears. Pores. She let herself dissolve into it, imagined disintegrating, cell by cell. She could actually feel it happening, so that after a while she was floating, submerged in nothing, was up or down, was up and down. It was like water.

Finally, when there was nothing left but absolute calm, when every last *Fuck Lena* had floated far away, Lily allowed herself to reach very slowly for the light switch by the door. She felt for it, found it, flipped it on. After a few moments of blindness, the bathroom—and her own body in the bathroom—reemerged. Cement walls, tile floor, tilted stall—all of it pink, a mottled mix of salmon and bubblegum. Scrawled with graffiti. *Lizbet rules. N.N. loves H.H. N.N. is a slut. If you sprinkle when you tinkle, please be neat and wipe the seat.* And, of course, various versions of: *There's no place like Almost Home.*

Lily checked inside the stall, behind the toilet, and sure enough, there was the bottle of Goldschläger she'd stashed. She unscrewed the cap with a little trouble—the sugar made it stick—and drank it, ignoring the burn, not bothering to catch the gold. It occurred to her that it couldn't be real gold anyway. They told you it was, but it wasn't.

A fly buzzed and bumped against the walls. "Good luck," Lily whispered, "there's no way out." She thought about putting it out of its misery, smashing it with her shoe. Her mother was a freak about rescuing bugs and wouldn't let Lily kill anything, not spiders or silverfish—not even the sugar ants that came, in a dark line, into the kitchen every spring. Lily was expected to sweep them into a paper towel and shake them out the window. It was a pain in the ass, they were so tiny. Took a million tries to get them all.

It's a long fall for an ant, she'd pointed out to her mother. They'll die anyway, when they hit the ground.

Maybe, her mother said. But maybe not. They're light, they might land easy.

Lily shrugged. According to the survival guide, they were edible, that's all she knew.

Lily watched herself drinking in the rust-speckled mirror above the sink, watched her face change not even a millimeter as the alcohol went down her throat. She looked into her eyes, concentrating on the dark middles, held her own stare without blinking for many seconds. You are getting sleepy, she thought. You are falling in. Dark centers into dark tunnels into dark. Rochelle swore that it was possible to hypnotize yourself, that she'd seen a whole TV show on it once. What's the point? Lily had asked her, and now asked herself. She let herself blink a few times—her eyes were getting dry—and then tried it again, stared straight in, let her vision go furry. To make yourself do things, had been Rochelle's answer. Anything, she'd said. Whatever you want.

It's working, Lily thought. The room felt hazy, all the pink pooling together. I'm going going going going. . . . Only, she couldn't think of what she wanted to do, where she wanted to go, and it was distracting. There were so many possibilities. It was hard to think of just one. I want to go home, she thought. It was stupid, but it was the first thing that came to her. Home. The real deal. Not the apartment they were living in now, which was small and cold, right beside a recycling plant that made noise all the time, night and day. And not Lena's apartment, of course.

But maybe she wasn't thinking about the old house either, the house she'd grown up in. 243 Center Street. The address and phone number and zip code still beat familiar tunes in her head. It was home, more home than anything else, but it mostly made Lily think about moving away. About unhappy endings. About the reception they'd had for her father—which is how her mother had put it at the time. Her mother hadn't been able say the word *wake*. Or *funeral*. Or *dead*. She called it a reception. She stayed up the whole night before, cooking things: frittatas and dumplings and little rolled-up appetizers stuck with toothpicks. She made dishes Lily had never seen before, from recipes in big, stiff books, recipes that had a million steps and took up whole pages. She wanted Lily to help, woke her up to sift ingredients, to stir, to taste things.

Something small scurried on the floor behind her, but Lily didn't turn around, just kept staring and took another drink, then rescrewed the Goldschläger and set it down on the sink. She got up close to the mirror, so close that her nose touched. She turned her head, pressed her cheek against the cold, then turned again so that her lips were touching it and she kissed it, opened her mouth a little and touched her tongue to the reflection of her tongue. It tasted metallic and dusty, but she did it more, kept her eyes open and stared into them and kissed again. Oh Denny, she whispered. Oh Lily.

Back in the hallway, she closed the door behind her, rebalanced the paper clip, and considered sneaking back upstairs and escaping through the kitchen. But it was such a long walk to their new apartment. All the way down Colfax to North Chambers Road. Colfax, the longest street in the world. Rochelle swore it was true.

And then there was the apartment itself. That too was depressing. Going in alone and turning up the heat, standing by the vent. Lying awake in bed, waiting for her mother. Getting up and sitting in the kitchen, waiting for her mother.

Someone'd left an empty beer bottle on the floor in the hallway, and Lily rolled it back and forth with her foot. She might as well go back into the bathroom—the only room that didn't feel like here—and curl up on the floor, go to sleep. Or just sit down. Right here, against the cool cement. Wait for the sounds of everyone finishing up. The music being switched off, the last chair stacked. Upstairs, she could hear "Tainted Love" playing, her mother's favorite stupid song. She was probably bobbing in place, flailing her arms.

But then it hit Lily: Marna was expecting her.

Just because she'd bailed on work and the others didn't mean she'd bailed on Lily.

Praying that no one would want something downstairs, that they were all too drunk and lazy to move very far, she went into the break room. The taxicab number was written in nail polish on the wall beside the phone.

"Could be an hour," the man said. "At least."

"That long?" Lily sighed. She sat down on the end of the couch. Her mother might be even longer. Hours. Plural. Hour singular was better than hours plural, it was better than nothing. "Okay," she said. She hung up the phone without saying good-bye. It felt good, a little dangerous.

Lena's locker was on the very top row. Lily had to drag the couch over to reach it. It was locked, but she knew the combo; she'd memorized it off a list of important numbers in Lena's dresser drawer. Lily swung open the door and pulled out a shallow wire basket crammed full of papers and junk: to-go menus for nearby restaurants, a cartoon off the Internet about why men like sports, boxes of mints, a lipstick, a bottle of aspirin. Lily almost laughed. Lena thinks it's a *desk,* she thought, in her *office.* She picked through the pile, found a twenty and a couple of ones, which she pocketed, and a glittery lighter, which she also pocketed, and a disk of birth-control pills, which she snapped open. She popped a few out. She tossed two into an empty locker and ate the other, let it dissolve bitterly on her tongue, then flipped through receipts and sidework lists and some photos. There were two of Lena's cat, Jiggers, and one of her nephew. Lena had only seen the kid once, Lily knew that for a fact. That's how caring Lena was. Beneath the photos—and this was even better—Lily discovered a picture that she herself had doodled a long time ago, a dumb house-on-the-lawn thing, in ballpoint pen. The sun a spiky smile in the background. Lena had taken it off the fridge because she said it made the kitchen look shabby. And then she'd gone and saved it. Lily imagined Lena showing it to people, pretending it meant something, that it'd been drawn for *her.*

Lily took the picture and folded it, put it in her backpack, then decided to take the nephew as well. What the hell, she figured. He looked so small and blameless.

At the very bottom of the basket, Lily found what she was looking for: Lena's spare key ring. The plastic tag said *Bitch on Wheels* and had a cartoon of the Tasmanian She-Devil on it, fangs bared. No kidding, Lily thought. She flipped through the keys and worried for a moment that it wasn't there, that Lena had given it back—until she spotted one with a small chip on one corner. She slid the key round and round until it came off, then stuck it in her pocket with Denny's cigarette, tucked it in as far as it would go.

19.

Denny rolled back in the chair to the file cabinet and slid open a drawer, flipped through the papers that were crammed inside a folder marked *shift logs,* pulled one out. What a joke, he thought. Shift logs. Not a lick of management where it counted and then Bill got on you about things like keeping track of bev-nap stock or facing all the cash the same way. He went ballistic if you slipped in a backwards twenty.

Denny was feeling better. Looser. This was good. It was good, he decided, to face important moments with the right attitude, with a little *well what the fuck.* Like that dumb Tom Cruise flick: sometimes you gotta say, *what the fuck.* Maybe that'd been the problem in the past. He'd been *too* focused.

He looked for something to write with. The calendar had fallen again and he tacked it up. It wasn't even a good calendar, but every time it fell, someone would put it back. It was one of those low-budget deals, probably shot in some creep's basement. January was chunky, with manly shoulders, and she had a beer bottle in her hand and one on the ground she was preparing to sit on. You could tell that she was having trouble holding the pose. Her expression said, *Hurry up already and take the goddamn picture.*

He found a pencil in the top drawer and licked the tip, a habit he'd picked up from his father. It didn't help the writing as far as Denny could tell. He filled in the date. He copied the gross and net from the checkout, broke down the numbers for food and bar, calculated inventory versus sales. Beside *weather* he wrote, *January.* Duh. Next to general comments, he wrote, *Super Bowl, Broncos win*—then added a few exclamation points. *Fuck Falcons,* he wrote. *Fuck Marna.* He erased that, wrote instead, *Marna quit. Good-bye Marna.* Added, *Hello JJ.* Wrote, *Who is responsible for sending her in to train tonight.* Added question marks. Then: *Super Bowl. Broncos 34, Falcons 19.* Exclamation points.

It wasn't like anyone read the logs anyway, they were just shoved back into the drawer, in a different file. *Completed shift logs.* Pure genius.

Lena appeared in the doorway, all red-faced, in one of her rants. "Fucking Lily," she said. "Goddamn little snot. You might think she's cute—*oh look at little Lily*—but I'm telling you, she won't be so cute in a couple years. She's not so cute *now.*"

He lit a cigarette.

"I swear, Denny. It's impossible to talk to her, I don't know why I even try. She's downstairs *hiding.*" Lena sat down on a stack of soda syrup boxes by the door and rubbed her temples, asked, "You got one for me?"

He shook his head. "Last one. I have a couple packs downstairs if you want to run down." He smiled. "Unless Lily's smoked them by now."

"I'm not moving," she said. "I can't imagine ever moving." But she got up and took the cigarette from his hand and sat back down with it. "Fucking Lily," she muttered and took a drag.

He gathered up the deposit and got a bank bag from the drawer and folded the checkouts, stuffed everything in. "What'd she do?"

"She's a shitty rotten spoiled brat is what she did."

He dropped the bag into the safe. It had a rolltop that you had to crank around. Bill was the only one with the key and once it was in there you couldn't get it back. For some reason that made Denny nervous. He'd never fucked it up, not once—and if he did, no one would care, they'd just fix it. But it still put him on edge, the finality of it.

"You shouldn't encourage her," Lena said.

"To do what?" He took back his cigarette.

"Anything. You know how kids can misunderstand at that age." She paused. She took a breath like she was about to say something long and preachy, then stood up as if to leave. She didn't do either. She leaned over and retacked the calendar. "It was about to fall," she said and put her hands on the back of his chair. She'd taken her hair down and it brushed against his neck. He could smell her shampoo. "I might need a ride," she said.

"I'll call you a cab."

"You can be my cab."

"Not tonight."

There was a silence.

"Oh right," she said, "gotta get home to the *wife*."

He slid open the bottom drawer, pulled out the accounting book.

"I have an idea. Call her, Denny. Tell her you're going to be late. Tell her you got *detention* and you'll see her first thing in the morning."

He flipped through the pages, found the right day and copied the night's numbers, rechecked the totals.

She slid past him. "No problem," she said. "I'll call her." Out of the corner of his eye, Denny saw her pick up the phone. She was bluffing. It was the one thing she'd never do.

She punched numbers.

She put it to her ear, twirled the cord. Smiled.

Dumb stunt. He could hear the phone ringing. She was probably calling her own apartment.

But someone answered. He could hear noise.

Lena said, "Yeah, hi there, I'm sorry to bother you—"

"Hey!" He lunged, wrestled the receiver away from her, slammed it down. "What the fuck is *wrong* with you? God*damn* it, Lena." It felt like he'd been sucker-punched, all the blood rushing to his gut, replacing air. His scalp tingled. He thought, he could call back. He could explain Lena was drunk. He could say that *he* was the one dialing and Lena had grabbed it away trying to be funny. This might even work in his favor. He could tell Steph he was calling to say he was coming over—soon. He was on his way.

He turned to Lena. "Would you get the hell out of here?"

She didn't move. She said, "Who's the guy?"

"What guy?"

"At your place."

"You got the wrong number," he said, shaking his head, sitting down, glad to be able to breathe again. "Christ, Lena, you dialed wrong. Go have another drink why don't you."

"No. I didn't get the wrong number. I got the right number. *She* answered." Lena smiled. "I heard *him* in the background."

He sat there. Stared at January. It didn't mean a thing. It's the Super Bowl, he told himself. She's having a party. To Lena, he said, "It's a party. It's a free country."

"Oh yeah? What party. It didn't *sound* like a party. Not that kind of a party. It sounded like I woke her up. And then *he* goes, 'Who is it?'"

Denny sat there.

"Well oh my god." Lena gave a short laugh. "Whatdya know. Sweet little thing has a guy on the sly. And all this time you were having trouble deciding. Should I move out? Will I hurt her? Will I hurt her *feelings?*"

He watched her talk. He couldn't say anything. There was nothing to say.

"Look, Denny. I know you're upset. I'd be upset. Anyone'd be upset. You spend enough time with someone. But *screw* her. Seriously, Denny. Cheating bitch. And listen, I have plenty of room at my place, you know, until we find something for you. We can decide from there."

The room filled up with itself—the desk, the chair, the walls, everything swelling twice as big. He waited for the calendar to fall again, for everything to fall, just peel away, that's how it goddamn felt. All the lightness of not even an hour ago, a fucking sham. Some guy was in his apartment, in his bed.

Denny stared straight at Lena. With all he had left, he produced a laugh. He said, "I don't need your help. I moved out weeks ago."

. . .

Colleen danced. She just had it in her. It wasn't something people guessed about her, she knew, and maybe that made it even better. After a busy night, when it was all over and she was exhausted and her feet were aching, the body that always fought her—that normally felt so heavy and out of balance—lifted. Suddenly. The music bubbled from within, roiled in her gut, buzzed her bones, lit her skin, swung her to the beat. It was electric. Like a good sprint of painting. Like she always hoped making love would be.

The others didn't say anything or even look up. They were used to it. On her way back from the bathroom, JJ joined her, hopped around a little, but then Fran started giggling and JJ sat down.

"I wasn't laughing at you, JJ. It was at James."

"Oh. I know."

"I got another one. What's the difference between the Panama Canal and an Almost Home waitress?"

"What?"

"Would you quit encouraging him?"

"One's a busy ditch."

"Hey, Keith, where do you keep *going?* Getting up, sitting down. Can you please keep still? Go or stay, either one."

"Stay, Keith, stay. Sing us a song. It just occurred to me! You look like a guy with a really good voice."

"Hey JJ, your nipples are hard."

"Shut up, James."

"It's cold."

"It's not cold."

"You know what I just figured out? I'm like a chocoholic, except with *alcohol.*"

The voices were far away, floating by from somewhere else.

She didn't care that they ignored her when she danced. She preferred it. The bar was hers alone. The dark smells, the flashing beer signs—it was her own club, showcasing only her. She never danced like this anywhere else. Not at home like some people did when no one was looking. Not even at any of the school dances she'd been to as a kid. Not out on the town. Just here.

A flash of Lily: older, in college, also dancing—with friends, in nightclubs, the lights beating. Lily, all pale, liquid limbs and glinting hair. At ease anywhere. With anyone. She would do so well—Colleen was sure of it and was filled with a sudden sharp pride. Lily was smart. College, then graduate school. But not just textbookish smart. She was off in the world, driving a car, wearing a suit, something in natural fibers. Her hair combed back. A hand-dyed scarf. Glass earrings from Brazil. It's a warm day. It's always a warm day—she lives somewhere rich and tropical. She can choose anywhere in the world to live. She says, I'll live here. She presses down on the gas, lets it up. All the time in the world. Nothing begins without her. The sky is wide and bright. She stops at a roadside stand, buys figs and lemonade. She breezes into her office, alight with soft air, enters with a *whoosh*. Glass doors, skylights, a bouquet of daisies on every desk. People look up. *There she is,* people say.

Colleen felt a funny whir from outside her body and she stopped dancing, turned quickly to the bar, which was dark. He wasn't there. He'd been there a second ago, she was pretty sure. She was positive. He was watching her.

Denny pushed back from the desk. It wasn't like something had changed all of a sudden. Knowing didn't make a flying crap of difference. It was the same as yesterday and the day before that and the same as tomorrow, and now he was going home. He was getting out of this fucking office and this fucking bar and getting in his truck and driving straight to his shitty apartment—maybe not even stopping for the god-damn lights, just going right through, one after the other.

Or—he'd still do it, he'd drive over there. He'd use his key and pull the motherfucker out of bed, just yank him out and tear him apart, start with his goddamn legs. *Now* who's the coward, he'd say to her.

Or—or what?

He'd beg.

He'd do nothing.

He'd be his father: useless.

Denny stood up. His head was throbbing. It felt full of sand. He needed a cigarette. He could hear the others, out there, laughing. Clinking and chattering.

Two weeks, he thought. She couldn't even wait a fucking month.

He went downstairs to the break room, where the air was cooler and he might be able to think. He stopped when he saw her. He'd for-gotten she was down here. He almost turned and left, but didn't. It was just Lily.

"Oh," she said. "You scared me." She had a mess of papers spread out on the couch and she jumped up and gathered it all and stuffed it into a bottom locker. "I'm so glad it's you," she said.

He opened his locker and got a pack, smacked it on his arm. He took out a cigarette, then patted his pockets for a lighter.

"Here." Lily held one out.

"Thanks." He lit it, took a hard drag.

Lily sighed and plopped back down on the couch. Crossed her legs. "I called a cab," she said.

He nodded.

"I need to go up and wait for it. I just don't want to. You know. Go up. See all them."

"So don't."

"Oh right, and stay here forever?" She snorted. "I'm stuck," she said. "There's no way out." But she smiled. She looked at him. Her face open and light. Lily, he thought, the only one who didn't want something. Who could smile at you and that was it.

Upstairs, someone flushed a toilet. The pipes gave a creak and a groan.

He thought, *It doesn't matter.*

He thought, Here was the truth: Out there, somewhere else, your life could go to shit and you might not even know it. You could stand still and stay put and disappear. Denny felt himself smile, an easy twitch of muscle. One small change. He dropped the cigarette to the floor and ground it out with his heel. "You're not stuck," he told Lily. "I'll show you."

If Lena could do anything, she could remain calm. She could cool off. She could sit and have a drink and play a game and let things settle.

But of course they had to start right in.

"Where's Denny?" Fran asked as soon as she sat down. "And where's Lily?"

"Sulking," Lena said, "and sulking." She filled her beer with what was left in the bucket. They'd given up on the Bismarck, were just going around now, saying things. She'd missed favorite sexual position—they were on to most annoying '80s song. "'In Your Eyes,'" she said.

"Oh I like that one," JJ said. "Is that the one that sounds like, 'when you go away, you take a piece of meat with you,' because the beat hits on the 'me'?"

James said, "I'll give you a piece of—"

"Don't even," Fran said. She sighed. "You know, when I hear something that I hated a while ago, sometimes I just remember that I had a strong feeling for it and I forget and think I loved it."

"Oh yeah," JJ said.

Lena told JJ, "You were barely alive in the '80s." She was a mouth breather, Lena noticed.

Keith said, "Was anyone fully alive in the '80s?"

"You're all getting on my nerves," Lena said.

"Oh god it's late." Colleen was slumped in her chair. A lump. Everything that was wrong with the place, Lena thought, right here at this table. "It happens so fast," Colleen whined. "And Lily, I swear, just a minute ago, she was like a baby."

"She *is* like a baby," Lena snapped.

"Lily's a good kid," Keith said.

Fran said, "You'll be in trouble in a year or two, Colleen. All the boys. And that body. I think she's sweet on Denny." She laughed.

"Oh I know, I know. Boys. I'm in trouble now."

"You're an idiot, Fran," Lena said. "She's a *kid.*" She turned to Colleen. "Tell me something, do you think you're a good mother? I'm curious. Because no one thinks you are. Does anyone here think Colleen is a good mother?"

JJ raised her hand, then put it down.

"Hey," Keith said. "Easy for you to say, Lena. How many kids do you have?"

"I'm not a matador but I know *bullshit* when I see it."

"Speaking of bullshit," James said.

"Shut up, James."

Colleen had a distant look on her face—not pissed off, not even thinking, just like she was somewhere else, like she'd stepped away from behind it.

"Hey, where *are* Denny and Lily?" Fran asked. Fran. Another winner. Fran, who had struck it rich in a legal settlement some years back and was able to *quit working*—the Almost Home even threw her a going-away party. *The Great Escape,* the banners read, and Fran had given a speech—actually stood up on a table to do it—about going and getting done all the things she wanted, maybe buying a camper and opening a gourmet kitchen shop. But it never happened, none of it. Fran didn't go anywhere.

Lena wished *she* were somewhere else. She didn't belong here, this was the last place she belonged. She could have any job she wanted, at any place in town, so why was she *here?*

"What's your problem, Lena?" Keith asked. Fat slob. Master of all things restaurant. Lord of idiot assholes.

"You," Lena told him, "are my problem. Your fat ass following Marna around. It's embarrassing. Wake *up.* I can't stand it, none of us can. Holy crap. She's not your girlfriend, Keith. I know it, Marna knows it, even the goddamn *new girl* knows it. Everyone seems to know it but you."

They stared at her, the whole table of them.

Lily helped Denny push the couch beneath the coat rack, then stood back as he took hold of the side of the lockers—it was funny, she'd never noticed before that they were separate from the wall. He yanked. The lockers gave a loud squeak but didn't move. He paused, repositioned himself.

"Can I help?" She had no idea what he was doing, but she loved it. Loved watching him move, the way he frowned at the lockers, like it was a contest: him against them.

He shook his head, tried again.

We'll hide, she thought, he's making room. She felt a sudden spin of giddiness, imagined the two of them crouched back there for hours, doing whatever they wanted to, doing *It,* quiet, muffled, humping away until the others were gone and it was just them, the place was all theirs. "What're you *up to,*" she wheedled, but he didn't answer. Just gave another pull and then another, a big one this time that worked. The lockers came back from the wall with a low scrape and revealed not just a mess of garbage and dust—and a pair of jeans and a transistor radio—but a *door.* A big metal door.

"Oh my god," she breathed. "Where did that come from? Where does it go?"

He flipped the lock and turned the knob, swung it open, let in a huff of cold.

"You've got to be *kidding!*" Lily ran past him, outside. *Free.* There was a narrow flight of snow-covered metal stairs and she skipped up, taking them by twos, and found herself in the alley that faced the Quickmart. "But I never knew!" she called down. "I can't *believe* it!" She twirled. The wind was icy and hard, whipping the falling snow sideways, into her eyes. She ran back down for her backpack and got out her coat, put it on. "Come on, let's go! C'mon, Denny. Wait for my cab with me. You will, won't you? You have to." She stood just outside the door, stamping the snow under her feet, enjoying the crunch. She held on to both doorknobs and tipped backwards, swung her weight from side to side. *Incredible.* It was like a dream she sometimes had, where she's back in her old house and suddenly discovers another *room,* one she's never known about.

Denny stepped outside. She followed him back up the stairs and down the alley to a bench out front, which was, thankfully, away from the front doors. Lily wasn't taking any chances. She'd made it out. She wasn't going back in. "So why was it blocked off like that?" she asked.

"Bill's worried about drug deals. And I think one time someone forgot to lock it and Bill came in to open up and found James passed out."

"James is gross," Lily said.

The bench was covered in a smooth shelf of snow, rounded so it looked like a cushion, and they ruined it—swept it away with their arms and sat down. The wind felt good almost, cutting against Lily's face. It jolted her, made her feel ready for anything. *Let's just start walking,* she wanted to insist, *let's walk and walk until our legs collapse and we can't walk anymore and then let's see where we are.* Or not even insist—just grab his arm and pull him along. Maybe he'd go. Maybe he already wanted to go, was dying to go and just didn't want to ask. After all, he'd been watching her all night. Giving her little looks. Lily knew what that meant. She wasn't stupid. *Denny,* she thought, mouthing it.

"Take me home," is what she told him, using a lower version of her voice. "I'll pay for your gas."

He took out his cigarettes. "I'm not the safest ride right now, L-pad."

"I don't care. Hey, can I have one?"

"No."

"Because you care, right?"

"Right."

"If you won't drive me home, Denny, I wish you'd come with me then. We can hang out. I make really good macaroni and cheese. The real kind, not the stuff from the box."

There was not much traffic now. There were very few reasons to be out on these streets at almost 4 A.M. on a Sunday night, Super Bowl or no Super Bowl. People, if they were still up, were downtown or having parties in their homes.

Lily was freezing. Her coat was the crummy cheap kind with the lining that got all bunched up in places, leaving the rest of it thin, no better than a windbreaker. "Brrr," she said and huddled against Denny, who was fiddling with the transistor radio he'd grabbed from behind the lockers. She put her arm around him, buried her face in his chest. From the survival guide: *If you are not properly dressed for conditions, finding shelter is crucial.* Denny smelled sweet and smoky. She stayed there for a moment and breathed him in—and he let her, didn't move, stopped fiddling—then she reached into his jacket pocket and grabbed the pack of cigarettes and his keys and leapt back.

"Hey," he said.

She darted, laughing, behind the mailbox. "I can drive myself home now. I don't need you. I can drive. My dad taught me when I was ten, I'm good." She smacked the cigarettes on her arm and pulled one out, stuck it in her mouth, dangled it from her lower lip.

"Great, Lily, my luck a cop'll come by and I'll be arrested."

"For what? Bad influence?"

"Bad something."

"I don't want to light it. I just like the way it feels. How does it look? Sexy?" She pretended to inhale and blew out a cord of breath.

"Very. Now hand 'em over."

"Okay," she said. "I'll give them back. But first you have to ask me a question."

"What question?"

"Any question. The first thing that pops into your mind. Make it good." She stretched herself against the curve of the mailbox, reached up and over toward Denny, as far as she could, and held the stretch, the metal against her stomach burning cold.

"Fine. A question: Can I please have my keys and smokes back?"

"I said make it good."

"Shit, Lily. I'm not in the mood for this."

"Hurry up. Cab'll be here and I'll take off with your keys. You won't be able to drive or get into your house. You'll be out of luck. You'll have to come with me." *You want to come with me,* she thought, sending it to him. *You want me.* It often seemed unbelievable to Lily that you could think something, scream it in your head, and no one else around you could hear it or know it. That you could be smiling and saying, Hi there, what a nice day, and thinking, Fuck shit dildo cock cunt ugly fucking fucking fuck fuck fuck.

Or: *I love you.*

Denny smoked a couple more puffs and dropped his cigarette into the snow. "Fine. So what was that photo you lost?"

Lily straightened up, stepped back from the mailbox. "Oh," she said. "That. I have a better idea. I'll ask you a question."

"Nope. You first."

Lily tipped her head back. The sky was dark and murky, a strange boiled purple. The wrong kind of sky, really, for snow, for this time of year and night. It was a tornado sky, the way it glowed. "It was nothing," she said. "It's gone."

"That's too bad." He was looking at her, like he expected something.

What would he do, Lily wondered, if she started taking off her clothes? Right there, outside in the freezing wind, layer by layer. Lily imagined a crowd slowly gathering, cars pulling up and stopping, everyone watching, Denny in the middle of them, cheering her on. "Maybe it left," she said.

"Left?"

"The cab. Maybe it came early and left."

There was a pause, filled with snow. It not only cut sideways, it also swirled, danced, changed direction if you watched it closely. And if you relaxed your eyes, it seemed to go away, dissolved against the sky.

"It was of my father," she said then. "And me, riding a bike. It's the only photo I have of him." She waited for it: the small involuntary flinch people always gave when she talked about him. But Denny just stared steadily.

"The only one?"

"Yeah. Pretty much."

"Did your mom know that's what it was?"

Lily shrugged.

He pushed his hair, wet with snow, from his eyes. "Fuck, Lily. Why didn't you say? Maybe it dropped out or maybe James grabbed it as a joke."

"It wouldn't have mattered. My mother took it. She takes everything. Besides," she said, "stuff comes and goes. After a while, you realize that, you know?"

"Yeah." He lit another cigarette, cupped the fire against the wind. Lily liked the way his hands moved—the same as when he was pouring bottles—fast and light, like he only had to touch things to get them going.

He fiddled with the radio. It came on, crackled and popped and zipped. "Hey," he said, "look at that."

"What songs do you like?" she asked.

He shrugged. "Mostly old stuff. And talk isn't bad." He set the radio down and they listened for a bit. He skimmed through the channels. Something was wrong with it, the volume came in and out, gave a spooky feel to all the programs. An old guy talking about mango-tree rot. High-pitched voices in Spanish. A woman: *It's not that I don't get orgasms, it's that they never last.* Lily giggled. Denny smiled, then turned to a tinny, faraway-sounding interview—like it'd been recorded off the back of someone's truck. *I have with me here today the postmaster of Shale county. . . .*

"Do you miss Marna?" Lily asked Denny.

He snorted. "Fuck Marna. Leaving like that is not cool."

"But say, if she wasn't coming back, you know, if she really did quit. If she was gone and you were never going to see her again."

"It's hard to be gone in this town. You're always running into people."

"But if you didn't, Denny, just assume that you wouldn't see her again."

"Probably not." He took a puff, made the ash glow. The postmaster complained, *No one sends real letters anymore.* Denny said, "I mean a little because it's Marna—hell, I like Marna—but really, Lily, in this business people are always taking off. It's not such a big deal."

"I would," Lily said. "I would miss her."

Denny nodded.

The postmaster boomed-then-whispered, *I'm telling you, with your email and all . . . I'm telling you, the future is in the package.*

"Hey, Denny?" She couldn't look at him to ask it, instead played with the zipper on her coat, inched it up and down.

"Yeah?"

"Promise me you won't go home with Lena."

He gave a laugh, looked away.

The radio crackled. *So how can we prevent all those bills from arriving?*

Sure, the postmaster said, *that's a good one.*

217

Lily turned it off. "I'm serious," she said, "Promise, Denny. And not just tonight either, but ever. I talked to India, you know, and she said that it was really bad, the two of you. That something awful would happen if the two of you were together." She held her breath and waited for him to crack a joke, to tell her to quit being so nosy. But he didn't.

"Are you upset, L-pad? Are you in a crappy mood too?" His eyes were a funny, iridescent blue. They shimmered like the sky.

What was he talking about—the photo? Marna? Lena? But just as Lily was about to ask, Denny hugged her. "Hey, it's okay, L-pad," he said, wrapping himself around her, pulling her in. Lily squeezed him back. "Okay," she echoed, not so much sad as wanting to be sad. "Okay," she murmured into denim, then looked up and tilted her head so that her face was up to his, and she stood on her toes and kissed him.

She did it.

It was too fast to think about. They were kissing. They were kissing and then leaning back onto the bench, and his body was heavy on hers and his hand was in her hair and she was having trouble keeping up with him, with his mouth, which wasn't wet in a loose way like she was used to, but firm. Hard. It was like a dance she didn't understand fast enough.

He pulled back suddenly. "I can't, Lily."

"Sure we can."

He shook his head, got up. The distance between them was a rush of cold; it dropped her back in place.

The Almost Home windows flickered yellow then purple then blue. Beer signs calling: *Come in, come in.* A nasty trick. Mermaids of on-land.

She drew a breath. "It's not a big deal, really, Denny. I'm not a little kid. I can take care of myself." Another breath. "Take me home with you, Denny, or come home with me."

218

"Yeah, right. I'm sure your mother would love that scenario."

Lily felt herself losing it. The moment. She'd had it for a second and now it was gone. Beyond Denny, down the street, she spotted her cab stopped at a red light, chugging exhaust out and around in a cloud. Two blocks away. Any second the light would change. It was like watching a movie and knowing that the characters had only so much time. That something had to happen—and now. "Wait," Lily said, jumping up, grabbing Denny's arm. "Listen, no, listen. I know where we can go."

"What a *bitch*. Fuck you, Lena."

"Excuse me, Fran?" Lena felt her throat tighten around the words: "I'm pretty sure I was talking to Keith, not you. But please, join in. What. Did. You. Say?"

"I said fuck you. I said *bitch*. It can't be a surprise—isn't that what you're going for? I mean, isn't that your thing?" Fran snorted.

"Stand up and give a speech, Fran, isn't this your table? Where you get up and tell us how it's gonna be from this day forward?"

"Not only are you a bitch, Lena, but a damn good one." Fran clapped. "Good job, bitch. We all knew you could do it. I know it, *Denny* knows it, hell, even the new girl knows it!"

James laughed and then stopped laughing.

All of them looking at her—every one of them waiting to see what she would do. Lena had never in her life been in a fight, but they didn't know that. If she wanted to, she could make them think anything. And it was tempting—not just to shut Fran up, but to fight. To really give it to her. Every muscle in Lena's body felt pulled tight.

But then, out of nowhere, she thought of Marna walking in. *I'm back.* Of all the things to think of, Christ. Even when she wasn't here,

Marna was making herself the center of things. And then, just as quickly as all that anger had come on, it vanished. Fran was already getting a soggy look, would soon be hanging on her. *Sor-ry, Lee-nie.* She was the bratty sister you never wanted. And Keith looked crumpled. You had to know him to see it, it wasn't obvious, and Lena almost felt bad. But, she reasoned, she'd done him a favor. Like building muscle, you had to first break it down. Keith would thank her later.

Lena sat. She thought, whoever said you could choose your friends but not your family got it *exactly wrong.* Your family—you could move away from them, you could start a new one. But with friends there wasn't a choice. Wherever you ended up, those were the people you were stuck with. That's what it came down to. You made do with what you had.

Please please *please* don't let us get caught, Lily thought as they climbed back down the stairs and through the break room to the bathroom door, where she jiggled the lock. Please don't let him laugh or say, *Oh gross, not here,* or, *Oh wait, this is all wrong.*

She very rarely prayed because, really, what was the point? It seemed just as logical to wish on stars or practice witchcraft—which she'd tried once. There was a store on 14th Street. She and Rochelle went there once to make little satchels that were supposed to cause things to happen. You put herbs and crystals and things into velvet bags, different stuff, depending on what you wanted. There were mixes to make people go away and to make people stay. Rochelle made one to get Brian Delmont to love her and Lily made one to get Mr. Davis to hurry up and notice her—though she didn't tell Rochelle that's who it was for—and one to get her mother to stop taking pills. None of them worked. It was hard to tell, though, if it was the satchels that didn't work or if she and Rochelle had done it wrong. There were so many variables. Time of day and tone of voice—there were certain things you had to say. Or maybe they did work and just hadn't yet. Lily wished she had a satchel right now. *Please,* she thought. Make this happen. I'll be patient with my mother. Anything. I'll love Lena. Please.

They shut the door and locked it. Denny held her face in his hands and kissed her. This is so right, Lily thought, tasting the wonderful mingle of alcohol and smoke, the delicious cool of his mouth. This is it, she told herself. *Adult love.* Denny. Strong Denny. Tall Denny. In the almost pitch dark, with her eyes closed, Lily tried to redo it in her mind: how this was actually happening. She wanted to save it, memorize it for later.

Were you supposed to make noises? She'd heard of screaming, but that came later and was probably just a figure of speech. She wished she could ask Rochelle. They'd talked about almost everything else, though not in terms of Denny—who Rochelle had only met once, and only for a second, and that was before Lily realized that they had something.

He's creepy, Rochelle had said.

Do you think? I don't think he's creepy. He's mysterious.

He's creepy and in kind of a trashy way.

But what did Rochelle know? She still wore those ponytail holders with plastic beads. She'd only gone on one date ever and they hadn't even frenched.

Denny guided Lily down to the floor. It was hard and cold against her back, and Denny, understanding, spread out her coat and his jacket. He kissed her neck and slid a hand under her shirt. His fingertips were rough and warm. Lily gave an involuntary shiver. Not a bad shiver. She was no longer cold.

But then—oh god—she started thinking. About people. Rochelle. Maryanne Lucciano. The guy who killed her father. Who picked Lily up from school a couple of times, played Morrissey on the car radio, bought them fast food, which they ate in the car. He never made a move. She kept thinking he might, but he didn't. He didn't even apologize. They just drove and ate and talked about nothing. And then he was gone.

Her mind went to other people, other things. All the wrong things. The homework she hadn't done, the photo. Her mother. She tried to get it all out of her head, tried to imagine the thoughts like gray sludge—then pictured a shovel scraping it out, blob by blob. Only, she couldn't seem to get the very last bit. A tiny bit left. And the bit inflated, expanded again, bigger and bigger. In the blackness, all the thoughts seemed to be growing out of her head—actually appearing before her. Her mother standing there, asking, Do you mean it, Lily? Do you really mean it? Really?

Oh god.

She must have spoken out loud because Denny stopped moving for a second. Lily made herself relax and gave him a slow squirm to let him know she was okay. Calm down, she told herself. She was breathing into his chest; their bodies pressed together as Denny moved rhythmically against her. And then she felt *it.* First just as a pressure again her leg—then Denny reached down and undid his jeans, kicked them off. For a second Lily panicked: How exactly were you supposed to touch it? Just *touch it,* keep your hand there? Should she straightaway put it in her mouth? She didn't have long to worry: Denny took her hand and placed her palm on it, *on his dick.* Lily felt it jump, just a bit, a small beat—the skin smooth and surprisingly warm—and it didn't matter, then, what she was doing—or it didn't seem to matter, from the noises he was making.

She thought: Don't think.

Don't think.

Enjoy.

She worked to get that delicious slithery feeling back. *Strong, sexy Denny.*

But instead: her mother again, tucking her in at night. Her mother smoothing the blanket and telling Lily things she just didn't want to know. Like about the guy from the kitchen at work who she'd taken as an occasional lover. Lover. What an awful word to hear from a parent. Or, even worse, things about her father. Sometimes her mother apologized. That was terrible, her mother standing over her, stroking her arm, or sitting cross-legged in the doorway, saying over and over, I'm so sorry. The best thing to do was to pretend to be asleep. Lily had that down. She could feign sleep better than anyone. She could keep doing it until it was true.

Denny slid down her jeans and nudged her legs apart. Lily thought, if only they weren't down here in this bathroom. It had seemed like a good idea, but now the stale air was choking her. She was sure she could hear that fly still bumping around, buzzing to death. Denny had one hand on her thigh, and the other he slid behind her head, into the hair at the base of her neck, like a comb. He was gentle, but if he wanted to, Lily thought, he could crush her head like that. And then that too was suddenly before her.

He lowered himself and began to push inside her. It was the worst pain. The worst pain ever, the pain of splitting in two, red awful pain, worse than anyone had ever told her, than Lily had ever read or seen on TV, so that she barely felt the rest of it, the hard cold floor, his weight—

Until it stopped.

He was pulling himself off her and standing up.

For a second, Lily was confused: she thought he must've heard someone, that someone was right there, about to open the door.

But there was no noise.

Lily didn't move. In the light that had somehow, impossibly, emerged from beneath the door and turned the air a watery charcoal, Lily could either see or almost see him move around, pull on his clothes.

His voice came from a million miles away. "Shit, I'm sorry. I'm so sorry, Lily."

20.

What else was he supposed to do?

Vomit. He did that outside while she cleaned herself up.

When he came back, he called the cab company, said, "Where the hell've you been? We've been waiting. She's a kid, she needs to get *home.*"

Lily appeared in the doorway.

"They're coming," he said. "I took care of it."

He couldn't look at her.

She kissed him first.

The cab arrived quickly. They barely had to wait and while they did, there were things to do: put on coats, pull the lockers back into place behind them, trudge up the stairs. And then it was there. She got in and he paid the driver. She looked so small in the back seat, her purple backpack in her lap, her hooded coat.

"Hey," he said. What could he say? "Have a good night," he told her.

"Right back atcha," she said, and the cab drove off. Even her voice was small. It hung lightly in the air for a moment, like a bit of snow, then whisked away.

It was only when the cab had disappeared, down the block, around the corner, that Denny remembered: she still had his keys.

It was Colleen's turn. "Cabernet and Coke," she said. "Frozen." Dumbest drink request.

"Virgin martini," Lena said. "I gave him an empty glass with an olive."

"Johnny Black and grenadine," Denny said, reappearing, sitting down. He pulled out a pack of cigarettes.

"Masking tape," Fran said. It was the first time she'd spoken since the blowup, and everyone turned straight to Lena, who smiled and shook her head. "You can't play, you don't work here." Everything was fine.

"I can too play. But it wasn't a drink. The guy asked Marna for it. Masking tape. He wanted it to fix his *teeth*."

They all laughed, including Lena, and Colleen was sure they all felt it too: the tension dissolving. It was just about impossible to stay mad at Lena. Colleen never could. Or maybe it was the opposite: since she was *always* mad at Lena it kind of fell away—the nasty comments, how Lena would point out gross things about food, just to get a rise out of her. There were some things you just couldn't think about or they never went away.

What Lena didn't know was that it was the stuff Colleen *couldn't* see that scared her most. What accumulated when things collided. Strangers everywhere, touching things, leaving residue.

She heard another faint whir, this time by the front door.

She turned. Not there.

But she caught a nod this time. Motion. Something.

She was still finding him, in her clothing, in her pocketbook, in her papers. Just yesterday, a hair in her old bank book. The smell of his aftershave in her Christmas sweater. A black-and-white bird dropping in her jewelry box, from the month before he died, when he and Lily brought home that parakeet they found. It lasted a week before it dropped dead. It'd started shaking, just a little, a steady vibration. It's *happy,* is what they all first thought. Look, Lily said, he's purring. And it was true: he looked so cheerful, all puffed up, his little eyes closed. It was like something not real, that tiny thing, that beautiful, artificial blue.

Come to think of it, a lot of things dropped dead that month. The bat in the attic. The cat next door.

It was amazing they didn't see it coming.

Not long after Rick's death, Colleen quit her job as a respiratory therapist. She was making her rounds one night, checking up on patients, when she came to a woman in a coma. The woman was just in her forties, had collapsed one day with seizures from an undiagnosed tumor. Her family was keeping her on life support and it'd been nearly a month. She wouldn't wake up. If she did, who knew what'd be missing—talking or moving. Or thinking. Her face was white, the skin gone a little slack. But her hair was lovely. Someone must have just washed it for her. It was shiny spread out over her pillow, the same color as Colleen's. Colleen wondered if the woman used her brand, her exact color. Summer Breeze. Colleen stared at the woman. It seemed like you should be able to see something, Colleen thought, catch a difference.

And then, in the low flickery light, Colleen *could* see a difference: she saw the woman's head cave in, like a fallen cake. It stayed that way for a full few seconds before going back—before the woman was a woman again, her eyes closed. A nap.

It was the middle of the night. The respirator hissed and huffed. The man in the next bed sighed in his sleep. Somewhere, in another room, the TV was on, the laugh track twittering.

She had another floor to go, she was running late.

She reached out and touched the woman's hair, just lightly, felt its softness spreading through her fingers.

She stood there for a long time before walking out and never coming back.

Last Monday afternoon. After the employee meeting. They were at his place. When she wasn't up, fiddling with the blinds or getting more soda or going to the bathroom, Marna sat beside him on the couch, one leg over the arm. She'd scraped it bicycling, bad, all the way down the shin, and had rolled up her pant leg so it wouldn't stick. They were watching a movie—or had been. Now it was on pause, frozen, this time on De Niro, his mouth gaping midword. Every so often, it unpaused and went to TV, blasted some bit of music or dialogue, at which point Keith would hit the button again, like a snooze.

She kept getting up. She said, I've always wanted to go to Boston. Or maybe New York.

You haven't been to New York?

No, have you?

No.

Oh. She snapped a stalk from his aloe plant, stretched a long thread of jelly. Right.

He watched her rub in the aloe, circling the raw areas. He asked, Is something wrong?

He meant it rhetorically, but she thought about it. Not *wrong*, she said, I'm not upset. I'm restless. She extended her leg as if admiring her work. You know what, Keith? I've been here two years. Shit, is that right? It's like I've been in Denver forever. She squeezed her eyes shut.

Me too, he said.

You live here, she said.

So do you.

She opened her eyes. They were green. Sometimes they were gray, depending on the light, but now they were green. Pale, like road brush. The color of outside, rushing by.

She said, Yup, it's time.

He could barely breathe. He was afraid to move. He was afraid it might change something.

part three

The future is in the package.

21.

The apartment building loomed tall and white and made of stone. It glittered in the streetlamp light like a sandcastle.

She ran up the six flights. The hallway smelled of SweeTarts, the carpet was a dizzying checkerboard of orange and green. The heat was on full blast and she was sweating. Her whole body hurt. The only way for it not to hurt was to feel the pain from a distance. To think, Oh, there it is, pain. To let it in by choice.

She came to the door, the last one on the right, and stopped. She knocked. Called softly, then louder, *"Marna?"*

Colleen got up to use the bathroom and paused at the pay phone, held its side for a moment to steady herself.

He was hovering, following her.

"Rick," she said when she'd locked herself in the handicap stall—which wasn't any cleaner than the regular one but seemed like it should be. Colleen layered paper on the seat before sitting down. Two, three sheets thick. She'd do four, but she had to pee bad.

"Quit hiding. I know you're here."

It was an interesting feeling, never being alone. The glimpses here and there, the textured patches of silence. He certainly picked creative times to show. It was like he waited, planning to catch her off guard. Usually it was here, but not always. Once, when she'd brought home a man she'd met playing pool at Wynkoop, Rick appeared in the bedroom, right beside the bed. Sat himself down on the dirty clothes hamper. It ruined everything, of course—she hadn't even been able to fake it that night. Every time she got going, she sensed him. Grinning. He wasn't even jealous. He was *amused.* Leave me *alone,* she'd hissed, and of course the man thought she meant *him*—which maybe, in retrospect, she had.

Colleen was done peeing but she sat there. She bent down and felt for the back pocket of her jeans, dug in for the three pills she'd stashed there earlier. She picked off a couple dots of lint and swallowed the pills dry. One stuck and she coughed. She ran her fingers over her throat to coax it down. The feeling, though, didn't go away. A phantom pill. It'd be wedged there for the rest of the night.

"Rick," she said again, "you're not fooling me. I can hear you breathing."

It was faint: a swish of oxygen, a gentle rasp of asthma, the sound that still kept her up some nights.

"Jesus, Rick, when you were *alive* you weren't around so much."

More breathing. Funny light—she thought she saw it flutter, a fast strobe, playing tricks. The room seemed dimmer and brighter at the same time. The lime-green tile glowed. Bacteria, she remembered reading somewhere, could multiply like crazy. They could adapt. Figure out how to kill them and they would change—not over centuries, but years. Months. Maybe less.

And then there he was.

As clear as morning: standing in the corner by the sink, in that rumpled casual way that he had—and it was a full vision of him too, not a sideswipe flash, but him, actually him. If not in the flesh, well, then something very, very close. He leaned against the soap dispenser, his hands dug into the pockets of his faded khakis—pants that Colleen remembered leaving by the curb in a cardboard box.

"Well," she said, "it's about time."

"Well," JJ said, "thanks, everyone."

"You're welcome," James said.

They were rising and yawning, bringing their glasses to the bar, stacking chairs.

"Whose keys are these?"

"Mine."

"Anyone have gum?"

It felt odd to just leave, after all this time. To just walk out. JJ paused for a second, tried to think of something that might get a laugh. "I know a joke," she offered—though nothing came to mind. They'd probably heard Keith's goat riddle. There was a long one her college roommate used to tell, but the ending was tricky and the whole thing fell apart if you didn't get it exactly right. And then there was the bit about the string and the frayed knot, but everyone'd heard that.

"If you tell a joke," Lena said, flipping a chair onto a table with an easy swoop, "I'll have to kill you."

"Save it for next time," Denny suggested.

"Okay," JJ said, "next time." The words felt crisp and certain in her mouth.

Bleeding, it was normal, it was totally biological. The *hymen* was designed to rip—she and Rochelle had read about it in another book of Marna's. A biology textbook. The body was designed that way. Ridiculous or not, it was just true. A hymen didn't know what it was doing. A hymen didn't know what you had done—or why.

Or if, in fact, you had done anything at all.

When you saw or read things in a book they could feel round or flat. Facts, in particular, felt flat—not in a bad way, more of a smooth certainty. And now Lily felt the smoothness of that fact: first rip, then blood, then pain. In that order. There was always a gap between the last two, a space where you could feel nothing. *Rip, blood, pain.* If you deliberately felt the words instead of thought them, they became a chant. You changed them. *Rip, blood, pain.* Lily dissolved them into threads of sound, part of something strange and faraway, woven into one of India's magic quilts, a beautiful African ritual, a ribbon of *ripbloodpain,* right through her body, from that old secret spot behind her ear.

It hadn't even counted.

She'd left her panties in the cab. On purpose. It wasn't easy, but she'd slid them off and wrestled them out of her jeans—slowly, with her coat on her lap so the cabbie couldn't see—and balled them into one hand. Getting out of the cab, she just left them. It was totally gross, the cabbie—or, no, probably another customer—would find them later. It'd give them a sick-out story for years. It was an option and she took it. She didn't want them, not on her, not in her hand, so she left them. Now it was funny to think—her blood driving off without her. There was part of her in that cab.

She knocked again. Harder. *"Marna?"* Then felt in her back pocket for the key—which, as it turned out, she didn't even need. The door was unlocked.

Rick needed a haircut, it was falling down over his ears. He looked thinner too, though not as pale as you'd think a ghost would be. She considered getting up, going over to him—to what? touch him?—but that would mean struggling to pull up her pants, fumbling with the buttons. "I've gained a little weight," she told him. She folded her arm over her lap.

Sure, he said. *You look great.*

"You too."

Right.

Small talk, she thought. Was this what happened, was it all one big loop? All those years, all those late nights and early mornings, the time he got shingles and she had to smear on the salve, the time he took off for a couple days without even leaving a note and she hurled the blender through the window—all of it, the ugliness, all gone? Would they talk about the football game? The snowfall? Colleen tried to remember all the things she needed to ask him. How it had felt, that moment of impact. What was it like, being gone. Who was that woman, at his funeral, standing at the edge of the crowd?

"Why," she began, "are you here?"

He smiled.

"What?" Her spine prickled.

It wasn't an accident.

"What wasn't an accident?"

I stepped in the way.

"You're not making sense. Quit it, Rick."

Okay. Sure. Smile. Shrug.

"I don't get what you're talking about. That's ridiculous."

He scratched his neck. She could hear it, nails against stubble. She tried to catch her breath. He was still smiling.

There wasn't any accident, Colleen.

"Do you," she managed, "have any idea how difficult it is? Raising a kid alone? Do you know what it means that you're gone? To me?" He didn't answer. "To *Lily?* Nothing I could ever do could matter now, Rick. Nothing. After that." She had something in her throat—the pill, a question, maybe just a noise. She couldn't bring it out.

Wrong, Colleen. You're wrong. It's the opposite. It all comes back to you.

The light seemed to thin out, flutter downward this time, all the brightness sifting to her feet, to the floor—illuminating germs so that the floor came alive, the colonies upon colonies of microbes swirling across the tile, fingering through the grout. She managed: "I love you."

There was a fizzle of static—the sound of microscopic life as it boiled on the walls, on the tile, on her skin. The air in the bathroom fell flat for a few seconds and then, suddenly, was like the inside of a conch shell. It rushed her ears.

On JJ's way out, something on the kitchen floor caught her eye: a ball of newspaper. It was beside an overfull can of garbage. The way it was wadded up looked tight and intentional. She picked it up, uncrumpled it. An article. With a photo. Of Keith, smiling. *Best Server,* the caption said. The others were there too, blurry in the background. Lily holding a tray, pretending to be a waitress. It struck JJ that she'd seen the picture before. This same one; she'd read that issue. The Best of Denver issue. How funny, JJ thought. She'd paused to look at it back then and it hadn't meant a thing. And here it was, exactly the same. And totally different. She was proud now, of Keith, of the Almost Home Bar and Grill. It was like she had won something too.

Keith looked almost handsome in the picture. I could love him, JJ realized. Or Denny: she could love him too. How interesting to realize that. You could run into your future husband in an elevator and he would look like anyone else until you ran into him again on the street.

Or you could take the stairs that day and miss it all.

"Oh shit, forgot one."

JJ jumped. She hadn't heard anyone come in. It was Keith, from outside, the air around him icy. "I'm sorry," she said, without thinking, and quickly jabbed the clipping into the mound of garbage.

"Gotta dump it," Keith said, nodding to the trash can. "Missed it earlier. You busy with it? Done browsing?"

She blushed. "No. I was just thinking."

"What about?"

She drew a blank. Blurted, "I was thinking I could fall in love with anyone."

He didn't laugh. "Be careful," he said, "who you love."

"Okay."

"Don't ever trust restaurant love."

"Okay."

"If you learn one thing from this job, don't worry about taking orders or knowing the names of liquors—shit, anyone can learn that— but the thing you should really remember is not to trust restaurant love, not for a second."

"Okay." Had he seen what she was looking at? Did he think she liked him? "Well," she said, but he didn't move.

"Think of it this way," he continued, "if you put a bunch of rats in a cage, what happens?"

"They eat."

"Yeah, and what else?"

"Sleep?"

"And fuck, right?"

"Sure, and fuck." It felt strange to say it. She wondered if he could tell it was a word she wasn't used to saying out loud. "They fuck," she said again, trying to get it right, to say it stronger.

"They hook up. This one and that one, then that one with the other, trading partners, over and over, you know? It's all about proximity. And does it matter?"

"With rats?"

"Exactly. That's how restaurant love is. Ninety-nine percent of the time."

"Not a hundred, though."

"Well, no." He looked off. "Not a hundred."

"Are you and Marna that last percent?"

He seemed surprised that she would say this. For a second, JJ worried that he was angry. But his face softened. "You know, JJ, if you'd asked me earlier, I would've said yes."

"And now?"

He didn't answer. Maybe he hadn't heard her. He turned to go and then paused. "Hey," he said, "do me a favor, when you're done with the garbage, shove the whole can out the door. I'll get it on my way out." And he loped back into the restaurant.

I could love him, JJ thought. She couldn't help it.

"Look what I found." Fran'd come back from the bathroom with Colleen, who was staggering. Her shirt untucked. Face pale and loose in a way that made her smile seemed wrong, misplaced.

"Hi, Denny," she drawled. "You remind me of something."

"You okay, sweetie?" Fran asked. She was putting on her coat, a big furry thing, and James was helping her. James and Fran. If you looked at them just now you'd think, Isn't that a nice couple, I bet they take walks early mornings. Which maybe they did. Who the hell knew what happened away from here? And, Denny thought, who the fuck cared.

"I'm okay," Colleen said, "if you are. Have you ever eaten a fig? Fresh ones, not dried ones."

"Can you get her home?" Fran asked Denny. "It's a big favor, sweetie. I know it's out of your way."

"Sure we can," Lena said. "No problem."

What was he supposed to do? He said, "If Keith'll close up." He imagined them pulling up to Colleen's and him saying, Oh hey, could you run in and grab my keys?

Keith said, "Yeah, I'll close up. I've got nowhere to be."

"I love you, Leenie."

"Oh get off me, Fran, cripes. You're drunk."

"I am. And if I forget it when I'm sober, I want you to remind me. And, anyways, you love me too, I can see right straight through you. We all can."

"Love hurts . . ." James sang.

They'd find out. He knew they'd find out. Maybe not right away, but soon. Eventually. And then what? He was too tired to care. He saw

241

it far away, off in the future, with himself and all the others and Lily—shrunken down, like TV, like something so small it couldn't matter, not really, not in the end.

He looked at Lena. She wasn't so bad if you caught her in the right light.

For the longest time, Lena's fantasy had been to bring Denny back out to the country. A vacation would do them good. They could have drinks on the plane, look out the window, watch Denver get smaller and smaller, turn into constellations of light and then nothing at all. They could go to his place in Nebraska, or she'd take him to Indiana, to her parents' house. They'd stay in the back room, in the old bed that might fall apart as they fucked. They'd sleep late and go for walks down the dirt road. They could see it together: the land that stretched forever, met the sky in a single unbroken line. She'd take him to the spot where Bear had died. To the field behind the junkyard, where she lost her virginity. To all of it. She wasn't sure *why* she wanted to take him there, to that middle-of-nowhere-shit-wasteland—after all this time, after getting the hell out and swearing never to go back. She just did. Maybe because they were the same, her and Denny. They understood. It would be a single experience. Something would happen, Lena was sure of it. Under the right circumstances, things happened.

Keith locked the front door behind them and watched through the dark glass their colored shapes move away, then blend together, then disappear into the long, deep plane of night. He still had to stack the bar stools and lock up, but already he could see himself out there, also walking away, heading home. Just like the others. Just

242

like any other night. All the way up Middleton to 6th. Past Barney's apartment, where you could usually see his dog pressed against the window. Across Colorado Boulevard by Pete's Eats and the Texaco, to Keith's street, to his building, to his apartment. All of it, once again, his.

At the back door, JJ was hoisting out the garbage can when she realized someone was sitting on the steps, slumped over.

"Marna?"

But it wasn't. It was India. "I'm just leaving," she said, wiping her mouth with her sleeve. Snow had gathered in her hair, big milky flakes, like the fake stuff in school plays.

JJ asked, "Do you want me to call a cab?"

"My car's around the corner."

"Are you okay to drive?"

"I'm not going to *drive.*"

"So you're okay?"

India made a noise of disgust—or maybe just exertion—and got up and teetered, then started walking—fast for someone who had just been dead asleep. JJ followed. The ground was slick beneath the fresh snow; she took tentative steps, slid into them. They stopped in front of a small battered hatchback. India opened the driver's-side door and JJ could see that the back seat was heaped full. Blankets and clothing and cereal boxes and a few old suitcases, the hard vinyl kind.

"Are you moving somewhere?" JJ asked.

India frowned. "Well, you're here," she said. "You might as well get in."

JJ hesitated.

"Someplace to be?"

"No." She went around to the passenger side with the quick image of a newspaper headline: *Waitress disappears after long first night.* Her luck, there'd be a quote from Lena.

"Do me a favor," India said as JJ swept Styrofoam cups to the floor and sat down. "Reach back and grab my thermos. It's under the Chia Pet."

The car smelled like a cafeteria. JJ felt behind the seat, a little afraid of what she might touch. "Aha," she said. "Got it."

"Is it empty or full?"

She tilted it. "Full, I think."

"Pour me some, will you?"

JJ unscrewed the thermos and filled the cap. "Vodka?" she asked.

"Water," India answered and drank it down. "Give me your hand."

"I don't have any money," JJ said. "I don't get tips while I'm training." She put out her hand anyway, palm up. India didn't take it. The two of them just stared at it for a moment. It seemed like you should be able to understand it yourself, JJ thought, just from looking. She felt a need, suddenly, to cheer India up. She couldn't end the night, not like this. She took a breath and said, "I'm going to tell you something I haven't told anyone." India didn't look impressed but she didn't stop JJ from continuing either. "When I was a nanny, before? In Boulder?" India nodded. "Well, the reason I left was that they caught me. They—" JJ paused. "They caught me playing their piano. A Bösendorfer baby grand," she added.

"A what?"

"It's a really good piano." And she had a flash of it: jet-black and gleaming. *Oh god,* JJ had whispered when she first saw it, when she'd gotten the job and was given a tour of the family's gigantic mountain home.

Yes, the mother had said softly, it's stunning.

JJ had seen pictures of such pianos. But never like that, up close. Her stomach tilted one way and then the other.

It's not for playing, the mother added.

Oh no, right, of course not, JJ had agreed quickly, I don't play anyhow. Not anymore.

JJ told India, "Those pianos are worth a lot of money."

India said, "And you couldn't help yourself and you got caught."

"Naked."

"Naked? You were naked?"

"Yes. And dancing. First I took off my clothes and danced and then I played their piano. I'd had some wine," she added, lying.

"Playing their special piano naked, dancing naked, drinking their special wine—and they saw all of it."

"Cameras."

"Well," India said, she was laughing, "didn't you think of that, beforehand? Nannycams?"

"No." She had to admit: it was pretty funny—it was a horror story, sure—especially the part where she'd been woken up in the middle of the night and *shown the video*—but, okay, it was also funny. Or would be. She was glad India was enjoying it, in any case. "Seriously, what was I *thinking?*" JJ said.

She hadn't been thinking and that—it occurred to her now—was what had made that beforehand part so wonderful. What *still* made it wonderful—why not? Why did one part have to be ruined by what followed?

The little girl had been sleeping, the parents were out of town, and, alone for the first time in their big, beautiful, echoing house, JJ wandered around. She opened the windows for the wind, then, on a whim,

245

undressed in front of the window—it felt daring even though the closest neighbor was miles away. She stripped down to her socks and slid across the wood floors, skidded and spun and sang. The Beatles and the Pointer Sisters and campfire tunes. She made up operas. She belted out torch songs. JJ had never thought of herself as a singer, never actually tried. But maybe, she thought, naked and twirling, she *was* good and she just didn't know it—she just hadn't given it a chance. What else might she be good at? How funny to think that you might be talented—maybe even brilliant—at something and never even know. An expert weaver. A golf pro. JJ leapt across the living room and through the study and library, and then, just for a peek . . .

It was even more impressive at night. With only the moonlight coming down through the skylight, the wood glowed softly and smoothly, looked like a sheen of skin.

She approached it slowly, sat down. She stuck to the bench, but it was a good feeling to be naked—naked at a *Bösendorfer*. She sucked in her stomach. I'm not going to play, she told herself, but she opened the lid anyway and touched the keys, ran a few fingers from one end to the other, lightly, careful not to release any sound. Then just one note. Middle C. It echoed richly through the room. It was amazing the difference a good piano could make. She played it again, harder. *C.* Then *D.* Then a scale. Up and back again. Then a Bach minuet. She wasn't bad, really. You didn't have to be a virtuoso to be pretty good. You didn't need a specific degree. The music filled the room, filled the house. She imagined it floating out into the trees, into the mountains— wouldn't sound be lighter up here, in the high-altitude air? She played bits of songs, anything she remembered. It came through her fingers and rose from the Bösendorfer—not by some force of muse or talent but as simple, wonderful noise.

India broke in: "My aunt walked in on my brother masturbating in the bathroom. At church. At our uncle's funeral."

"Oh," JJ said. "Oh. Yikes. That's much worse."

"Yup." India sighed. She drank some more water, rescrewed the lid, and handed it back to JJ. For some reason it was hard to imagine India with relatives. "Remember, earlier, when you asked me about love?"

"Sure," JJ lied. She tried to remember. She heard Keith, about rats: *They fuck.*

"Well, I have another answer."

"Yeah?" The windows were fogged now. The closed-in air had gotten warmer, and JJ was suddenly stricken—it seemed horribly obvious, she was sure India was thinking it too—that any two people, in any car, alone, had the potential to make out.

India cleared her throat. "I thought of what it was. Love," she said, leaning in so that JJ could see the little dry lines gathered around her mouth—she had to will herself from shrinking away, she had to count to ten—". . . can't you just see that newspaper cartoon? I don't even know if they run it anymore. Beneath the jumble? The two kewpie dolls?" She hacked a laugh. "Love is. It's where everything you can't predict comes together. A crop circle. One gigantic black hole of hope and reason all sucked into one. The crop circle of the mind. There." India sank back and smacked her lips. Closed her eyes.

"Oh," JJ said. "Okay." She pressed the side of her fist against the window. Topped it with dots. Made a matching set.

Before getting out of the car, she checked to be sure India was all right, that she was still breathing. "Good-night, India," she said.

India stirred. Sighed. "Good-night, Marna."

.   .   .

You could tell she was gone. Lily had been right after all, she'd been right all along—Marna hadn't just ditched her shift like Big Keith and everyone said. Stuff was still around, the big furniture and lamps and posters on the walls, but you could tell. The whole place reeked of emptiness. Drawers pulled. The shelf of snow globes, bare. Bookshelves, bare. A scatter of empty cardboard boxes. Cupboards were open.

Marna was gone. Gone-gone.

Lily found half a loaf of bread and some cheese, made a sandwich, ate it wandering around. She picked things up, put them down. An old trophy with a chipped gold baseball player midswing. *Rayburn Little League '81.* A lamp with light-bulb boobs. Books. *War and Peace.*

In the bedroom was her father's chair. Lily sat down on it. She dug her notebook and pen out of her backpack, then opened to a blank page and wrote: *Things to remember.* Marna had given Lily the notebook one evening when they were hanging out, having fun. You seem like the type to keep a notebook handy, Marna had said. Lily liked how Marna had handed it over, like it had weight, not just physical weight, but something more. The first thing she'd copied into it was from her father's survival guide: *Don't forget your compass! When traveling into wooded regions, make note of where you entered—and, if you get disoriented, just return in that direction. Don't panic. Take it slow. Another reason to pack a good lunch!*

Lily tipped back in her father's chair. Spun around. She squeezed her eyes shut, thought of her childhood, tried to sense something, smell something, feel a color, anything. Nothing. It was just a chair.

In Marna's sparkling bathroom, the walls covered in bits of shattered glass, Lily found something. On the floor, in the middle. A square cardboard box, the size of a tissue box. White. Sealed with packing tape. On the top, in ballpoint pen, Marna had written: *What I left behind. For you.* Lily turned it over, looked for more. But that was it.

What I left behind. For you.

So Marna hadn't forgotten after all.

Immediately, even before opening it, Lily figured out it was a snow globe. She could feel the heavy slosh. Maybe it was Canada. Or Death Valley. Knowing Marna, this could be, Lily thought, a message. It was definitely a message. Marna was inviting Lily to join her. Wherever it is, Lily decided, I'll go. She had a little money. She'd pack up some food and get on a bus. Tonight. Right now. She'd really do it.

She ripped off the tape, opened the box, took hold of the top. Eased it out. Held her breath.

The cash-register-shaped building. The mountains.

Even before she saw the writing she knew.

Denver.

Well.

Lily set it down. She went through her backpack, found the jelly beans that James had broken into. The champagne-shaped bottle filled with white jelly beans. She ate a few. She remembered how, on that very first night she and Marna had talked—that awful Fourth of July— in the hazy twilight, Marna had said there were only two kinds of people: the leaving kind and the staying kind. You were either one or the other, you couldn't be both. And it wasn't as though the staying kind was bad, she explained. She wasn't saying that, not necessarily. In either case, you could be stuck. In fact, she told Lily, she was a little jealous of that many-layered connection some people had with where they lived. But she was not that way. She was the leaving kind. I have to keep moving, she said.

Like sharks, Lily had exclaimed, excited she knew this—she'd just seen a TV show on it. She told Marna, They need to, they can't stop, they have to swim even when they're asleep.

Really?

Yes, it's true.

Huh, Marna had said, breathing out sweet smoke. But, wait, we're *all* moving when we're asleep, aren't we? I mean, in a way? It's awake that most of us get stuck?

And, stupidly, at the time, Lily's mind had wandered on the *sharks*—on how it would be beautiful and exhausting, both, to keep going like that. She'd imagined a whole school of them, slicing endless curves through water. She didn't even consider the stuck part. She didn't think to ask Marna if she could come along—to tell her that she was the same, that she was the leaving kind also.

And now it was too late. Now it didn't make a difference *where* Marna had gone off to. Marna herself, Lily thought, no longer mattered. Sure, she was out there, findable even—another flat, physical fact: *matter can't be created, matter can't be destroyed, matter can't disappear.* Marna was in one part of the country or another, in California driving the coast or sitting in a Southeastern, un-air-conditioned Laundromat, listening to the *swish swish* of the machines. She could be in Fort Collins buying mint cigarettes.

Lily rescrewed the cap to the jelly beans and drifted into the living room, to the big window. It went from floor to ceiling, a single pane of glass. The prettiest window ever. Lily stood close and looked out.

She thought back to the night her mother had run away, made an attempt to go from here to not here. When she quit her hospital job and drove so many miles—and then called Lily from a motel. I'm so sorry, she gasped into the phone. Please. You have to. Come get me.

So Lily did. Half asleep, she found her father's keys and unlocked the '79 Datsun two-door her mother still hadn't sold. Lily could drive; her father had taught her on this exact car, his car, patiently, not even yelling when she ground the gears.

Lily started the ignition, got the Datsun coughing and chugging, and then eased it into the old familiar, metallic purr—all the while hearing her father: *Clutch, gas, clutch, gas—that's right, Lily, perfect, light and easy.* She drove into the hot, glistening night. Slowly, then faster. There was no one else on the highway at 2 or 3 in the morning, and Lily hurtled through the light-dazzled darkness, the road ahead of her shiny and slick like a streak of mercury. But what Lily remembered most wasn't the road or the feel of the ride—or how the air inside the car still almost smelled like her father—*almost.* If she breathed it casually, she was able to catch him: his spicy cologne, his hair cream. Breathing deeply didn't help. Then all she got was old car upholstery. Chemicals and rain.

But that wasn't what stood out most clearly—nor was what she found when she got there: her mother, on a twin motel bed, curled up, crying, eating cookies, her pill bottles set up neatly and familiar on the nightstand, in a way that was almost comforting to Lily, like a still life her mother was planning to paint.

No, what Lily remembered first and clearest of all was the single instant before she slowed her father's car and flipped the signal and turned into the Starstruck Motel. That instant when she realized she could keep going. *She could pass the motel right by.* She wouldn't even need to do anything. It was a matter of *not doing*—of not slowing down, of keeping her foot from the brake.

Off in the distance, something was on fire. Lily could see fire engines and the clouds of smoke rising into the dark sky—only, from here, it didn't look so bad. More busy than anything else, the clumps of cars, the commotion. Kind of social.

Lily leaned against Marna's beautiful wide window, tilted into the glass, pressed its coolness against her forehead. Glass, she'd learned in shop class from Mr. Davis, was really liquid. Over the years it dripped down so that the bottom got thicker than the top.

There was nothing but liquid between her and the ground, all those floors below.

Seemed so easy.

A splash.

Rip, blood, pain.

You could trick your body. Disorient it. Dismantle your internal compass. Even if just for a little while, even if you couldn't hold on to it, not against all that endless fact. It was still possible. You could melt everything liquid, float in it, lose yourself in your own motion even while perfectly still. Dissolve every cell into the swirl of speed—of driving or biking or rolling downhill—or of swimming upside down underwater, right under the surface. One easy flip changing everything. You could pull a fast one. The sky is no longer just sky. You are staring up into something entirely new. You are flat against a dazzling infinite.

In the distance, the Wells Fargo Bank flashed 4:52.

Right now, her mother was worrying about her.

Lily lifted herself away from the glass. She gathered her stuff to go home.

When she was half out the door, she paused and took it in—one last sense of *Marna*. In all that emptiness, there was still a little of her left, hanging in the air.

Colleen sat at the kitchen table drinking a cup of water. It was really late. Or really early. Both. Pretty soon, the dark would spread into light and things would take shape. Get ordinary again. Here it was, Colleen thought, the best hour, and most everyone was sleeping. A waste. She'd had a bit too much beer, and every so often the room began to spin, but, basically, she was fine. She'd survived another night.

She remembered, how, not long after she quit her hospital job, she'd heard a news story about another hospital where an unusual number of terminal patients were dying in the middle of the night. They couldn't figure out why, so they hooked up a video camera and discovered that the cleaning woman had been unplugging the life support, just for a second, to plug the vacuum in.

Colleen had heard it on the radio. The radio hosts couldn't stop laughing.

She put the cup in the sink and climbed upstairs. It was amazing how much restaurant smell you could absorb, in your clothes, in your hair and skin. She was still wearing her apron, she'd forgotten to take it off, and it kept hitting her knees. She reached Lily's room and paused, then leaned against the door frame and slid down to sit. Just for a moment. Lily's bedroom clock flashed 4:52. Colleen sat there in the doorway, her back against the frame. She didn't want to disturb Lily. After the long night, it was the last thing she wanted to do.

"I don't want to bother you, honey," she whispered into the darkness.

Lily didn't answer. Her daughter. Off in some dream. Just like JJ had said, kids were so hardy. They were amazing, Colleen thought, they were stronger than anyone.

"Lily?"

Nothing.

"Can I ask you a question?"

. . .

JJ was almost to her car when she saw Keith. He was sitting on the back steps, right where India had been, and JJ trudged over. She wanted to say good-bye. She wanted to make sure, doubly sure, she was working again. She wanted to see Keith.

"I thought you'd left," he said.

"Did everyone else?"

"Yup. Just me. You forget something?"

Yes, she thought. "No."

"So. Ready to call it a night?"

No. "Yes." She paused. "Are you still working?"

"Just need to turn out some lights and lock up. I wanted some fresh air. The nice view and all."

"I was in India's car," JJ said, then felt stupid.

"Oh yeah?" Keith said. He was looking past her, out into the lot. "You get a fortune?"

"Kind of."

"So what did you think of your first night?"

"I really liked it."

"You did?"

"It was okay." Somewhere off in the distance a siren wailed. JJ rubbed her hands together. Her lips felt stiff in the wind.

"Well," Keith said, standing up, brushing off the seat of his jeans. He sighed. "You ever have a hot toddy?"

With everyone gone, the bar seemed strange. Shrunk down. Keith did something in the office, then switched off lights JJ hadn't noticed were on and went behind the bar and fixed drinks in two coffee mugs. They sat at 14, the only table that hadn't been wiped off. Keith relit a candle. They stirred sugar into their drinks. It smelled strong. The mug felt good in her hands. Hot and perfectly curved for holding.

"So I wanted to ask," Keith said. "What was that joke?"

"Joke?"

"The one you were going to tell. Good idea to have a few ready, make people laugh. They don't even have to be that funny because people are drunk." He smiled. "Sometimes I forget that. Sometimes in the middle of everything, I forget that people have been drinking. I've gotten a new definition of normal."

"Me too," JJ said.

"So bring it on. I told you one. Your turn."

"Oh." She tried to think. "Did you hear the one about the string walking into the bar?"

"That was your good joke? Shit."

"No. No, I know that's bad. Okay, here. What's the difference between three hundred sixty-five tires and three hundred sixty-five blow jobs?"

"What?"

"Well, one's a Goodyear, one's a great year."

He smiled. "I wouldn't expect that from you."

"Thanks."

"If you want to know who can really tell a joke, much as I hate to admit it, is James."

"Really?"

"Well, not all the time, and they're kind of all about Kentucky, even when they're not. You know, Did you hear they found a new use for sheep? *Wool.*"

"Is he from Kentucky?"

"No, or, I don't know. It does seem like it, doesn't it? Actually, that's not fair to Kentucky. I've never been to Kentucky. It's probably a great state." He paused. "What does it make you think of?"

"What?"

"Kentucky."

"Oh. Um. The Derby?"

"Sure." Another pause. "That's true."

They drank.

"Is everything okay?" JJ asked.

"It takes a while," Keith said, "at the end of the night, for everything to fall back into place."

Already she knew what he meant. "Are you going to be okay to drive?"

"I'm okay to walk."

"I can give you a ride."

"Thanks, that's nice of you." He stirred, clinked his spoon. "I walk everywhere. I don't mind."

"It's snowing," JJ said.

"I sit around a lot, so I like to walk."

"What if it's across town and you're late?"

"Then I'm across town and late." He gave her a long look, like he hadn't grown used to the idea of her, like he was still taking her in, then asked, "Doesn't it bother you? All that shit in your eyes?"

"That shit is my hair." She tucked it behind her ears.

"It's nice but why do you cover up your face like that?"

"I don't."

"Yeah, you do."

"My skin breaks out. I'm hiding it." She couldn't believe she was saying this to him. Was he easy to talk to, she wondered, or did she just want to talk?

"Well it breaks out because your hair is on it. Wait." He went back behind the bar and fished around for something, returned with a hair scrunchie.

She laughed. "Keith, I'm not putting someone's dirty hair scrunchie—"

"It's not dirty." He buffed it on his shirt like you would an apple, then handed it to her. She obliged: tied back her hair, leaving a few strands loose in a way that looked sexy in magazines.

"Much better. You can see your eyes."

Then it was quiet. They stood there, facing each other in the semi-darkness. Blind people, JJ'd read, developed their other senses and could actually feel something before they touched it, before they made contact.

She said softly, "So I'll give you a ride," then made herself do it: she moved closer. She could feel him, the particles around him pushing against the particles around her.

But he stepped back. He picked up their mugs and smiled. Said, "I'll walk you out."

"Sure," she said. "Okay." It wasn't embarrassing. She wasn't embarrassed. It was a matter of deciding. The moment came and went.

He set a security alarm, which began to beep, and they rushed out the back door—though on the way, he ducked into the cooler and grabbed a plastic bag.

Outside, it was getting light. The air felt exposed and pale. JJ's eyes were puffy. She was off balance, buoyant. "Not even half a ride? Are you sure? I could drop you off. . . ." She realized she had no idea where he lived.

"I'm sure."

"I'm not sure," she said, laughing, meaning it to be funny, "that I'm ready to be alone."

He nodded. Handed her the bag. "Here," he said. "Welcome wagon."

"Thanks." It was heavy. She could make out a candy bar and an orange through the plastic.

"So," he said. "You work tomorrow?"

"I don't know," she admitted.

"Come in. Either way."

"I will."

"Hey," he said. "I meant to ask. About your name. What's it stand for?"

She smiled. "Nothing."

"No really, I won't tell."

"Nothing. The ultrasound was wrong. I was supposed to be a boy and my mom wanted Jason and my dad wanted Jeremy."

He smiled. He didn't say, That's too bad. Or, It's a nice name. Just smiled. Then turned and walked away, slopped through the alley slush and took a right, headed down the sidewalk with that lumbering grace that he had, and disappeared.

One last chance, he thought. But she didn't appear and he didn't expect her to. He thought about leaving anyway. His shit was all packed. Or gone. He could still take off. He had cash. He could take a bus or hitchhike. It was safe if you were careful, if you arranged yourself into the kind of guy they wouldn't mess with.

He thought about his LPs, if they were still at Planet Spin, if he could buy them back. And JJ, how pretty her face was when you uncovered it. And Lily, who reminded you that, in the end, everything would be okay. He thought about going home and maybe running a hot bath and opening the window so the cold air came in. Poor man's hot tub.

He took a right onto 6th and felt, as he always did, the bar receding. Back there, no matter what, the crew would soon arrive. They'd show up, some of them cranky, filled with morning, others still half asleep, and one by one, they'd go inside the bar—which was quiet now, emptied of all its texture and sound—and take down chairs, and turn on lights, and wipe tables, and pour drinks. They'd fill it up, all over again.

She climbed into her car feeling the strange, slow lightness of no sleep. She started the engine, felt it blow cold, then get tepid, then finally warm. She sifted through the bag of food and took out a sandwich and unwrapped it. Ham and cheese. She ate it quickly, not chewing it enough, then opened another and ate it too. It had gotten all-the-way light, without her noticing when. She waited for a long time, watched the sun stream down from the clouds and touch on specks of wind-stirred snow, and felt a tug. For no reason. Like a memory that wasn't hers but she remembered anyway.

Tomorrow she'd be back. And maybe next month and maybe next year she'd still live in Denver. Or maybe not. There were people out now, walking, holding paper cups of coffee. Any one of them could be Marna.

acknowledgments

I am deeply grateful to my family, and to my friends and mentors at Indiana University, the University of Colorado, and the University of Virginia.

A special thank you to the Henry Hoyns Foundation and the University of Virginia's Young Women Leaders Program—and to the many restaurants and bars across this country that took me in, including Garcia's Pizza and Yogi's Grille and Bar (for giving me a start), Legends, and Ludwig's (for seeing me off).

I am forever grateful to my editor, Greg Michalson, and the rest of the team at Unbridled Books, and to my agent, Alice Tasman (who went above and beyond—and then *beyond* beyond).

Finally, this book would not be possible without the support and guidance of Tony Ardizzone, Luisa Cannon, Julia Casey, Norman Casey, Jeremy Clarke, Laura Ellis, Andy Fox, Kristin Girten, Lisa Grocott, the Goldsteins, Scott Handy (who I would mention twice if it wouldn't read as a typo), Cecilia Johnson, Helisa Katz, Dana Kerker, Mary Kerker, Molly Kerker, Shelly Kerker, Chip Livingston, Jill Maio, Elizabeth Maupin, John Munden, Cornelia Nixon, Greg Owens, David Pantos, Nancy Pate, Dennis Reardon, Nathan Roberts, Kathrine Ross, Sherry Spurlock, the Sullivans, Rhea Tresh, Dahn Warner, Michael Weiner, Tony Winner, Mrs. Woodbury, Jay Yellen, and Marty Yellen.